D1147558

The
BLESSED
HALLOWED

Also by Tonya Hurley

The Blessed
Passionaries

The
BLESSED
HALLOWED
TONYA HURLEY

Hodder
Children's
Books

First published in the U.S. in 2015
by Simon & Schuster Books for Younger Readers

First published in Great Britain in 2016
by Hodder Children's Books

A Catalogue record for this book is available from the British Library

ISBN 978 1 444 90477 2

Typeset in Berkeley Book by Avon DataSet Ltd, Bidford-on-Avon, Warwickshire

Printed and bound in Great Britain by Clays Ltd, St Ives plc

MIX
Paper from
responsible sources
FSC® C104740
www.fsc.org

The paper and board used in this book are made from wood from responsible sources.

Hodder Children's Books
An imprint of Hachette Children's Group
Part of Hodder & Stoughton
Carmelite House
50 Victoria Embankment
London EC4Y 0DZ
An Hachette UK Company
www.hachette.co.uk

This book is dedicated to
my mother Beverley Hurley

I thought of your beauty,
and this arrow,
Made out of a wild thought,
is in my marrow.

W. B. Yeats

Eve of Agnes

We are forged
Licked by fire
Our bond
Like iron
Our love
Anointed with smoke and green water
Washed in blood
Our skin made of thorns and stars
Purified
Burnished
Branded inside
On our hearts and minds,
Each wound etched more deeply than the next
Upon souls skin
Ashes to ashes
Dust to dust
Donec mors ex parte?
When all there is has ceased to be
What still remains is
You and me
Eternally

1

Afternoon Suicide

'Don't touch me!' Cecilia's voice bounced off the white walls and tiled floors of the Perpetual Help psych ward, rattling the grimy windows. Her plea echoed loudly down the hall reaching Agnes, who was grabbing frantically at her locked door and banging on her window shouting Cecilia's name. Completely in vain.

'I said, hands off,' Cecilia demanded once again.

'You're insane,' the burley male recovery nurse said, laughing off her request and shackling her right wrist to the dirty exam table.

'Wow. You should've been a goddam detective,' CeCe said. 'If you haven't noticed, we're all mad here.' She struggled,

1

ripping her hospital gown. With one arm strapped to the bed, she swung blindly at the attending doctor.

'Calm down, bitch,' he shouted, grabbing for her sinewy arm. His hands were large and calloused. More like a construction worker's paw, or a hit man's.

'Not much of a bedside manner you have there,' she snapped, gathering all the saliva in her mouth that she could before spitting it in his face. She thrust her free elbow swiftly into the soft part of his throat and brought him to his knees. He gasped for breath, and his dignity, and eventually for his consciousness. 'I hit like a bitch too, don't I?'

He pulled at the alarm on the wall next to him, signalling for help as he collapsed at her feet. The site of the beefy health aide struggling like that satisfied her immensely. She looked down at him and laughed.

'Help,' Cecilia mocked. 'I've fallen and I can't get up. They should have gotten a chick nurse to do this job. Oh, that's right. They did.'

An orderly came running down the corridor, his rubber soles squeaking on the newly waxed floor, arriving within seconds of the distress call.

'Grab her,' the nurse demanded hoarsely, rubbing at his sore and reddened neck. The orderly was stunned at the sight of her – one arm fastened to the bed with her legs and free arm swinging wildly. No one would have guessed she was semi-dazed from the cocktail of meds she was forced to take that morning. Cecilia stared him down and could tell he was shell-shocked at the sight of her – whether it was because of her reputation, which she was used to now, or her current state. He stood there, watching her flail like a live butterfly with its wings pinned down to a mounting board. He looked like a scared little boy drafted to do a man's job.

'Come on, Billy. Do it . . . now,' the attending said to him while picking himself off the floor.

'Bill . . .' Cecilia muttered, her mind suddenly drifting a million miles away.

'You want to get out of here, don't you?' Billy asked, trying to stabilize her.

'Don't you worry. I'll get out, one way or another, even if it's in a box,' she said. 'Come with?'

The recovery nurse made it to his feet, still a little wobbly, and leaned on the bed to steady himself. He reached for a leather strap affixed to the bottom of the bed and tied one of her legs down.

'Aren't we going to administer the anesthesia now?' Billy asked out of breath, finding the sight of her so helpless unsettling.

'She's not getting anesthesia. Orders from upstairs. This bitch is going old school.' He pulled a decades-old rubber mouth bit out of the stainless-steel drawer. It was deformed from overuse and reeked of bad breath and disinfectant. Her

3

eyes widened. Half of her body out of commission. Her fate now lay out on a rusty tray in front of her.

'It's a *relic*,' the nurse taunted. 'You know what those are, right?'

'I'm surprised you do, dipshit,' Cecilia snarked. 'That's an SAT word.'

'Look at you, all tied up and still talking smack,' the nurse said. 'Who the hell do you think you are?'

'I'm the worst kind of a bitch,' she whispered. 'I'm a bitch with nothing to lose.'

'Based on my experience in this room, you do have something to lose,' he said, getting supplies from the rusty cabinet. 'Your mind.'

He fastened a bib around her long neck and took the rubber bit off the tray. Cecilia focused her gaze on the young orderly, looking for some piece of a soul that she could connect with, that she could reach.

'You don't want to do this, Billy.'

He swallowed hard.

'Don't listen, kid. She won't have much to say in about fifteen minutes. She'll be left staring off into space, trapped inside that hot body. Lights out, nobody home, ya know what I mean?' A perverse smirk washed across his face. 'Hot but defenceless, just the way I like 'em.'

Billy reluctantly nodded, trying to fight the sick feeling that was rumbling up from his gut.

'Strap her other leg down!' his superior barked.

Billy grabbed her thrashing leg with one hand and held it down as he scrambled to open the remaining leather strap with the other. She kept her eyes fixed on him the whole time, trying to find the human part of him, the believer, the part that she knew was in there, that he might not have even recognized himself.

'What the hell are you waiting for? Strap this bitch in!' the recovery nurse ordered. 'Now!'

The attending affixed white pads to each side of the metal headpiece he grabbed from the stainless cabinet and placed it over her temples.

Cecilia retreated into herself. She knew this was it. There was no use delaying the inevitable, she thought. She closed her eyes and began to talk to him. To Sebastian. She desperately recalled his face to her memory. She was completely calm, emptying her mind of fear and terror and replacing it with thoughts of him. Only him.

As the nurse rushed out to get the doctor who would be pulling the switch, Billy took her leg that he'd been holding, and began to strap it in. It was all so final.

'I'm sorry,' Billy said, buckling the strap.

His apology fell on deaf ears. Cecilia was with Sebastian deep inside herself. Suddenly her leg got warm. And then hot. Burning hot.

'Shit!' Billy said, trying to keep hold of her, while hearing the sound of his own skin sizzling.

'My hands!' Billy tried his best to keep her in his grasp. He couldn't believe what was happening, thinking it must be faulty equipment.

Cecilia kicked out of his hold and slammed the door shut with her foot; her eyes still closed as if someone or something inside of her flipped a switch and activated her only free extremity. Billy grabbed for her leg again but she kicked him in the face, knocking him to the floor. Cecilia spit out the mouthpiece, freed her hands, and gasped for air.

'He was right, I do have a hot body,' she whispered.

Her eyes popped open and she scanned the room for a weapon but saw none. There was nothing but grimy windows slightly ajar, machinery that looked like some vintage modular synthesizers she'd fooled around with in a recording studio, a spare set of electrodes and several half gallons of conductive salt solution.

She thought about running for the window, diving through it, setting herself free. For good. Instead she smashed the windowpane with her hand, grabbed one of the fallen shards and cut herself out of the ankle strap.

The orderly was dazed but still reaching for one of the shards that now littered the floor before him.

'Don't do it, Billy,' she warned. 'I don't want to hurt you.'

He picked up a jagged piece of glass and thrust it upward toward her. She kicked it from his hand and pinned his wrist down with her foot.

'Life is choices, Billy. I gave you one. You gave me none.'

Cecilia reached over to a counter next to the table she was perched on and twisted the cap off one of the jugs. She poured it out on the floor. First one half gallon, then another, and watched the liquid pool around the orderly's feet, nearly covering them, the cuffs of his pants as well as a large portion of the room. She flipped the door lock to keep him from running out, trapping them both inside.

'That's the problem with old buildings,' she mumbled. 'Floors aren't level.'

Blood from her stigmata flowed freely down her arms, on to her smock and to the wet floor, mixing with the solution one drop at a time.

She ripped the metal headpiece off and the pads, exposing the ends of the wires, and turned the voltage dial on the transformer to maximum and hit the switch. She felt the heat rise as the current flowed through the wire. And the mild stench of burning skin filled the room as the temperature rose around the open wounds on her hand.

The rumble of techs grew louder as a scrum of attendants arrived at the door, peering through the tiny rectangular reinforced window and banging on it to be let in.

Cecilia smiled at them and held the exposed wires up for them to see, taunting them. The panic in Billy's eyes was evident to his colleagues.

'Back off or I turn this fucker into a sparkler,' she demanded.

'What do you want?' one attendant shouted to her, trying to talk to her through the psychotic hostage situation.

'Get Frey. Get him now.'

Before she could even get the words out, the doctor stepped forward from behind the crowd, with the paperwork orders in hand. Next to the nurse.

'I knew it was you who would pull the switch,' she said, his angular face framed perfectly by the window like a profile photo for the hospital web page.

'I was the only one who volunteered,' he said, reaching in his lab coat for a key.

She watched as the handle turned slowly upward at a 90-degree angle to the floor, the latch clicked and the door gradually opened.

'Just you!' she barked.

He nodded and waved the others off. Frey's expression was impassive but the deliberateness with which he entered told her he was worried, if not frightened. Like an animal catcher approaching its unpredictable, rabid prey. He noted the hot wires and the solution slicking the floor. Billy ran out of the room as Frey entered.

'For a dropout, you're quite resourceful,' the doctor said.

'A lot like Sebastian. At least that's what you once told me.'

'Yes. Like Sebastian,' Frey mused. 'He also put up quite a

struggle in this room. Maybe better for you and the others if he hadn't. Ever considered that?'

'Before him I was flat on my back. On a stretcher. Downstairs.'

'And now you are upstairs.'

The doctor's condescending look – one she'd seen before – was galling.

'At least I'm moving in the right direction. Like him. Like Lucy.'

'Sebastian is dust. And Lucy is a statue now. Calcified stone. Cold and lifeless. Encased in glass,' Frey opined. 'It doesn't have to be the same fate for you and your girlfriend Agnes down the hall.'

'Right, just as long as I let you fry my memory and rip my soul from me,' Cecilia laughed derisively holding the wires near her temple. 'I'd rather die on my feet than live on my knees.'

'What a noble quote to use at such a time,' Frey said. 'Cecilia, haven't you had enough? Let this nonsense go. Renounce it. You can get out of here. I'll even testify at your trial.'

'A deal with the devil? How trite, even for a prick like you.'

'Just an observation, my dear. You haven't got many friends. Is it a good idea to alienate the one person who can help you?'

'I'm always amazed at how you manage the balancing act of doctor and demon,' she scoffed. 'You disgust me but the fact that you've fooled so many people for so long is quite the accomplishment.'

'We're all frauds, Cecilia, in one way or another, aren't we?' he rejoined. 'The essence of performance. Pretending. All of us.'

'How long are you planning to keep me here?'

'Well, the court said I can keep you here as long as it takes. You're an accused murderer after all.'

'I didn't kill that kid and you know it.'

'That's not what Captain Murphy thinks. Or the prosecutor.'

'That was *your* letter opener sticking out of his chest.'

'With *your* fingerprints on it.' Frey reminded her.

'You're a goddamned liar.'

'There were witnesses who saw you barge into the hospital and my office. Murphy himself overheard you threatening him in front of New Life the night Jesse was, ah, injured.'

Cecilia remained silent.

'You're a danger to yourself and others,' he said. 'You're delusional. Diagnosed.'

'By you.'

'You're lucky. They placed you with the best psychiatric care in the city.'

Frey produced a tight, mocking smile.

'So I'm getting out of here never,' she spat.

'That depends on you,' Frey said. 'Besides, the alternative is a lot less . . . pleasant.'

'Depends which alternative you mean,' Cecilia replied coldly. 'Jail or . . .'

Frey sensed a renewed tension in the girl. He stepped closer, bringing the tips of his shoes in contact with the liquid. She leaned over and lowered her arms and the live wires to within a hair of the floor.

'Are you testing me?'

Frey stood, silent. She let both her legs drape down from the table letting her feet hang nearly but not quite skimming the floor, about to step down. She held the wires out in front of her delicately as if about to drop them at any second.

'Suicide?' he said sceptically.

'No, murder. You're coming with me.'

Cecilia looked at the doctor, waiting for his next move, and was surprised at what she saw behind him.

It was Jude. He was standing right there in the doorway. Shaking his head *no*. He pointed straight behind her. At the window. Cecilia sat back up and turned towards it. Suddenly she heard the faintest sounds coming up from the street below. Her name. Chanted. Frey remained still unsure of what she might do next. She leaned over towards the window and saw a small crowd gathered below. At the main entrance of the hospital. Just a few people. Holding signs and candles. Singing. Speaking her name. She paused for a second, smiled at Jude. He smiled back. She looked outside again and there he was. Outside with the others, singing.

Cecilia turned off the transformer and dropped the wires on the table. Surrendering herself. A group of orderlies rushed in sensing their opportunity and grabbed her, pulling her towards the doorway. Frey walked to the window and spied the scene below, momentarily disconcerted.

'It's inevitable,' he said, as much to himself as to her. 'Stop fighting. You can't stop this, Cecilia.'

'They can,' she said pointing at the window. 'They will.'

2

Unbeliever

Agnes pressed her face against the glass in the door window so hard she could barely get air. Her breath visible before her, fogging out her view until she sucked it back in again. The sounds of struggle coming from down the hall were disturbing enough but it was the eerie silence that followed that Agnes really feared.

She could just barely see Cecilia approaching, surrounded as she was by a pack of goons in scrubs. Not actually walking but being half carried down the hall toward her, her newly shorn locks barely moving as her chin hung almost lifelessly to her chest.

'Cecilia!' Agnes banged on the door and screamed to her

motionless friend, distraught. Her worst fear realized – Cecilia was a shell. Gone.

Agnes broke down in tears, wetting strands of her long copper hair, still banging on the window, hoping this was a bad dream. As Cecilia passed Agnes's room, doing the Thorazine shuffle, she lifted her chin slightly from her chest and opened one eye. She paused and looked at Agnes. Agnes was paralyzed. Subtly, Cecilia cracked her most sinister *I'm just fucking with you* smile and winked before dropping her back head down. Agnes exhaled, momentarily relieved, tears of relief mixing with the ones of sorrow. She sat down on her cot and felt the springs push up into her backside through the cotton covering that they called a mattress. She stared at the shiny white walls and milky tiled floor and swore she could almost see herself in them. Just as she'd seen herself in the glass of Lucy's encasement in the chapel. But this time it was not so much a reflection of herself but more of a ghost of herself. And she wasn't even dead. Not yet at least. She laughed a little at the thought before bursting back into tears.

She cried for Sebastian and Lucy. For herself and Cecilia. They were caged. Imprisoned. Via different protocols but nonetheless under Dr Frey's total control. At his mercy, which was something he had none of. Just as he'd planned. Just as he'd arranged. She began to wonder if the whole thing hadn't been orchestrated from the start. The attacks clearly had been. Finn's *suicide*. Of those she had no doubt. But what about the rest of it, she wondered. Sebastian's 'escape'. The 'chance' meeting at Precious Blood. Even Jude and Sister Dorothea were feeling more like breadcrumbs than people, like cheese for a trap the doctor had set long before the mice had arrived. Paranoia was setting in and it was hard for her to tell if it was real or induced by the meds she was being force-fed.

And then there was Jesse. Languishing in a hospital bed down the hall in the next ward. In a light coma, Frey had told his parents and the newspapers. And as far as Agnes was concerned, he planned to keep it that way, judging from the snide whispers among the nurses about Jesse's long-term 'treatment' plan. A sudden turn of her door handle interrupted her internal monologue.

'You have a visitor,' the floor nurse advised.

Agnes stared at her blankly.

'Who?' she whispered suspiciously, looking past the sour-pussed woman for a few of Frey's minions.

'Who else? The only person who ever comes to visit you,' the nurse advised snidely. 'Your mother.'

'You mean the only person *allowed* to visit me,' Agnes challenged.

'Are you coming or not?'

Agnes exhaled and stood slowly, her joints aching much too much for a person her age, and she dragged towards the doorway, her feet sliding slightly in the hospital-issued slippers she wore. The nurse led her to a familiar spot down the hall to two empty chairs. Both positioned right outside of Dr Frey's office. His door was cracked and she could see him busily juggling phone calls and shuffling files, seemingly unaware of her presence.

Agnes sat and stared straight down the hallway towards the reception area and watched her mother enter and approach. Appearing bigger and bigger as she got closer and closer. Like a monster from a horror movie. Martha appeared harried to her. Bothered. As usual. There was nothing calming about her gait or her greeting.

'What on earth was that commotion about?' Martha complained. 'They had me waiting in reception forever like some kind of pharmaceutical salesperson.'

Martha ducked her head into Frey's office and smiled. Frey stopped what he was doing, hit the mute button on his phone and acknowledged her. 'Mrs Fremont.'

Martha beamed as if she'd just seen a celebrity in her local restaurant.

Agnes was disgusted at the cosiness between the two of them. 'Nice to see you too, Mother.'

Martha fiddled with her purse, straightened her skirt and jacket and sat down, legs crossed at the ankles.

'I hope it wasn't you causing trouble,' Martha chided.

'It was Cecilia,' Agnes said, knowing full well what to expect in reply.

'I should have known,' Martha said tersely.

Agnes found herself looking back through the doctor's

office door nervously like a convict's lawyer worried about being overheard.

'You have to get me out of here,' Agnes growled, reaching for her mom and digging her nails into Martha's wrists.

'Agnes!' Martha shouted, attracting stares from the floor nurse at the desk down the hall. 'This is not like you.'

'No, Mother. I'm not myself at all. That's just the point. Not with the shit they're pumping into me every day.'

'Agnes,' Martha whispered in the most sympathetic tone she could muster.

'Something's gotten a hold of you. You can't see it but you will. With therapy, medication and Dr Frey's help you'll be as good . . . as new.'

'Fuck him,' she spat. 'He's the reason why I'm here. And you.'

'Quiet!' Martha reprimanded. 'Don't you think he can hear you?'

'Oh, I'm sure he can. Why do you think we meet outside of his office?'

Martha pulled away from Agnes's grasp and noted the small scar that remained from her suicide attempt.

'I hope you're not getting paranoid again,' Martha said, the judgmental tone in her voice not even thinly disguised. 'Who knows? Maybe this *is* you now. Maybe I've been blind. All this started with your trip to the ER.'

Agnes was ready to unleash when the nurse's voice blared over Frey's speakerphone and spilled out the office door.

'Dr Frey,' the nurse said. 'Daniel Less for you. Line 1.'

Martha was way too pressed for Agnes's liking. They both heard Frey stand and walk towards the door. He smiled at both of them and closed it.

'Daniel Less? Friends in such high places,' Martha whispered giddily. 'You should be happy, Agnes. I've got you with the best there is.'

'You're fangirling a psychopath,' Agnes said under her breath.

'What's that?' her mother asked.

'I'm getting tired, Mother.' Agnes knew this visit was going nowhere and sought to cut it short.

'Just as well,' Martha said, fidgeting once again for her phone. 'I'm already running behind thanks to that stunt your friend pulled.'

'Oh you mean that fighting not to have her brain fried and her body shocked into torturous spasms? Having her soul ripped out? That stunt?'

'She's an accused criminal. A murderer. She killed Finn, for God's sake. No matter what you said he tried to do to you, no one is a judge *and* jury.'

Agnes glowered at her, chaffing at her hypocrisy. 'Except for you, isn't that true, Mother? And Frey.'

'Stop resisting, Agnes. You have to let go of these delusions if you're ever going to be well.'

'Why can't you understand that I'm perfectly well,' Agnes shouted in frustration.

'Mentally ill people never think they're sick, Agnes.'

'Is that what Dr Frey told you?'

Martha was dismissive of the jibe. 'Remember, they didn't build that ECT room just for Cecilia. If this keeps up you might find yourself there.'

'Are you threatening me?'

'I just don't know what I ever did to deserve this. I'm trying to help!'

'That's the problem. You don't know what you ever did. Well, all you have to do is just get me out of here!'

Agnes turned away from her.

'I don't want to fight, Agnes. But I'm not signing any papers until I have my daughter back.'

Agnes's frustration had reached the breaking point. 'Can you at least do me one small favour before you go?'

'That depends,' Martha answered in tough love mode.

'Walk me to Jesse's room. They won't stop me if I'm with you.'

Martha looked at her intensely, considering her daughter's request. Agnes saw some sympathy in her mother's eyes for the first time in a long time.

'Well, OK, I don't see what harm it can do.'

Martha escorted Agnes to the other side of the ward where Jesse was recovering, the floor nurse eyeing them each step of the way. They entered and Agnes left Martha in the doorway as she approached him. Gone was the battery of life-saving machinery she'd seen attached to him following the savage attack. What remained was a single IV stand dangling a bag of salt solution to keep him hydrated and a bag of sedative.

'Such a tragedy. A young man doomed to life as a vegetable,' Martha said, as she looked on impatiently at the unconscious young man in the bed. 'All self-inflicted.'

She heard her mother's comments, knowing they were meant for her, but didn't listen. Agnes stood by his bedside and brought her hand to his forehead, pushed aside his hair and brushed the tips of her fingers along his cheeks. He was thin and pale, but warm. Breathing. His hands were clasped, resting on his chest. She grabbed them gently and entangled them with hers. She brought her mouth to his ear as her copper hair fell about him, blanketing both their faces, hiding them. 'Wake up, Jesse,' she whispered. 'Please wake up.' She began to weep. 'We need you now. We need you so badly.'

Martha was uncomfortable witnessing such a scene, starring her daughter.

'All right, Agnes. There's nothing you or anyone can do for him and I've really got to go.' Martha coached Agnes up to a standing position slowly and, as she did, she saw Jesse's finger move ever so slightly. Agnes saw it too.

'Mother?' Agnes said.

Martha was silent for a moment. 'Agnes, don't do this to yourself,' she said, brushing over what they both just saw.

'You saw his finger move,' Agnes said. 'I know you did.'

'That sometimes happens, I guess,' Martha said.

'You guess?' Agnes asked. 'You saw it with your own two eyes.'

'Reflexes, Agnes,' Martha said. 'Why do you always have to go . . . there?'

'Where?' Agnes asked. 'To *hope*?'

Martha ignored the slight. 'I have to go. I'll never get out of here. I have to fight through that crowd down there. Ugh, it's going to set me back even further.'

'What crowd?'

'Jesus, I'm surprised you can't hear them from up here. The same idiots that were hanging around our house. Praying. Carrying signs. Yelling at passersby. Blocking the entrance. I think even Hazel was down there.'

'Why?'

'Trying to get you and your partner in crime out of here. Lot of good it will do them. They should throw the bunch of them in jail if you ask me.'

Agnes smiled a knowing smile as the first ray of hope crossed her face since she'd been admitted.

'I'm ready to go back to my room.'

'OK sweetheart,' Martha said, leaning in just far enough for an air hug as they parted ways. 'Will you be all right?'

'I'm going to be just fine now, Mother.'

The Pope prayed, on his knees, elbows positioned on the kneeler armrest, eyes shut tight, one hand gently fingering his

brow, the other a rosary. Except today he prayed even more fervently. He prayed for guidance and for strength. He prayed for calm in the face of the visitor he was expecting momentarily.

Some footsteps and then a quiet voice alerted him. 'Holy Father, he is here.'

The Pope concluded his prayers with a faint amen and nodded to the young attendant. He rose to greet, if not welcome, his guest, the weight of his office showing in the weariness of his expression. The former Cardinal DeCarlo, pale and weakened from confinement in his quarters, entered the cavernous room and approached the Pope slowly, trailed by two Swiss Guardsmen. He appeared to the Pope to be extraordinarily frail and spent, as if he was beginning to wither now that his nefarious purpose had been revealed.

DeCarlo stopped a few feet from the Pope. The two men, once friends and colleagues, eyed each other suspiciously. The Pope waved off the soldiers.

'Leave us please.'

The Swiss Guard departed.

The intense silence between them was not empty or even awkward, but preparatory. After a while, DeCarlo spoke, a note of defiance and sarcasm in his voice. 'I thought when the soldiers came for me, they would be bringing me to one of your newly minted exorcists.'

'You're defrocked, confined to your quarters and without authority any longer. The evil within you cannot spread.

I am satisfied.'

'Yes, Vincenzo. Complete authority is now with you. I should know, pezzanovante. I made sure of it.'

The Pope bristled at the visitor's insulting informality. DeCarlo did not address him with either the formal titles or endearing ones to which he had become accustomed but with his given name, signalling his contempt for the man whose papacy he'd once fought for.

'Mi ricordo,' the Pope replied in Italian, acknowledging DeCarlo's efforts on his behalf as a fact well known to them both. 'What has turned you against me? Against God?'

'Against God? That is quite a presumption.'

'You were my closest advisor, my friend, and you betrayed me. I trusted you.'

'And I trusted you. And you betrayed me. And your office. And the Church,' DeCarlo railed, his voice echoing off the marble floors up to the vaulted ceiling.

'You are mad.'

'I am mad? You elevate trash to the Throne of Heaven and you accuse me of insanity? It is you who eviscerate our traditions, cede the authority conferred upon us by celebrating the unworthy, making sinners of saints, hallowed of the hell-bound.'

'You consorted with our enemies, those who would undermine us,' the Pope chastised. 'Who would turn the people against hope, against faith.'

'I think we've done a good enough job of that on our own, Vincenzo.'

'Institutions are run by people, DeCarlo. Good and bad.'

'It is a matter of opinion, is it not, my one-time friend?'

'Those that do evil are punished and do not tarnish the good that is also done.'

'I do not need to justify myself to you. The world is ever changing and so too must traditions. These girls bring a new and powerful message, heard by those who've stopped listening to us, whether you choose to accept it or not.'

The Cardinal raised a finger, wagging it disrespectfully in the pontiff's face. 'What you refuse to accept is that they are not here to help you. They are here to replace you!'

'If that is His will, so be it.'

'God works in mysterious ways, is that it, Vincenzo?' DeCarlo queried. 'It is precisely because we have forsaken our traditions, lowered our standards, sought to be loved rather than respected, that abusers of all sorts occur.'

'You mean feared, don't you? If it was up to you, our respect would be found at the end of a hot poker.'

'Yes. Right where it has always been.'

'Thank the Lord it is not up to you any longer,' the Pope retorted. 'You are a man of the past, DeCarlo.'

'Past is prologue, Vincenzo. Now if it's all the same to you, I'll return to my room now.'

'You may have immunity from the law of this world, but

you are not immune from Final Judgment.'

'Nor are you, *Holy Father*.'

'The Lord will judge. Not you.'

DeCarlo's gaze hardened and the eyes appeared to be nearly set ablaze with anger, burning like the last bits of flame shooting out from a log just before it dies.

'The doctor did us a favour. He identified these charlatans. These pretenders,' DeCarlo fumed. 'I was only doing my job. *I* should be praised. Sainted!'

'Doing your job? The excuse of every scoundrel!' the Pope replied with anger of his own. 'You misinterpret all we are and stand for. And now a girl is dead.'

'Not by my hand. By her own,' DeCarlo declared without apology.

'More excuses,' the Holy Father said.

'On the positive side,' DeCarlo wheezed snidely, 'at least you have a new saint to worship.'

'Leave me!' the Pope commanded. 'I won't see you again.'

'As you wish.'

As DeCarlo turned towards the enormous double doors in the back of the Papal quarters, the Pope called back to him.

'Is there anything else you can tell me about the situation in New York?'

'No, but I do know this. You should be prepared to make two more saints.'

3

The Murder Ballads

Jude looked on silently at Cecilia who was inhaling deeply on the cancer stick dangling loosely from her pale lips, dripping with a cold sweat and doubt. He sat nearby, his eyes never leaving her. Like a little guardian angel, a piece of Sebastian.

'People come and go. Some are cigarette breaks,' she said, blowing a smoke ring in the air. 'Others . . .' She took the tip of her cigarette and poked through the smoke ring violently breaking it up. 'Others are forest fires.'

Cecilia didn't look back at Jude. She knew he understood, more importantly, she knew he was there. Just as she never looked back at the bodyguards who protected her at shows or high profile events. She didn't need to. Ever vigilant. Jude, she knew, even with her eyes closed, was there and would always be.

She had the look of a convict who'd just escaped the hangman's noose. But like all executioners, she thought, they would try again. All she'd bought for herself was temporary reprieve, not freedom. Freedom, the more she thought about it, might actually be death. Would Lucy stand being there for five minutes she wondered? It was an upsetting thought for Cecilia, but maybe, she thought, Lucy *was* the lucky one.

She continued to stare pensively out the large, dirty windows of the penthouse to the world beyond, chain-smoking. There wasn't much else to do in the *looney lounge* as it was called. Not very politically correct terminology, but it definitely fitted. Cecilia, Agnes and Jude weren't officially kept segregated from the other patients, but they didn't need to be. Interaction was pretty unlikely, and pointless, in Cecilia's case, except to exchange small pleasantries or cigarettes. In fact, to her surprise, they weren't kept apart from each other either.

She would have thought that Frey would worry about them plotting or planning their escape or even just commiserating, but she'd guessed he was much too arrogantly overconfident for that. He'd brought them there. And there they would stay. Warehoused. Sequestered. Away from their Apostles. Their lives. In an earthly limbo, which right now, felt to her worse than any hell she could imagine. This was Frey's plan apparently and he'd worked it to perfection.

Cecilia heard the sound of muffled, paper-covered footsteps falling just behind her. She didn't look. She knew who it was.

'Hey,' she said, between drags.

'Hey,' Agnes whispered back.

'You OK?'

'Sort of. You?'

Cecilia reached out her hand, still without turning. Eyes fixed on the windowpane. Agnes grasped it and sat down next to her.

'Don't worry about me, Agnes. These bastards aren't going to break me.'

Agnes wasn't able to put on as brave a front as her soul sister. She swallowed hard and took a deep breath, sweeping back her long, greasy copper fishtail braid off her shoulder.

'I just don't know how much longer I can stand it, CeCe. I feel like I'm waiting around for my head to be chopped off or something.'

'Yeah, it is a kind of terrorism. Teasing you by threatening your sanity or your life. Scaring you into submission. Compliance. Same with the meds and ECT,' Cecilia said, looking up and flipping off the omnipresent camera lens mounted in each corner of the lounge. 'Well, fuck that. And fuck you, Doctor.'

'Aren't you afraid?' Agnes asked, almost embarrassed,

voicing the one thing Sebastian had expressly warned them against.

'No,' Cecilia said. 'Only the unknown can make you afraid and I'm pretty sure I know how this story is gonna end. For better or worse.'

'How do we rewrite it?' Agnes anguished.

'I don't think we can, or should, Agnes.'

'We're kind of at his mercy here. Who knows what he's really planning.'

Cecilia lowered her finger and her head and turned to make eye contact. She laughed a scornful laugh. 'Yeah that's exactly right. Look at what happened to Lucy.' She paused. 'Mercy? What mercy? And as for his plan? *This* is the plan. The game.'

Agnes was sceptical. To her, it just didn't seem elaborate or sadistic enough for Frey. 'What? Keeping us here worrying? Smoking?'

'It's a kind of death, don't you see, but without actually dying. Removing us from the world. From its consciousness. People are sheep. Without leadership, they'll stray. Forget, Agnes. That's what he's betting on.'

Agnes considered what CeCe said carefully and came to a conclusion of her own. 'It's more than that.'

'What?'

'Rejection.'

'Very high school, but very true,' CeCe said, matter-of-factly, her eyes widening. 'He's not stupid enough to really think he can talk it out of us after all that's happened. After Lucy. After . . . Sebastian.'

'Life is high school after all, isn't it?' Agnes asked rhetorically.

Cecilia continued to muse, not really responding but more thinking it through out loud. Thinking about why she dropped out to come to New York and try to make it in music in the first place. The sort of emotional vertigo that comes with being misunderstood. A misfit in your own hometown. In your own mind.

'It's at the core of every fear. In high school, on stage, in life,' CeCe mumbled, almost trying to convince herself.

'In love,' Agnes agreed, citing the one thing that mattered most to her. 'That's what there is to be afraid of, CeCe. It's all about rejection.'

'The more accepted we are, the stronger. The more dangerous to Frey.'

'Yes. We can't forget it. We can't falter, Cecilia.'

Jude walked over to them in a sign of solidarity. Cecilia picked up her head and smiled at him wanly, then turned it to process her grim, colourless surroundings.

'I don't know anymore. What kind of game is it when you have to die to win?'

Agnes sensed despair in her tone, a note she wasn't used to hearing from the rough and tumble rocker.

'You know, rejection isn't just about others rejecting us.

It's about rejecting ourselves. I think that's what this is really all about.'

Cecilia snuffed out a butt on the tiled floor and lit another, exhaling as much of the smoke out of her lungs as she could. She waved her hand quickly in front of her face, fanning the fumes away from Jude.

'You keep believing that, Agnes, but...' she cooed, taking Jude's sweet face in her nicotine-stained hands. I'm not so sure it's even about us anymore.'

'Then who? What?'

'The future,' she said, pointing out the window towards the chanting crowd and then gently kissing Jude on the cheek.

The mental and emotional exhaustion on both CeCe's face and in her words was obvious to Agnes. He might not have been able to shock the fight out of her but Frey was getting to her nonetheless. She was in a funk for sure, dispirited. And who could blame her, Agnes thought. Agnes could feel the nurses moving closer, silently warning the three of them to split up.

'OK, break it up. Party's over,' one nurse ordered.

Cecilia and Agnes complied, not from fear of the consequences they might suffer but to shield Jude from any more unnecessary pain or punishment. They'd almost gotten used to the inhumanity they faced each day, from forced druggings and solitary confinement to strip searches and straightjackets, but he was just a child and needed whatever little protection they could provide. Some days that meant not making things worse. Cece ran her hands through his hair gently and Agnes nodded towards his room. The boy blinked, signalling he understood, and left.

The girls exchanged a few final comments in whispers as the nurses looked on impatiently.

'My mother said the papers are reporting some gossip that Daniel Less is trying to get you out of here.'

'Yeah? Well, whatever,' CeCe said, wiping the ash from her pant leg and forcing her lean frame upright. 'I'm not leaving here without you.'

Agnes turned atypically stern and took Cecilia by the shoulders, startling both her and the boy, almost holding her up. It was a steely side of the free-spirited girl that rarely showed itself. 'If you get a chance to get out of here,' Agnes insisted. 'You take it. Do you hear me?'

Cecilia stared hard into Agnes's eyes. 'Do you know what you are?' Cecilia said sweetly.

'I'm not sure I want to know,' Agnes said with a smile, bracing herself.

'You are an unframed masterpiece.'

Agnes was flattered but suddenly saddened, thinking of Lucy. If ever there was a masterpiece it was her.

'I think that's what the chapel is for,' Agnes said. 'Framing. Do you know what I mean?'

'I do,' CeCe said.

'I meant it, Cecilia. If you get a chance to go, you go.'

'Not without you.' The determined look in Cecilia's eyes told Agnes she meant it.

'You can do more good on the outside.'

'Outside will take care of itself, Agnes,' Cecilia said, removing Agnes's hands and placing one hand on Agnes's heart. 'It's what's inside that matters.'

Sister Dorothea approached the front desk of the Perpetual Help psych ward as she always did, with extreme caution and suspicion. The well-lit but tiny foyer was not welcoming and not really suited to visitors. It seemed to her this might be intentional. If not entirely discouraging loved ones from visiting, making it as uncomfortable as possible. The trend in psychiatric care was clearly away from that kind of sterile environment, especially when it came to treating children with mental health issues, but there was no arguing with Frey's reputation and success rate, so little fuss was made about the general unpleasantness.

'I'm here to see Jude,' the sister announced.

The desk clerk pretended not to know exactly why the nun was there and went through the formal 'just a moment' perfunctory platitudes and buzzed the floor nurse in the back of the ward. It was taking longer than usual to reject her request, which the nun found disconcerting.

'Is there a problem?' she asked.

The response the nun expected came back to her. It was the same each day.

'No, I'm sorry but Jude is in session right now and is not allowed visitors.'

'Can I just leave this bag of treats for him with you?' the nun asked politely.

'I can't accept gifts for patients.'

The no-nonsense look in the nurse's eyes told Sister that sympathy was not this nurse's specialty.

'Groundhog Day,' the nun mumbled sarcastically, to a blankly indifferent stare from the desk. 'I'll come back tomorrow. You can count on that. Bless you.'

The nun felt as if she'd entered some sort of real life Twilight Zone. The same questions asked, the same responses given as if it was the first time. Neither acknowledged the redundancy, preferring to play the game by the rules. The visit ostensibly had accomplished little, just as her previous visits had. Though she might not have gotten to see the boy, she was quietly putting Frey and his psych ward minions on notice that someone was watching.

As she turned to leave, she spied the boy at the end of the hall being ushered into Frey's office. He walked slowly, staring straight ahead, frowning. Whatever joy there had been in his childhood, and there was precious little she knew, was gone or had been taken by Frey. Jude looked up and down the hallway towards her as if he could sense her presence. Their eyes met and his lips curled into a smile, a sign she felt, to let her know that he was OK. It was all the nun could do to hold back her tears. Seeing him standing there, so helpless, so alone. But the smile spoke volumes. It spoke the words he could not. Or would not. She only hoped it might soften the doctor's black heart as Jude disappeared inside the office. But that would be a miracle and they were in short supply, she reckoned, in this literally godforsaken place.

Frey was buzzed over the intercom from reception, notifying him that the nun was departing. He walked over to his door and looked out towards her as she walked away, closed his door and returned to his chair behind his desk, and stood behind it.

'Good morning, Jude.'

The child was his usual silent and unresponsive self. Frey pulled the shades on his office windows, allowing the sun to shine through, nearly blinding the boy. It wasn't exactly the hot lights interrogation depicted in noir detective film squad rooms but it was close enough. Jude could barely make out the doctor's silhouette in the glare.

'Such a lovely day, isn't it, Jude?' Frey observed snidely, as the squinting boy remained impassive and motionless. 'The sun is out. Children are outside playing. Roaming free. Where you should be, son, don't you think?'

If he was tempted, Jude didn't show any sign of it. He remained stoic.

'I hope you weren't too upset by the commotion Cecilia caused on the ward earlier. She's a rebellious one.'

Jude sensed that the doctor referenced the incident not to reassure him, but to remind him.

'You, young man, seem to me to be far more rational than either of your friends. Wise beyond your years.'

Jude was unmoved by the doctor's flattery.

'Do you know why you are here? Why all of you are here?'

Jude slowly turned his head from side to side.

'The short answer is because I want you here. In fact, though you might find this hard to believe, you are better off here. In my, ah, care. Safer.'

Jude remained poker-faced, unimpressed by Frey's claims of magnanimity, but it was clear to Frey that he was at least listening.

'Make sure the girls know. They trust you, Jude. All this is for their own good. And for yours,' the doctor suggested ominously.

Jude smiled. Guilelessly, innocently, as he had at the nun a few moments earlier, but Frey's reaction was not a benevolent one. His persistence bordered on obsession. Jude was no longer sure if the doctor saw him as a source of irritation or whether he was simply using Jude to taunt himself. Either way, his displeasure in Jude's indifference was evident. His words began to flow more quickly. Manically. As if he was running out of time at a college lecture and trying to get every thought out.

'What you are suffering from is a kind of child abuse. A deep psychological and emotional trauma foisted on you first by Sebastian, then the church,' Frey opined, foamy white spittle collecting at the sides of his mouth. 'This is the power of religion. It makes saints of the confused and the vulnerable and glorifies them through the stupid and superstitious. It amplifies the young person's penchant for make-believe and naiveté with disastrous results.'

Jude dropped his chin to his chest, almost as if he'd gone to sleep on the doctor's scathing dissertation. Frey had barely noticed and continued with his speechifying.

'. . . Bringing with it guilt and shame and eternal damnation. I bring you relief from such supposed morality. Freedom.'

Jude's head suddenly snapped upright. His pupils widened and eyes focused squarely on Frey's. 'But no soul, Doctor,' the boy said, in a voice that was not his own. 'Nothing inside.'

Frey was stunned. Not only that the mute boy had spoken, but at the familiarity of the tone. The doctor recognized it. He held up a prescription bottle of psychoactive medications, rattled them and twisted off the child-protective cap, opening it.

'Don't bother looking too deeply inside yourself for a soul, Jude. It's right in here.'

Jesse's Delirium

*T*he wind blew gently across the patient's face, caressing it. The smell of roses hung thick in the breeze invading his nostrils, rousing him.

'Wake up, Jesse.'

The familiar voice seemed to come to him as if from a subway speaker in the darkened room. Crackling with static in the black night that spilled through the windows, barely comprehensible.

'I can't,' he moaned.

'You have to.'

'I'm so tired, Lucy.'

'You've been asleep a long time, Jesse.'

'My whole life, is that what you mean?'

'Weren't we all?'

Jesse stared up at the ceiling, wincing in pain, unable to move.

'My hands hurt.'

'I'm sorry.'

'It was my own fault.'

'No. It was brave.'

'It was stupid.'

'You did it for me. For all of us.'

'For what? I'm lying here like a cadaver.'

'You're still alive.'

'Always so hopeful. And confident, Lucy. I wish I had more of that.'

'Get up, Jesse.'

'Help me.'

'I can't.'

'You mean you won't. I think you like this.'

'No.'

'Come closer. I want to see you.' Jesse watched a shadow on the ceiling above him grow larger but could not hear her approaching. He turned his head to the side and she was there.

'There is work for you to do, Jesse.'

'I'm shot, Lucy. There's nothing left inside me.'

'I don't believe that. You're a fighter. A survivor. Remember all we went through.'

'You mean what I put you through. I shouldn't have.'

'You didn't make me do anything. No regrets, Jesse.'

'I was angry and jealous of those other kids at school. I wanted to show them what I had.'

'You did. We did. Now you need to show everybody.'

'I feel like I'm dreaming but not, you know.'

'I know.'

'Are you even here?'

Lucy shook her head no.

She reached for his injured hand and took it in hers. His pain subsided and his body strengthened at her touch.

'I don't understand. I see you,' Jesse said, tears welling in his eyes. 'I feel you.'

'I'm nowhere and everywhere.'

'They killed you didn't they? Frey and those fucking animals.'

'No, Jesse. I did what I had to do.'

Jesse began to shake in anger and frustration.

'This is all Sebastian's fault,' he wailed. 'I hate him!'

'Don't, Jesse. There is no blame.'

'He took you away from me!'

'He brought me to myself. He brought us together. Forever.'

'But you're gone, Lucy.'

'I am more here than I ever was. I am not forgotten. That's what matters.

That's your job. Your mission now.'

'Tell the story?'

'Write what you know.'

'I can't do it without you.'

'You can. You will.'

'We're a team.'

'And always will be.' Lucy smiled a never-ending smile. Bright and magnificent and contagious. Stars appeared about her head in an almost blinding headpiece, creating an otherworldly glow in the room.

'You're a star now, Lucy.'

She lowered her head and her blonde mane hung over his face. Tears of gold ran down her face and mixed with his. She brought her hair to his eyes and dried them, kissing his cheek three times.

'Please don't go. If you stay then it's not true that you're dead.'

'I died so that I could live, Jesse,' she said. 'We'll be together again someday, Jesse. Believe it. Laughing. Fighting.' He squeezed her hand tightly. 'And then I can tell you…'

'Tell me what?' Jesse pressed.

'How much I love you.'

It was growing faintly light. Jesse opened his eyes. Lucy was gone. If she was ever really there to begin with. He started to rise. Determined. He struggled up to a seated position despite the degenerated muscles in his arms and legs tightening. The pain was intense but he refused to cry out. The electrodes monitoring his heart rate and breathing pulled away as he sat up, sending out an alarm to the nurses' station.

He heard calls for Dr Frey made over the ward's PA system and the rush of nurses and orderlies coming towards the room. They looked at him, astonished. He looked back, thinking only one thing. With only one question in mind.

'Where's my laptop?'

4

Hardcore

Cecilia could only hear the argument going on outside her door in muffled strains.

'Step aside.'

'This is completely against all accepted medical practices,' the nurse declared defiantly. 'Against medical advice and not in this patient's best interest.'

'Step aside,' I said.

Cecilia put on a black tank, leather leggings and wrapped herself in a vintage see-thru embroidered black kimono. Down the back of her arms and across her back was the word S-A-I-N-T handwritten in black lipstick on her skin – showing through her frock.

'This patient was remanded to treatment here under Dr Frey's care before a trial. What you are doing is against the law.'

'I have a court order,' the officer said, producing a few sheets of paper and waving it under her nose. 'Take it up with the judge.'

'We'll see what the doctor has to say about this.'

The head nurse rushed down the hall to her desk and fumbled for the phone on her desk, pushing angrily at the dial pad. The men were not bothered by her threat.

Cecilia closed her eyes and smiled. She looked badass and beautiful. She looked ready.

The door was unlocked and opened.

'Miss Trent.'

'The one and only.'

'Please come with us.'

'From the crazy house to the big house?'

Cecilia was ushered out of her room. She stopped briefly at Agnes's door and planted a kiss on her window. Agnes jumped up and ran to her door, meeting Cecilia's lips with her own through the glass barrier. Cecilia continued down the hall past the front desk to angry stares. She returned them. As she waited for the elevator down from the penthouse, she looked repeatedly over her shoulder to make sure this wasn't some sort of set-up. She caught Jude's eye and blew him a kiss, mouthed "It's cool", and waved goodbye as the elevator doors opened.

He nodded but did not smile.

The elevator ride seemed to take forever and, as grateful as she was to the hunky escorts riding down with her, she felt uneasy. A feeling confirmed by the sweat beading suddenly on her brow and the droplets of blood pooling in her hands. The elevator car bounced to an uncertain halt and the doors opened. Cecilia was grabbed by either arm and whisked through the Perpetual Help lobby and out the front doors. The crowd that had gathered in her honour, to keep her name in the news, on the lips of the neighbourhood gossips, to free her from Frey's loony bin slash penthouse dungeon, seemed to need a minute to process that their mission, or at least half of it, had been accomplished. Her Apostles were screaming, waving signs, crying and chanting her name with joy at the sight of her, even as the body guards shoved past them, scattering them like bowling pins. A single voice stood out from the melee. 'Cecilia!'

'Catherine,' she called back, reaching for her friend.

Their outstretched fingers almost touching like live wires separated in a bundle of old ones.

'I tried to come see you,' Catherine yelled. 'But they wouldn't let me.'

'It's OK,' CeCe said, smiling at her, their eyes meeting though their hands could not. 'I'll find you.'

'C'mon,' one of the handlers ordered, nearly dragging Cecilia to the kerb. 'The car is here.'

All Cecilia could see was a black roof, approaching, like a lifeguard eyeing a shark near the surface of the water. The crowd parted. The rear door of the limousine was pushed open from the inside and Cecilia was pushed in, head first, like a perp in police cruiser. The cool clean smell of treated leather flooded her nostrils, forcing out the stench of piss and puke that had filled them since she'd arrived in the psych ward. She breathed in like a deep-sea diver coming up for air, oblivious to the man sitting directly across from her in the jump seat.

'Hello, Cecilia.'

'Mr Less?'

'How are you?'

'You did this? You got me out? How?'

'Frey is not the only man in this city with friends in law enforcement.'

'Apparently not.'

Cecilia was suddenly very aware of her appearance and began fussing with her hair, staring at her pale skin, licking her chapped lips and wiping at her bloodshot eyes. She felt her body tense up reflexively. Being in the back seat of a limo was a circumstance she was far too experienced with.

'Don't bother, you look great,' Less complimented.

'I look like death, and not in a good way,' Cecilia all but snarled.

'No, really, you look naturally beautiful.'

'For a mental patient.'

'You're not buying in to that nonsense are you?' Less asked, his lips curling into an uncommon smile. 'You're no crazier than the rest of the artists on my roster.'

'I wouldn't be so sure about that if I were you,' Cecilia warned, looking once again over her shoulder at the acolytes that had gathered for her.

'You're the real thing, Cecilia,' Less opined. 'What you have, money can't buy. All the publicists, marketing experts and A & R people couldn't manufacture it if they tried. And believe me they try. Every waking hour, they try.'

'You pay them a lot of money to try, don't you?'

'You see those people standing out there. Waiting for you. They are dedicated.'

'They are,' Cecilia mused.

'If they'll go to those lengths to get you out, imagine how many albums, tickets and T-shirts they'll be willing to buy.'

'I don't want to seem ungrateful, but I'm really not interested in any of that,' Cecilia explained. 'The only thing I want is the chance to play my music, to sing my songs to as many people as I can.'

'I can make that happen for you,' Less said, reaching into the breast pocket of his suit jacket. 'If I'm not mistaken, we still have some business to conclude.'

'Yeah, we do,' Cecilia agreed, changing the subject. 'My friend Agnes is still in there.'

'From what I understand, she was committed by her

mother,' Less explained. 'There is nothing I can do. I wish there was.'

The record man handed over the pages of a contract. Cecilia felt his approach a little insensitive but not insincere. She knew he was right and in both the case of Agnes' confinement and her own record deal.

'You don't fuck around, do you?'

'No time like the present.' Less smiled and handed her a pen.

Cecilia didn't bother to look it over. She grabbed the pen from his hand, signed her name and handed the contract back.

'Congratulations,' he said. 'You're mine now.'

'I'm not sure I like how that sounds.'

'On the contrary, now that you're one of my artists, it's more important that I like how you sound.'

The banter was playful, but Cecilia sensed seriousness in his tone that was all business, even when he was kidding around.

'I'll do my best,' she said.

'Just a little warning, Cecilia. The contact is standard, for seven years, but most artists don't make it that long. Maybe you'll be the exception.'

'Probably not,' she said matter-of-factly. 'I'm gonna use the time I have to maximum effect.'

As he folded the paperwork, she noticed him noticing a blotch on the contract. It was a bloodstain. She looked at her palms and saw her blood seeping out from them.

'Sorry,' she said. 'My hands have been bleeding since they took me to the hospital.'

'I wouldn't be the first executive to ask for a contract signed in blood,' he smiled, stashing the contract in his pocket with one hand and giving her a fresh, clean white handkerchief with the other. Cecilia balled it up and clasped her hands together.

'You haven't asked me anything about the charges or about myself. Why?'

'I know all I need to know, Cecilia.'

Less nodded and reached into his jacket pocket once again and produced a brand new smartphone.

'For you,' he said. '64 gigs. Apps loaded. Paid for.'

'Thanks but I'm not big on technology.'

'Well, I am. It's completely private. Only I will have the number.'

Cecilia accepted the phone. There was something exciting about it to her. An older, rich and powerful man pursuing her, rescuing her, courting her. She'd been in this position before, but never with anyone so respectable.

'Keeping tabs on me, Mr Less,' she said, the flirtatiousness in her voice a throwback to her old self.

'I always keep a close eye on my investments, Ms Trent.'

There was a long silence as the car sped over the bridge and worked its way up the lower east side into Alphabet City.

'Where are we going?' she asked.

'Home.'

'Whose home?'

'Yours.'

The limousine stopped near the corner of Avenue A and 2nd Street in front of a loft building. Less reached into his pocket and produced a set of keys.

'Apartment 13C,' he said. 'Make yourself comfortable.'

'Is this a joke?'

'No,' he said. 'It's a corporate apartment. A place where you can live and work. Where you will feel safe.'

As she stepped out of the car, she looked back at the mogul and then muttered, 'I'd give anything to see Frey's face right now.'

'Dr Frey!'

The nurse's shouts startled the doctor, who'd been carefully reviewing Cecilia's release order at his desk.

'What is it?' he called back.

'Come here, you need to see this.'

Frey strolled calmly down the hall to the room Cecilia had been in. The nurse was standing in the doorway nervously, seemingly afraid to walk in.

'What?'

The nurse pointed inside. At the wall over the cot where Cecilia had been sleeping. Frey stepped in.

Another man might have been stunned, aghast even, at what he saw. But Frey was not.

'What is that?' the nurse said, a shiver in her voice.

Frey studied the image on the wall. It was drawn vertically in blood. Like some odd mash up of graffiti and fresco. Three icons. A burning heart. A sword with a bow. A pair of eyes. Cecilia had been gone for hours but the blood was still bright red, not brown and dried, as he would have expected. The doctor imagined Cecilia dipping her fingers into her bloody palm like an artist swiping paint from a palette.

He stared long at hard at the images, especially the eyes. The longer he stared the wetter the blood on the wall became, until it began to drip like tears. The deeper he looked, the more they appeared to him to look back. Unblinking. Accusingly. Mockingly. Defiantly.

'Madness,' he said quietly, as much to himself as the nurse.

5

Beautifully spoken

Cecilia's limo sped off with a screech while Catherine stayed behind, not so much mingling with the crowd as observing them. The smell of fumes from the limo exhaust still lingered in the air at the kerbside of the Perpetual Help entrance. It was a noxious mixture of burning fuel and burning rubber but the artist in Catherine experienced it differently. It was the byproduct, what was left behind of something combustible. And if nothing else, Cecilia and the reaction to her, both on and off stage, was always fiery. Which is exactly what this crowd was, milling around with their signs and their chants now that Cecilia was gone.

She noticed a few of Cecilia's most rabid followers, the ones who were always closest to the stage at her gigs and had gotten closest to her just now, waving away the petrol gases frantically, covering their mouths. Catherine sucked it in. Let it burn her throat. Make her eyes water. It might have literally been the tail end of the experience, but it was still a part of it. A reminder that you had to take the bad with the good. Sometimes even the most beautiful things leave a stink, she thought. Like a decaying flower or a dead body.

Signs and placards rose over the throng like umbrellas on a rainy day, fighting for airspace, sporting words and phrases and symbols drawn out in bold letters in black, blue, purple, and red markers.

Some traditional and uplifting.

'Free Our Everyday Saints'
'Not your Grandmother's Saints'
'Pr@y 4 Us'
'Subway Saints'
'Have Mercy On Them'
'Justice for the Blessed'
'Faith will set you free!'
'St Cecilia Is My Homegirl'
'HELL No We Won't Go!'
'Don't let them Frey!'

Catherine shook her head and continued to wander

through the protest, rubbing shoulders with all types from true believers to rubberneckers. Some on their knees in prayer, some shouting in the direction of Frey's penthouse office and the psych ward, others preoccupied with their smartphones, posting pics of their own or photobombing someone else's, busily updating their statuses and instagramming whatever shots they could get of the fleeing saint. It was a 21st Century crowd and whatever their attention span, their motivation or depth of the commitment, they were there – and this was the thing that impressed Catherine the most. And the fact that the crowd had not dispersed, in fact, it had only grown, as if Cecilia's release had given them a collective shot in the arm. A shot of confidence. They'd taken time from their day, their lives, called off work, skipped school, put aside their chores, to do something they felt was important. Cecilia, Agnes, Sebastian and Lucy meant something to them, even if it was unclear exactly what.

Someone had obviously tipped off the news media about Cecilia's release. News teams had been dispatched from throughout the city. Print and broadcast. Bloggers. Network, local and cable. Everyone. Catherine stopped to listen to some of the interviews underway. First to the musings of an older white-haired couple, and from the crosses dangling from their necks, obviously religious.

'I just think it's a sign from God,' the elderly woman replied, her gentle voice catching with emotion. 'A reminder that there is good all around us. The world is becoming such an awful, dangerous place.'

'You can't deny it. The miracles and everything,' her husband added. 'Restores your faith.'

'In humanity?'

'In God,' he replied with both hope and cynicism. 'Humanity has a lot more work to do.'

Catherine smiled at their sincerity. If they really knew Cecilia and Lucy and Agnes, she mused, they might not approve of them one bit, but in the abstract, from a distance, they were on the same page. Her attention quickly turned to a crowd of young girls sporting Team Sebastian shirts, sacred heart chaplets stacked by the dozen on their wrists and milagro rosary necklaces. Saints of Sackett Street fangirls for lack of a better description, decked out in dime store accoutrements that seemed to be springing up in every bodega and gift shop window in the city. It wasn't so much their spiritual appeal, the empowerment message that inspired such devotion from the kids, Catherine thought, but their celebrity, the virally-fueled fame that powered this part of the movement. And it wasn't just Cecilia either, for better or worse, they were all rock stars now.

'This isn't gonna go well,' Catherine mumbled.

The reporter jutted the microphone into the girls' faces and started peppering them with questions.

'Why are you here?' the correspondent quizzed predictably.

'To show, like, our support,' one said overenthusiastically.

It could have been an Earth Day or animal rights or breast cancer event or a football game, Cat thought, and the answer would have been the same. The total flipside of the earnest elderly couple she'd heard interviewed a few moments earlier. But then a facile question deserved a facile answer. She could tell the newswoman was barely listening, waiting for the next question from the producer in the satellite truck to come into her earpiece. 'What do you say to people who think she's a murderer?'

'I think they're jealous,' one girl said, wearing an embellished sacred heart hoodie.

'She's totally being thrown under the bus,' another girl said, already copying Cecilia's look – writing S-A-I-N-T in black lipstick across her arms and chest.

'By who?' the reporter asked.

Silence and then a collective group shrug.

'Do you believe these girls are really saints?'

'I don't know,' said another girl, the arrow piercing in her eyebrow changing directions as her facial expression tightened. 'But I saw one of Cecilia's concerts online and I really love her music.'

'And Lucy is and will always be a style icon.'

'They're just like me and my friends. Especially Agnes. All my friends say she's my twinnie!' a third girl blurted, fixing the fresh flower crown atop her gorgeous red locks.

'So you're fans more than anything?'

'Yeah, we're fans. Of course we're fans.'

Each had a reason.

'*I* can't wait for Cecilia's album.'

'*I* was hoping to get a picture with her but they moved her along so fast.'

'*She dresses so badass.*'

'Are you happy that she was released?' the reporter probed.

'*Soooo* excited,' one replied, cheesing hard at the camera through her pricey orthodenture.

'I see you're wearing Sebastian on your T-shirts. Why?'

'He's *hot!*' they screamed, jumping up and down.

Catherine just smiled and moved along as the reporter ended the interview. There was a lesson in this for her, she thought. You don't really have a say in who your fans or followers are. But then, who was she to judge? Without much of a following of her own, she'd just as well cross that bridge if she ever came to it.

This was inevitable, this change in the sorts of followers they attracted as the crowds grew larger and attracted more and more attention, but just as inevitable was the fact that a less benign element would begin to infiltrate. Catherine could feel the menacing presence, like a serpent silently winding its way through tall grass surreptitiously seeking a victim.

A muffled cry and loud shouts rose unexpectedly from

behind her, the space she'd just left.

'Oh My God!'

'Jesus Christ!'

Catherine turned back towards the direction of the anguished voices but could barely move. Panic had already set in and the stampede begun. She was knocked to the ground, kicked and trampled. An avalanche of arms and legs pelting her. She couldn't tell whether any of it was intentional or not. The sounds of fear and fighting were all around. Sirens began to wail in the distance and bullhorns crackled with official commands. She felt for her forehead, which was cut and streaming blood.

Several masked and hooded men brandishing knives ran past her, knocking her sideways and laughing. Catherine locked eyes with one and could've sworn his pupils were burning. She couldn't be sure but she'd seen a look like that before from Ricky's crew when they held her down and assaulted her. Demons possessed by the same monstrous spirit.

'Don't we know each other?' he asked, bringing his blade to her eye.

Cat shook her head *no*.

'My bad.' He kicked her in the ribs as he passed and took off.

Dazed and bruised, Catherine tried to stand and limped towards the centre of the melee as the crowd thinned. She didn't run away, she ran towards the ones that might need help, despite any danger to herself.

A few yards closer to the entrance and Cat saw the reason for the panic. Bodies were strewn across the sidewalk and bleeding out. The old couple and teenagers who'd been interviewed. A cameraman and the frustrated reporter. All injured, or worse. Bloodstained, Some gasping for breath, moaning in pain. Clothes turn and stained. Sitting upright, looking blankly off in the distance. Shellshocked. Others, the old couple, hadn't moved at all. She got close and could see they were already ghostly pale and turning blue. Blood from their wounds pooling around them. She turned her attention to the girls.

Catherine leaped into action, kneeling before them and reassuring them until help arrived.

'I don't want to die,' one of the girls cried. 'Please don't let me die.'

'I won't,' Catherine swore.

She pulled off her jacket and tore at the bottom of her T-shirt, trying to staunch their bleeding. She screamed to the stunned hot-dog vendor for water, which he tossed over to her. She picked up the girls in the Team Sebastian shirts one at a time and gently washed the blood from their faces, and offered them a drink. Following Cat's example, strangers began to offer comfort, sympathy and help to other injured strangers. Runners stopped and picked up a few girls, darting them through the ER doors at Perpetual Help. Blood-soaked Sebastian shirts and all.

Emergency room personnel soon burst out from the ER entrance with gurneys and medic bags as fire trucks, police cruisers and EMTs arrived. Some officers began to cordon off the scene, using police tape stretched from light post to light post down the block, some began to interview witnesses, others took off in hot pursuit of the vandals who were responsible for the attack. Some in the earlier crowd began to slowly return, ashen-faced and with tears in their eyes, but nevertheless they had returned. Most, praying.

'Hey! You! Nurse Jackie!' a gruff voice shouted almost directly in her ear.

Catherine turned only to see a beefy male hand reaching for her shoulder. She froze for a second and then swung awkwardly at him in self-defence.

'Get away!' she screamed.

'Sorry,' he mumbled, pushing a camera in her face, 'I've got a live shot right now and I need a warm body to talk to.'

'I'm a mess,' she said, holding up her bloody palms and brushing away her matted hair.

'It's not a beauty contest. People need to know what just happened here.'

Something about the genuineness of the request touched Catherine, even in her disoriented and dishevelled state.

Somebody, she thought, had to be a witness and Fate had chosen her.

'OK,' she nodded. 'I'll do my best.'

'That's all I can ask for,' he said.

Just as the cameraman turned on the camera light to begin the interview, a human wedge of blue burst through the bystanders, clearing a path for Detective Murphy who'd only just arrived to take control of the crime scene.

'Back the fuck up!' a sergeant shouted, nearly knocking the newsman off his feet as he passed.

Murphy surveyed the carnage and then looked up purposefully towards the penthouse floor of Perpetual Help and stared accusingly for a good long while. He then began yelling instructions and commands to his subordinates. Catherine, whose ears were still ringing, could hardly hear any of what he was saying except for a single word that seemed to sum up the whole horrible situation. A truer word she thought, had never been spoken.

'Goddamnit!'

6

Saintitorium

Agnes sat impatiently, lifting her thighs up periodically to keep her bare skin from sticking to the pleather seat. It was chilly in the room so she had a chunky, oatmeal-coloured, hand-knitted cowl around her neck.

She crooked her neck and squinted, trying to see inside Frey's office, but the door was not far enough ajar. She'd been waiting for a while, same as usual. Same as since she'd been remanded to his care. Five-day-a-week sessions that were torture.

But the waiting was the worst. A not-so-subtle kind of power play reminding her that she was basically more prisoner than patient. Agnes was on the doctor's schedule. And the nurse's and the orderlies'. Even the janitor's. In the penthouse pecking order, she was at the bottom of the barrel. Scraps. Especially today, where everyone seemed preoccupied with yesterday's rioting outside.

No wonder, with the story on a seemingly endless loop on the local and cable news channels, fanning the flames of the division. They were headlines now, screaming from the front page of every tabloid in town from the looks of things, and though she should be used to it, Agnes still couldn't avoid a petty thought or two, bristling at unflattering pictures of her lifted from her social media sites by lazy news editors and producers to illustrate their sensational stories. They had papers to sell, and this was their business.

She thought about the victims, prayed for their recovery and couldn't help feeling responsible. Still there was nothing she could do but wait and hope that Cecilia would be safe.

The idle wait did, however, give her plenty of time to reflect. And she did. Not so much on events of the recent past, but on the hours and minutes that had brought her to Perpetual Help originally. It had all seemed a blur to her until recently but gradually she'd begun to make sense of it. The ambulance, the gurney, the stitches. Her own bad relationship decisions. Her mother blaming her for everything. Very little had changed apart from the wounds on her wrist, which had healed almost entirely. She pondered over her scar and imagined it now as a zipper. The place where

Sebastian had been able to enter her and where her old soul had departed. An escape hatch of sorts. She smiled at the idea and stretched her head out to see down the hall, but instead saw Jude. He was sitting right next to her. He'd come up on her silently.

'You shouldn't be here with me,' Agnes whispered. 'The nurses will tell. Frey will be furious.'

Jude shrugged indifferently. Agnes admired his fearlessness.

'Have you seen the crowds outside?'

He nodded *yes*.

'It's unbelievable.'

Jude smiled as if to say it wasn't.

'I heard the staff buzzing that it was probably pressure from the people downstairs that got Cecilia out,' Agnes enthused. 'I'm so happy for her.'

Jude's expression turned sombre. He shook his head *no*.

'What do you mean?' Agnes leaned toward him anxiously. 'Is something wrong?'

Frey's office door opened and Jude suddenly began to flap his arms and wave his hands. His head titled backwards and his eyes turned upwards. He was nervous.

'Hello, Agnes. Sorry to keep you waiting,' the doctor apologized. 'Hello Jude.'

Agnes eyed Frey with contempt and took Jude's shaky hand in hers, soothing him.

'It's OK,' Agnes said to him.

'Yes, Jude. It's OK. Run along now. You don't want to miss your therapy.'

The boy stood up and shuffled away, turning his head occasionally back towards Agnes and Frey as he meandered down the hallway.

'Please, come in, Miss Fremont.'

Frey stretched his arm out formally like an usher, guiding an audience member to her seat. Agnes got up, stepped inside his office and sat down in the chair across from his desk. Frey followed behind and closed the door.

'I want out of here,' Agnes insisted.

'Well that's no way to begin a conversation,' Frey opined. 'With a demand. We leave that for hostage-takers and bratty children.'

Agnes didn't take kindly to the slight. 'What happened to Cecilia?'

'She was released. I'm sure you've heard.'

'So you can kill her?'

'I had nothing to do with her release or the rioting I assure you, but if you are trying to say that she would have been safer in here with us? Judging from the events outside, you are both perceptive and correct.'

'Admit nothing, I get it. Just a little old-fashioned crowd control,' Agnes scoffed. 'It won't surprise you that I don't think of this place as a refuge.'

'For sick people, that is exactly what it is. Here we specialize in rehabilitation, not annihilation.'

'Sounds like a great tagline for your next brochure,' she said. 'But you're full of shit.'

'I appreciate your honesty, Agnes. I think we're making progress.'

'Can we *please* stop this game now?' Agnes snarked. 'You aren't talking to my mother. You're talking to me.'

'To Saint Agnes you mean?'

'Things are not the same as when I first came in here.'

'Clearly not,' Frey observed dryly.

'You've gotten away with a lot but not for much longer.'

'I might have expected those threats from Cecilia or even Lucy, but you surprise me.'

'Why, Doctor?' Agnes asked. 'I know who you are and you know who I am.'

'Yes, I know who you are. And I am not the only one.'

'You can't keep me in here forever. And even if you try, you can't stop what's happening outside.'

'Yes, outside,' Frey mused, looking down from his office window. 'That's the problem, isn't it?'

'For you. Not for me,' Agnes informed.

Frey paced behind his desk, continuing to stare downwards at the throng gathered in front of the hospital.

'Do you know who those people are, Agnes?'

'They believe in us, Doctor. You can't scare them away. That's all I need to know. And everything you need to fear.'

'Are you sure?' Frey suggested cryptically. 'Do you really want to place your freedom, your future, your, pardon the pun, *faith*, in that hashtag militia out there.'

'Can we stop pretending you actually care about me or any of us at all?' Agnes asked. 'I'd rather take my chances with them any day.'

'Sheep. Waiting to be led over a cliff by you three. With so much time on their hands they can spend their aimless days protesting in front of a busy hospital?'

'You missed your calling, Doctor,' Agnes conjectured.

'How do you mean?' Frey asked cautiously.

'You would have made an excellent high-school girl,' Agnes snarked. 'You have all the attributes – phony, undermining, backstabbing. Somewhat less appealing in a grown man though, I must say.'

'And for a high-school girl you make an excellent doddering old fool. Naïve, oblivious, stuck in the past, blindly loyal.'

'I'll take that as a compliment.'

'I'm sure you do,' Frey replied, making a quick conversational pivot. 'Have you ever heard of the Dunning-Kruger effect?'

'No,' she said dismissively, rubbing the spot on her wrist where her chaplet once hung. 'Should I?'

'It's a cognitive theory, recently developed. In essence it suggests that people suffering from illusory superiority seem to be incapable of accurately rating their own inabilities or even to recognize their own ineptitude. It wasn't meant to diagnose would-be saints and martyrs but I think it applies to Sebastian, Lucy, Cecilia and yourself quite nicely.'

'Did you discover it looking in the mirror, Doctor?' Agnes sassed. 'You're in *such* denial.'

'No, but you are making my point without even realizing it. You see the miscalibration of the incompetent, or in our case, the delusional, stems from a fundamental error about the self.'

Agnes was unimpressed with Frey's theorizing.

'Sounds like cherry-picking, Doctor,' Agnes said scornfully. 'You aren't the only one with a theory today. Have you ever heard of bikeshedding? Look it up.'

'You are indeed a clever girl, Agnes. Perhaps a bit too clever.'

'You mean a wise-ass, don't you? Disrespectful and condescending of your authority, your age and experience.'

'It's part of your illness, Agnes. I don't take my patient's criticisms personally.'

'Patients? We're your prisoners.'

'Not *my* prisoner dear. A prisoner of your own making. Not mine.'

'You talk about illusions. This whole charade. Treatment. Therapy. That's the illusion. We both know why you corralled us here. But Cecilia's out now. And the crowds outside are growing, Doctor, despite your best efforts.'

'Narcissists just like you all,' Frey replied imperiously. 'How many among them should be up here instead of down there?'

'Every single one of them, if you have your way.'

'Angry mobs can be unpredictable, Agnes, and crowds are the perfect place for dangerous people to hide, as we have just witnessed.'

'What are you implying?'

'Nothing more than what must be obvious to you. Not everyone wishes you and your supporters well.'

Agnes laughed out loud, unable to contain her derision. 'Including present company.'

'Believe me, it could be worse, Agnes.'

'A prediction, Doctor?'

'No,' Frey answered bluntly. 'An observation. Outside, you are beyond our protection.'

'You mean your control.'

'I may not be the worst you have to fear.'

Agnes lifted herself partly out of her chair, bringing herself closer to Frey. Confronting him as she hadn't ever before.

'Do I look frightened to you?'

'If you had any instinct for self-preservation left, instead of a perverse death wish, you might well be.'

'I'm not afraid, Doctor, because I know the difference between my friends and my enemies. There is a certain comfort in knowing your enemy. Being able to look him in the eye.'

Frey smiled dismissively, increasingly mystified by the girl's steadfastness. He took her in. The pale skin, the amber curls falling and twisting downwards over her cowl, the delicate hands. She looked the same as the first time they'd met. Except her eyes, which seemed to burn with clarity, with a steely confidence. With faith, if not in a higher power, then in her own self. The emotional wreck, barely held together with nylon stitches and gauze wrapping, who had once washed up in his office had been salvaged, repaired – but not by him. Not by his expertise as a therapist, by his prescriptions, potions and powers of persuasion. She'd been saved, though he was loathed to admit it, by love.

'I envy you in some ways, Agnes. How blithe you appear. Sitting here, in your hospital gown, committed involuntarily to a psychiatric ward, looking as if you don't have a care in the world. I never imagined Sebastian could have such a hold on you. On any of you.'

The doctor spoke those last words more as an aside to himself, she thought. Comments not really meant for her ears yet too honest for him to keep inside. Cecilia had slipped from his grasp and now the truth too was slipping out. It was all slipping away.

'You underestimated him and us, Dr Frey. You underestimated what love can accomplish.'

'Yes, it is plain to see what love can accomplish, said the girl in the straightjacket,' Frey replied snidely. 'Any other greeting card wisdom to share?'

'I think you're feeling pressured, Dr Frey,' Agnes proffered. 'And more than a little irritated that a few teenagers and their fan mob might just be responsible for pulling the curtain back on your whole fucking shady network.'

'Can't you see, I'm trying to save you, sweet, dear girl.'

'I'll save myself.'

Frey balked at the phrasing, a bemused expression crossing his face.

'Ah, the man of the hour rears his head,' Frey said. 'You risk your future, your life for a total stranger. A lost ghost. I don't know why I should be surprised. You're suicidal.'

'Then let me go?' Agnes offered slyly. 'No matter how many pills, bull sessions or shock treatments you prescribe, I won't change.'

Frey stared hard at the young girl across from him. He noticed her curls flowing down over her patient's gown, her vulnerability, but the girl he'd met not long ago was gone. The look of determination in her eyes told him what he needed to know, confirming his worst fears and reaffirming his worst instincts. It was time, he'd decided, for a new strategy.

'As you wish. Since you are determined to see this through to the end. I'll sign the papers and have a word with your mother.'

There seemed to her something unusually and increasingly resigned in the doctor's tone, as if he actually meant the things he was saying. Perhaps, she thought for just a fleeting moment, the loss of Cecilia had chastened him. But then she remembered. Frey was cowed by nothing and no one and, if anything, he'd come back stronger from each setback.

She refused to let down her guard.

'You'll release me?'

Agnes's face with filled with joy and then suspicion. She knew Frey too well to believe that he would just let her go without some ulterior motive, that in letting her go the doctor was not granting her freedom but almost certainly replacing a life of incarceration with a death sentence.

'I think we've covered everything,' Frey said without actually answering her.

'Yes, we've covered everything.'

'Don't say you weren't warned.'

Frey closed her file and tossed it casually to the windowsill behind him.

'What about Jude and Jesse?'

'You will all be free to go.'

Frey's frustration was evident to her but deep inside she couldn't help but feel that she'd been invited to a dance, a *pas de deux*, carefully choreographed, and the music had just stopped. It had reached a conclusion. Their session and their patience for each other.

'Thank God,' she whispered simply and turned her eyes toward the office window to the relentless, unwavering crowd outside. 'And them.'

'Spare me the piety, Agnes,' Frey snapped, removing his glasses and placing them on his desk. 'Those stragglers outside aren't there for *you*. They are out there for themselves. For the

71

cameras. For the attention. For the parade. And once it passes, so will they, on to the next big thing, and you will be forgotten. That is at best.'

Agnes stood up and backed out of the room, her eyes locked on Frey's like a wary opponent. Neither blinked.

'Like they've forgotten Lucy?' Agnes said as she left. 'You're losing, Doctor. Did you ever think the parade might just be starting?'

7

Username

Jesse gathered his things, zipped up his bag and walked out of his hospital bedroom under his own power for the first time since he'd arrived. He was still sore. His head still hurt every time he put his foot down and the puncture wounds, mostly healed now, in his hands ached as he grabbed for the strap. He walked slowly, cautiously to the reception area to fill out his discharge papers and noticed a beautiful girl standing there in a vintage emerald-green mini-dress and leggings, already waiting at the desk, 'Agnes?'

'Jesse!' Agnes leaned in and held him tight. Jesse dropped his bagged and hugged her back, with all his strength he had in him.

'I heard you were here,' he said, a worried tone in his voice, only vaguely aware of what had transpired since his arrival there.

Agnes looked at him sympathetically, sad for the time he'd clearly lost and things he'd missed while in the coma. Jesse had always been so on top of things, it was odd for her to see him appearing so fragile and uninformed.

'Yes, my mother is picking me up. Frey released me.'

Jesse raised an eyebrow and Agnes shrugged, seconding his scepticism.

'Cecilia?' he asked.

'She's already out, against Frey's wishes.'

Another sceptical expression crossed Jesse's face, this time it was mixed with trepidation.

Agnes brushed a comforting hand along his cheek.

'You're going home, Jesse. For a minute there we didn't think you were going to make it. You're alive. And you're going home.'

'Lucy's not,' he said.

'She's bigger than life now, Jesse,' Agnes whispered. 'No one can delete her. She's forever. You understand?'

'Sorry but it's not a very comforting thought to me,' he said. 'All I know is she's dead.'

'She knew what you did for her Jesse, we all did. She was the first one at your bedside when you were taken here.'

'She let her guard down because of me. They got her

because of me.'

Jesse's lip began to quiver.

'Miss Fremont,' the nurse said, calling her to the desk.

'Yes,' she said, taken aback by the charge nurse's politeness.

'Everything seems to be in order. Dr Frey has signed your paperwork. You're free to go.'

Agnes took the paperwork and half expected the nurse to pull it back, but she didn't. The nurse gave her a large tote bag made out of teal, red and gold vintage carpet with leather straps, Agnes's boho bag, and then handed her a plastic baggie with her green turquoise, crystal and gold gypsy jewellery – rings and bangles.

'Thanks,' Agnes said politely, glancing back over her shoulder at Jesse.

'Be careful out there,' the nurse said with a smile.

'Be careful in *here*,' she warned. 'The lunatics are running this asylum.'

The nurse just smiled condescendingly.

'Your mother is waiting for you in the lobby downstairs.'

Agnes should have been cheered by that thought, but she wasn't. She turned back to Jesse and gave him a soft kiss goodbye on the cheek.

'I'm glad you're OK,' Agnes said, some tears welling in her eyes. 'Call me when you're settled,' she said, putting on her jewellery like armour – bangles up her arm and rings on almost every finger, some had more than one. She took out a black enamel brush with red, blue and yellow roses on it, and brushed her long gorgeous copper hair for the first time since she could remember.

'I'm not sure we should be together for a while, Agnes, any of us. We both know this is bullshit. Whatever reason we are being let go, it's not an act of kindness. Frey won't give up.'

'I'm not afraid,' Agnes said, throwing her brush back in her bag.

'Yeah, well, I've heard that before. You should be. We should all be.'

'Never. Not as long as we have each other,' Agnes insisted, kissing him on the cheek once more. 'And we'll always have each other, no matter what. I love you.'

Agnes smiled sweetly and headed for the elevator. She waited for it to arrive more patiently then she would have thought, glancing back again at Jesse in relief, watching him finish up his paperwork, almost in disbelief that he was upright. He looked weak and frail to her, broken, and not just physically. Beyond his own trauma, it was obvious to her that Lucy's death was weighing heavily on him. She felt for him. He appeared lost and vulnerable, like a widow grieving a longtime spouse. More than that, it seemed to her he felt responsible in some way. Much more. Neither he nor Lucy had ever discussed their relationship with her, but one thing was for sure. It was complicated. In so much as Jesse could love anyone, she believed he loved Lucy.

There was definitely a practical side to it, she thought. Without Lucy neither of them would have existed, and vice versa, not in the way that they did. She remembered before she'd ever met Lucy that night in the church, she'd read about her on Byte. All her friends had. They dreamed secretly and not so – secretly of being her, of having someone be so obsessively into them that they could force them as a topic of conversation. Lucy and Jesse were a team, professionally, but it was the personal side that drove the entire thing, Agnes could now see. And this was at the heart of Jesse's problem with Sebastian. He was jealous of him. It was something Lucy had that he didn't arrange and promote. Something bigger, which Lucy sensed right from the start. And apparently so did Jesse. The fact that his jealousy turned into resentment and scepticism was normal under the circumstances, but offering himself up like that against the vandals, sacrificing himself, was an act of pure unselfishness. He fought not just to save her life, but also to prove his bona fides to her. His sincerity. His love. Now it was obvious to Agnes that he was blaming himself.

The elevator doors slid open and Agnes got in. She rode it down to the lobby where her mother was waiting, as she'd been told.

'It's about time,' Martha groused. 'I've been standing around here for an hour.'

'Hello, mother,' Agnes said snidely.

'Well, you got what you wanted, Agnes. I hope you make

the most of it.' Martha took her firmly by the arm and tugged. The crowd noise from outside was nearly maddening as they approached the hospital exit. A swarm of people, mostly followers, nearly blocked the doorway, but the police were now out in full force and cleared a partial path to the kerb for them.

As Agnes exited, a loud cheer of gratitude went up from people excited to see her but also thrilled to know that they must have played some part in her release. They threw rose petals at her feet, placed gorgeous flower wreaths on her head, and slipped her notes, pleas and wishes, and artful sacred heart milagros in every shape and size, were given to her, made for her. They reached for her, to take her hand, and she reached back for them.

'Thank you,' Agnes said as she passed her supporters. 'I'm free because of you.'

'Crazy breeds crazy,' Martha groused resentfully. 'You're free because of me.'

The crowd parted for Agnes as she walked around her mother's car to shouts of encouragement and solidarity. She grasped the door handle to open it and paused for a moment to survey the swelling crowd and to look up at the hospital building, to the very top. To the penthouse where she'd been held captive. In the window of the corner office she could barely make out the silhouette of a man. More shadow than substance. Looking down at the scene below him. At her.

She got in the car – beautiful, thoughtful, handmade gifts being thrown inside up until the last second, and closed the door. Jesse was right. Frey was watching.

Cecilia pottered around her new pad restlessly. Moving from the tufted beige sofa to the modern kitchen to the pimped out mini-recording studio that had been set up for her in one of the three bedrooms. She peeked out the living room window and was both relieved and surprised to find that there was no one on the street below. She was safe here, just as Less had promised.

She wasn't used to this kind of luxury. Luxury of any sort, in fact, and it was making her uncomfortable. She flipped open the gleaming stainless-steel encased laptop and noticed a card sitting on the keyboard.

Life is short.

Enjoy,

Daniel

The note brought a smile to Cecilia's face, the first one she could remember in a long while. *Life is short.* He had no idea how right he was or what he was getting himself into, she thought. Life might well be short. Especially in her case. And she still had a lot to do. As motivational maxims went, this was as good as any. A call to action, both practical and, now, contractual as well. He'd made an investment in her, she concluded, and he needed to stay on top of it. The phone, the furnishings, equipment, technology, the apartment. It cost money. Lots of money. He was betting big on her.

A sudden and familiar wave of anxiety raced through her mind. The sort of feeling she used to get before Sebastian came into her life, whenever a big opportunity presented itself, be it a hot guy or a hot gig. Less was touching something deep inside of her. Something she'd buried. Her desire for success, for the big time. Here it was, offered to her on a silver platter. Where once she might have jumped into Less's arms or into his bed for such an opportunity, for even the promise of it, she was now torn. Between who she was then, who she'd planned and struggled to be, and who she was now. A girl on a different kind of mission, on a different career path. Careers in the music business could be short, but not as short as the journey she was on.

Maybe it was the fact that he'd saved her from Frey that conjured up such deep feelings of gratitude and, if she were being honest with herself, affection. It was the same with Sebastian. He'd freed her too, but in a whole different way and she was struggling not to imprison herself again. She felt herself slipping.

Cecilia sat down at the computer and booted it up. All the music software she knew by heart was pre-loaded. If there wasn't any inspiration for her in this situation, in the conflicted feelings raging through her, she might as well hang it up.

She began to tinker at first, making random drum loops

of beats. Building the track in her imagination from the bottom up. She'd had a song in her head for weeks now but getting it out was a whole different story. She teased out her feeling, her thoughts into separate rhythms, bass and melody, like woollen strands from a tangled ball of yarn. She grabbed her guitar and recorded a riff to add to her mix, fashioning each part into a whole.

Cecilia channelled what she was feeling for Sebastian and everything he meant to her. And her sadness and anger and pride at Lucy's death. There were so many conflicting emotions to draw from about so many things. Her confusion about the future and the gratitude she was feeling for the executive and for the crowds that had stood outside day and night on her behalf. The music flowed freely from her now, like blood from a wound. The beats were powerful; booming so loudly she worried her high-end neighbours might be disturbed from their night's sleep. The keyboards and guitars were spare and dreamy, translating her feelings into an atmosphere of sound. It all came together quickly and organically, as the best songs always do.

Cecilia was bleeding from her heart now, it was pouring into the recording console drop by drop. It was the sound of her soul.

You are my agony.
You are my joy.

You are the part of me,
They can never destroy.

No sooner had Agnes and Martha sped away than a shrill voice burst suddenly through Dr Frey's speakerphone.

'Dr Frey, your call has come in.'

'Hello, Captain.'

'You called?'

'Yes, I wanted some explanation as to the release of Cecilia Trent. Are you in the habit of letting psychotic murderers walk the street?'

'It wasn't my call,' Murphy said abruptly.

'But you didn't fight it either?'

'No, I didn't. I arrested her. We did our job. The evidence is thin.'

'That never stopped you before.'

'There are powerful forces at work on her behalf, Doctor. You understand how these things work.'

The sarcasm in the police captain's voice was not lost on the doctor.

'And by powerful forces you mean Daniel Less?'

'He's a billionaire media mogul with connections, Dr Frey. And a colleague of yours, isn't he?'

Like a good cop, Murphy was prodding. Frey was perturbed.

'He's a pimp, detective.'

Murphy let the characterization go unchallenged as he had

little use for either the doctor or the music man, but he was nevertheless curious about the rivalry, at the adversarial relationship that existed between the two men. It was the first he was hearing of it.

'Pressure was put on and the judge signed the order. It's out of my hands.'

'Unless she kills someone else.'

'It's not clear to me that she killed anyone. And you weren't beyond pulling strings to get her held at Perpetual Help instead of the jailhouse,' Murphy reminded him.

'She's mentally ill. Observation and treatment was, and still is, the best course.'

'There were a lot of other fingerprints on that letter opener, Doctor. Some traceable to patients in your ward and at Born Again.'

'Are you implying something, Captain?'

'I don't imply, Doctor. I deal with facts and the facts are contradictory,' he said.

'Aren't they always?'

'All I'm saying is that Less, or whoever sprung her, did you a favour.'

'I'll be sure to send a thank you note.'

'You know, it's not clear that preppy kid that was killed didn't try to rape your other patient,' Murphy posited. 'Maybe we were looking at the wrong girl.'

'I don't find Mrs Fremont to be homicidal, Detective.'

'With all due respect, she had motive and she's good with a blade, if you catch my drift. Any half-assed lawyer would get Cecilia acquitted in a heartbeat. Not to mention the pressure being put on by those groupies and news crews lining up outside the hospital.'

'So now we make our legal decisions based on public opinion? A lot of so-called *witches* got burned in town squares that way.'

'And sometimes it's the townspeople that get burned,' Murphy said. 'When they get in the way, create an embarrassment, cause too much of a fuss?'

Frey had been waiting for Murphy to connect him to the violence outside the hospital and the Captain didn't disappoint.

'Another insinuation, Detective? That situation had nothing to do with me. You should really try being more direct. Maybe some therapy would be helpful?'

'I'll consider it, Doctor.' Murphy said sarcastically. 'Know any good psychiatrists?'

Frey dismissed the jibe. 'Back to the reason for this conversation, Captain. Cecilia is your problem now. Mark my words.'

'Thanks for the tip, Dr Frey. Frankly, I don't think the case will ever go to trial.'

'Finally, something I think we can agree upon, Detective. She won't make it to trial.'

* * *

Hazel sat in the back of the class at the end of her final period, nearly dozing off until the phone in her oversize faux fur fox bag began to hum. She reached for it stealthily, while the teacher's back was turned, punched in her security code and tapped on her message list.

'Yay,' Hazel whispered almost inaudibly as she read Agnes's text.

It was short but sweet as could be: *I'm home. Come cuddle.*

Another girl sitting just behind glanced over at Hazel's phone message and nodded to yet another classmate. Hazel had a weird feeling. She felt their eyes on her, but then that was nothing new these days. Her friendship with Agnes, her loyalty to her, had made her a sort of pariah, not just in her classes but in the school. The other girl's suspicion, Hazel had decided, wasn't such a bad thing. In fact, it was oddly liberating for her. She no longer needed to seek their friendship or their approval. Invites to parties had stopped coming long ago, but whatever the impact on her social life, Hazel knew that Agnes was worth the sacrifice. She subscribed to the age-old axiom of life, of relationships and of parties: you dance with the one who brought you. And in this regard, Agnes was her life partner.

The bell rang but Hazel took her time leaving as the class and the school emptied out for the day. She texted Agnes back and returned a few emails, reached for her bag, slung it across her shoulder and walked back toward the classroom door and out into the hall. She'd all but passed the last girls' bathroom before the exit when she felt a sudden urge to pee. Her classmates, the two that sat behind were standing outside the door. They'd changed out of their Catholic school uniforms and penny loafers into tattered low-rise jeans and crop tops.

'You guys waiting?' Hazel asked politely.

'No, go ahead in,' one offered, even holding the door open.

'Thanks,' Hazel replied and stepped inside.

She went inside the stall and relieved herself quickly, anxious to get home, change and then to Agnes's place for some vegan grub and gossip. She walked over to the sink, washed her hands, dried them and looked down into her bag, rummaging around for some lip gloss. As she brought it to her lips, she suddenly saw the reflection in the bathroom mirror of the two girls, standing right behind her. A little too close for comfort.

'Can I help you?' Hazel asked the two girls in the mirror.

'On the contrary, you're the one that needs help and it's gonna take more than a little lipstick.'

'Yeah,' the other girl said. 'You should really do something about those gumby shoulders of yours.'

'And those flabs.'

'*Flabs*?'

'Give it a goog, fat ass.'

'Oh, abs. *flabs*. I get it, asscrack,' Hazel mocked, snapping the cheesy thong riding up the girl's hip. 'Hey did a pole come with that dress?' Hazel asked of her whorish outfit.

The girls moved closer together, shoulder to shoulder, blocking Hazel's path. One of them produced a cigarette lighter, the other a joint.

'You smoke?' one asked rhetorically, taking a deep toke on the fat blunt.

'Course not,' the other said, reaching for the spliff. 'She's too good for that.'

'Listen,' Hazel said calmly. 'I don't know what's up here but I got no problem so I'm gonna go now.'

The girls didn't budge. Hazel tried to push through them but they pushed her back towards the sink.

'Who texted you?'

'None of your business,' Hazel snapped.

'Was it your virgin bae from the mental ward?'

'Lying ratchet skank,' the other laughed, exhaling.

'Shut up, you fucking trolls,' Hazel yelled, ready for the fight that was coming whether she wanted it to or not.

'She better not be coming back here,' one of them warned.

'Yeah, she's making us all look like fucktards.'

'If the tampon fits . . .' Hazel said.

Hazel looked both girls in the eyes. 'Get outta my way,' she shouted, rushing them again, hoping that a teacher, janitor or student leaving detention would hear.

She was cracked in the jaw by an elbow and fell backwards. One of the girls grabbed a handful of her hair and slammed her face into the mirror. It shattered on impact cutting her cheek, the bridge of her nose and eyebrow. She wanted to fight back but dropped to the floor, dazed and still under assault. They kicked her ribs from each side with their hard leather ankle boots. She felt herself ready to vomit. Her attackers screamed like banshees and lifted her to her feet.

'Now *she* looks like a martyr,' one of the girls observed heartlessly.

'Hang on, I want to gram this.'

She took Hazel by the chin, steadied her and snapped a few pictures.

The bullies let her go and Hazel dropped once again to the floor. She was dragged over to the toilet bowl by her hair.

'Look at yourself and ask yourself . . .' Hazel's head was dunked in the toilet, four times, punctuating each of the following words: 'Is. She. Worth. It?'

Hazel coughed her lungs clear as the attackers laughed at her distress. Drenched, she could smell the ammonia from the janitor's pail and the mildew from aging pipes fill her bloody nostrils. She crawled on her hands, sliding along the mouldy and urine-stained tile floor.

'Well, is she?'

One last kick to the face and a question and the girls snuck away. Hazel grabbed the edges of the white porcelain sink. Pulled herself up. She looked at her cut and bruised face and swollen lips in the cracked mirror and answered their question.

'Yes.'

8

Devil's Mirror

Daniel Less arrived at the dimly lit Bushwick joint to find Alan Frey already seated at a table in the back of the neighbourhood cafe. To see such well-dressed and well-known men would not have seemed out of place in midtown or the Upper East Side of Manhattan, but here nobody knew them. Exactly as they'd planned. Less strode to the table, his usual confidence on display in every fibre of his being. Frey watched him warily as he approached.

'Alan,' the executive greeted, taking a seat across from Frey.

'Daniel, thank you for coming.'

'My pleasure.'

'I ordered an espresso for you.'

'Very kind, thank you.'

Both men sipped at their coffees, eyes locked on each other over the rim of their cups. Less looked away for a moment, over Frey's shoulders towards the open and overfilled burlap sacks of espresso beans that lined the shelves along the back wall of the cafe. Just above the shelf, impossible to miss, were religious portraits – Saint Jerome holding a skull, Virgin Mary stepping on a serpent, Jesus with a sacred heart bursting from his chest, Saint Theresa surrounded by gorgeous flowers, and others. They appeared to be old, more than likely brought over from the old country and still a common sight in family businesses in these immigrant Brooklyn neighbourhoods. Old, familiar portraits, except for one. A new one. A portrait of Lucy. She was dressed in a gold gilded gown, a crown of thorns and stars around rested on her head over her coiffed blonde locks; her eyes were closed and dripping blood. She was standing on red roses and holding her penetrating blue eyes on a hot pink plate. A turquoise votive candle was flickering wildly beneath it.

'Couldn't you have found an organic market for us to have a cup of coffee and a chat?' Daniel asked, pointing indifferently towards the back wall.

Frey didn't need to look. He knew what Less was referencing.

'The coffee is better here,' Frey answered. 'And it's easier to focus on our, shall we say, issues.'

'I didn't come for a therapy session, Alan. This is a strategy session.'

Perhaps not, the doctor thought, but between Les and Murphy he could hardly think of two men more in need of care.

'Yes. Strategy. That was quite a stunt you pulled.' The doctor was in no mood to mince words.

'Cecilia, you mean?'

'Yes,' Frey said.

'Something had to be done, Alan. As I told you in our gathering, your approach was failing and time is of the essence.'

'Surely you don't think you need to lecture me on the efficacy of my treatment plan for her or the others.'

'Your plan as it were yielded nothing, in fact it was doing more harm than good.

'And your expertise in psychiatry derives from all of those psychotic wannabe pop tarts you date and dump?'

'If you're implying that my interest in the girl extends beyond our mission, you are wrong.' Less smiled, his teeth big and gleaming white in contrast to the salt and pepper goatee surrounding them. 'Mostly.'

'I'm not here to evaluate you, Daniel. That would take too long.'

'Then why are we here, Alan? For you to vent at losing Cecilia? To cover for your own incompetence?'

'Incompetence? I had all of them in my care. Under my control.'

'Yes, quite famously in your care, unfortunately. While the

crowds outside grew larger and more and more media trucks parked outside the hospital door, which, by the way, were undeterred and grew larger still when your minions went on the attack. It's a grassroots groundswell. The most dangerous kind.'

'Since when are you afraid of the press, Daniel?'

'I'm not afraid, nor am I stupid,' Less griped. 'It doesn't take a shrink to see the effect these girls are having on the public, and the media taking up their cause does us no good whatsoever. Quite the opposite in fact.'

'Weak-minded, looking for something to latch on to,' Frey groused. 'To feel part of.'

'Maybe so, but we can't take that chance. I warned you I would take matters into my own hands.'

'You *warned* me?'

'Even the police are becoming suspicious of you, am I right? Cecilia would have been released sooner or later and you might have become a target of the investigation. I did you a favour.'

'In my own way, in my own time, I would have achieved the desired result.'

'Have you taken a look at the wall behind you, Alan? Do you recognize that girl at the end? Memorialized in the pantheon of misfits they worship as saints.' Less growled. 'They are winning. We are losing.'

The irony that Less would echo Agnes's sentiments was not lost on Frey.

'Your way, we may win the battle. But we lose the war. It's short-term thinking. They need to be re-programmed.'

'The war analogy is a good one, Doctor. The problem is that Generals are always fighting the last war. For centuries now we've been content to let the culture do our work for us. A few steps forward, a few back, but always moving ahead, leaving the old ways in the dust without anyone ever noticing or powerless to do anything about it. Customs, laws, rules all changed in our favour. But it's different now.'

'Yes it is, Daniel. We have the tools. We control the levers of power. How we proceed will be the difference between our survival or extinction.'

'We live in an attention deficit society, Doctor. You of all people should know this,' Less continued. 'Out of sight, out of mind. They don't need to be persuaded they are deluded, nor does anyone else. I am interested only in their extinction. They need to be eliminated. People will forget soon enough.'

Frey pointed back at the old portraits on the wall.

'No, Daniel, people don't forget.'

Less backed off only slightly. 'We don't have time for twelve-step programmes and drug therapies, Alan. It failed with Sebastian and you gave no indication it would be any different with the girls.'

'You don't give me enough credit, Daniel. You never did, and yet it was I who identified the threat from Sebastian and from the girls and confronted it. Not you nor any of the others.'

Less took a long sip of his espresso.

'Yes, I see now that was a mistake. One I won't make again.' Less insulted. 'Do you know what your problem is, Doctor?'

'Now this is a consultation? All right, you tell me what my problem is.'

'I think you have a martyr complex of your own.'

Frey laughed loudly enough to attract the attention of the cashier at the front of the store.

'I hope you didn't lose any sleep dreaming up that theory, Daniel.'

'You appeal to the head. The mind. I appeal to the gut.'

'Sorry, but I don't follow you.'

'Of course you don't. You have been trying all this time to persuade Cecilia of what she isn't. That's a fight you can't win. What I have given Cecilia is what she most desires.'

Frey shifted uncomfortably in his chair, irritated at the umbrage his colleague had taken.

'She doesn't want to be what she was, can't you see that?'

'Wrong. She wants it as much as ever. It's just buried. I'm going to dig it up. Make her face it. You want to change people Alan, convert them to your view. I want to encourage her to be who she really is. And that will be her undoing.'

'The rock star is no longer who she is or wants to be, Daniel.'

'Wanna put money on that?'

'Temptation? That's your strategy?'

'Time-tested. You were a priest, you should know better.'

Frey bristled at the characterization and the reminder. 'We aren't betting a few bucks here. We are betting on our future. On *the* future. This is not a hand of blackjack, Daniel.'

'Isn't it? She will be weakened. Her loyalty divided. Her spirit broken. Her mind confused. Vulnerable,' he said sipping the last of his espresso. 'The heart wants what the heart wants.'

'You don't know Cecilia.'

'You want to fix her, Alan. I want to break her,' Less advised. 'One side is going to win and the other is going to lose. This isn't the Little League where everyone gets a trophy. I'm making sure the deck is stacked in our favour.'

'You've interfered in my work.'

'*Our* work.'

'Well then you'll have *your* work cut out for you.'

'How so?'

'I released Agnes yesterday and that irritating blogger. It's in your hands now.'

'Taking your ball and going home, Doctor?'

'There's no spite in it. All theories need to be tested including yours. The scientist in me, you understand.'

Frey was goading Less, challenging him. Releasing Agnes and Jesse was a petulant act but not an impulsive or irrational one. Less understood this was the doctor's way of pushing back, of staking out his territory against a threat even more repugnant to Frey than the girls: loss of his own position and relevance. Less remained cool and didn't bite.

'You seem to be taking this rather personally, Doctor.'

'On the contrary, it's strictly business, Daniel.'

The executive eyed the psychiatrist sceptically and prioritized the task at hand.

'Agnes can wait. The boy can be managed. The blogger is a sideshow. Cecilia is at the top of my agenda now.'

'You approach everything as a business, Daniel. I think the music industry has finally gotten to you.'

'And your analytic, therapeutic approach to things has gotten to *you*, Dr Frey,' Less hissed with contempt. 'You are trapped in the process.'

'There is an order to things. First a problem must be identified and understood clearly.'

'It is not enough to identify problems. They must be solved.'

'I have people to solve them.'

'How has that worked out for us so far?' Less sniped. 'You rely too heavily on those minions. They are erratic and attract unwanted attention. Instead of scaring the crowds off, they've only emboldened them. There are some things one must do personally to be sure they are done properly.'

'I knew you were a devious and deceitful man, Daniel, but even I didn't suspect that under the expensive suit and manicured fingernails was the soul of a Mafia hit man.'

'Coming from you I'll take that as a compliment, Doctor. I

learned early on there's no good in being a backstabber unless you're willing to put the knife in yourself.'

'It's quite a business you're in, Daniel.'

'Indeed, Alan,' Daniel said. 'It's cut-throat.'

9

Cult of You

Jesse walked the Brooklyn streets he'd known for years now as if it were the first time. All the clichés about the feel of the sun on his face, the concrete ground beneath his feet, rushed through his head. Unlike the reception waiting for Cecilia and Agnes, his departure from Perpetual Help was barely noticed. He'd left through a side entrance undetected, which, he thought, was fine with him.

He was wobbly from pain and moving slowly. Like an elderly man instead of the young guy he was. Jesse carried along down the streets of Cobble Hill into Carroll Gardens until the spire of Precious Blood came suddenly into view, piercing the dark, gloomy sky with its righteousness. He thought about continuing along the way to his apartment, given how badly he was feeling, but made the turn and walked towards the church. It looked very different than it had even a few months earlier when he'd last seen it. Grim scaffolding and broken windows had been replaced by sandblasted granite and stained-glass. Paid for he suspected by the generosity of their legion of devoted followers. He looked up and couldn't believe his eyes as his heart sank. Two ornate windows in the bell tower. One of Saint Lucy and the other of Saint Sebastian. There they were, together, etched in glass. A tragic love story. Timeless. Iconic. Eternal life. Eternal fame.

Jesse approached the wrought-iron gates at the entrance and noticed an old, neighbourhood woman locking up. 'Can I help, young man?'

That was a big question and he wasn't sure exactly how to answer. Right then, he felt he needed all the help he could get. Any help would do.

'I came to visit.'

'I'm sorry but daily mass is over and the church is closed.'

'*Please.*'

The old woman looked carefully at the young man. He was thin, barely able to fill out his clothes, unrecognizable even to those who'd followed the story in the daily papers. He might as well have been a junkie or a vagrant, she thought, there to steal whatever he could to sell on the street for a few bucks and a quick high. But the look in his eyes told a different story, especially when he was looking up at Lucy's window. She took pity on him. She removed the key from the lock and the chain from the gate and waved him in. 'Did you know her?'

'Yes.'

'All right. Just for a few minutes,' the woman said with a sympathetic smile.

'Thank you,' he said softly, holding out a shaky hand in gratitude.

She clasped it with both of hers and felt his unsteadiness as she led him up the stairs to the main doors of the building.

'She's inside.'

Jesse hobbled into the darkened vestibule and down the centre aisle, looking off to either side. The hollow echo of his footsteps provided the perfect, solemn soundtrack to his memories. He was in a holy place but felt haunted nevertheless. He headed for the sacristy door and pushed gently on it. It opened without resistance. A few steps further and he found himself at the door to the cellar chapel and pulled on the handle. The smell of roses, frankincense and candle smoke filled his nostrils. He placed one hand against the cold stonewall and guided himself down the staircase, the faint gleam of yellow, red and violet candle flames lighting his way. He took a deep breath and held it as he reached the bottom of the stairs, composing himself. He entered the chapel full of blue smoke and black shadows.

The small room was aglow. Bones hanging like sculptures

from the walls and the chandelier. The fog of incense shrouded the room and made it hard to see. In the back, surrounded by a floor to ceiling canopy of flowers and greenery, was a large glass case on a pedestal, a statue of St Sebastian positioned directly over it. He walked over to it, closer to it, and saw her.

Lucy was lying still, a slight smile on her lips, dressed in the most beautiful finery he'd ever seen. She was wearing a gown of gold and she was crowned with an elaborate bone headpiece dripping with pearls. It fit loosely over her long blonde hair, which flowed down around her shoulders. Her hands were clasped over her chest; her bone chaplet with double eye Milagro was visible. Shadows flickered and danced across her face like the strobe lights in the clubs where they'd spent so much time. She was dead, but there was not a hint of death in the room. It was ablaze with her beauty, filling the space with her presence. He wanted to pray, but didn't know how.

Jesse had never seen a dead body before, not like this, but to him it looked as if she were sleeping peacefully. He hoped so because as he gazed behind her at the statue of Sebastian he was feeling anything but peaceful.

'You,' he whispered like a jealous suitor. 'You took her from me.'

He brought his face closer to the glass, closer to hers, grabbed hold of the translucent casket, hugging it and spoke, chanting her name, 'Lucy, Lucy, Lucy, Lucy.' Over and over

again, until his hot breath had fogged over the cool glass lid, leaving a film of condensation and desperation upon it. He moved in closer to her still and kissed the glass directly above her mouth, leaving the impression of his lips, hoping against hope to conjure her back to life like some medieval magician or fairytale prince.

He sat down in the front pew and stared ahead at her. A cascade of feelings swept over him – feelings of resentment towards Sebastian, of vengeance towards Frey and his Vandals, of fear for Cecilia, Agnes and Jude, and guilty loathing for himself. But as he closed his eyes, all he could see and hear was her. His ears filled with her laughter. His eyes filled with her eyes. His heart filled with peace and love.

Jesse broke down into tears.

10

Spirit and Teeth

'They're back,' Martha said snidely as she pulled the curtain away from the parlour window.

'Who's *they*, Mother? Half of those people who pray beside you at church on Sunday.'

'Damn mindless zombies,' Martha spat. 'At least I was able to get some peace while you were . . .'

'Away? Is that where I was. On vacation or something? Or was it a vacation for you?'

'Stop it with your attitude, Agnes. You were there for your own good and I'm still not sure Dr Frey did the right thing letting you go. Or the other one.'

'Dr Frey never does the right thing, Mother.'

'You've got to stop with these fantasies of yours, Agnes. You're scaring me. Those other girls have filled your head up with such nonsense you can't see through it.'

'Not girls, Mother. Not anymore. One of us is dead.'

'And Dr Frey killed her?'

Agnes was silent.

'If you really think that, why don't you take it to Captain Murphy?'

Agnes bit her lip. 'He doesn't believe us.'

'Well, let's think about that for a second. Why don't people believe you? Could it be because the boy you claim to love was an escaped mental patient?'

'Please don't play psychiatrist. I've had enough of that shit.'

'And your friend Lucy was a suicide from everything I've heard. No wonder, with the kind of empty life she was living.'

'Shut up.'

'Well, it's true, isn't it?'

'Sure. Just another rich girl, club-hopper tragedy. Is that it?' Agnes mocked. 'A teen celebrity gone bad?'

'Every girl wants to feel special, to feel loved, to be worshipped. Believe me, I get it. But life doesn't always work like that. It rarely does.'

'You're blind.'

'I wish you were as blind as me, Agnes,' Martha said, wringing her hands just a little. 'I see perfectly what you're doing to yourself.'

Agnes drew the curtain back, exposing the crowd. 'Don't you see what's going on out there, see what's happening?'

'People with too much time on their hands looking for something in the wrong place,' Martha griped. 'The only thing happening is in *your* head.'

The doorbell rang bringing the conversation to an abrupt halt.

'What now?' Martha spat. 'If it's one of these crazies I'm calling the police.'

She brought her eye to the peephole, exhaled and opened the door. 'Hello, dear,' she said sweetly, until she got a good look at the girl. 'What in hell happened to you!'

With intense scepticism, Martha noted the black eye and split lip and the purple brownish raised scabs over her brow and on her cheek.

'Hi, Mrs Fremont. It's nothing. Got into a fight with a kitchen cabinet. I'm clumsy.'

Martha couldn't believe the sight before her. 'Are you OK?'

'Hazel!' Agnes shouted, running into her friend's arms.

'I thought those creepy people were going to ask me for my autograph or something,' Hazel huffed, taking Agnes by the hand before she too could ask any uncomfortable questions.

'Thank you,' Martha grumbled, raising an eyebrow as she walked off to the kitchen. 'Finally a girl with some sense. I think.'

Agnes stepped back from the embrace. 'Not you too?'

'I don't judge, I'm just sayin',' Hazel added, slipping off her jacket. 'Not everyone is so supportive, you know.'

Agnes led Hazel back to her room and closed the door loudly to be sure Martha heard it.

'You look terrible,' Agnes said, worse than you described in your text. 'How are you?'

'Gee thanks. Yeah, it was a stupid accident.' Hazel replied. 'More importantly, how are *you*?'

Agnes shrugged, tears continuing to well and slip from her eyes. 'That's a big question.'

'Did they give you shock treatments and shit?'

'No, why?'

'A lot of kids at school were, you know, talking.'

'They're always talking, Hazel,' Agnes sniffed.

Agnes turned her back and opened her desk drawer, eyeing her tear catcher. She picked up the flute-shaped glass, removed the top of the bottle and held it to her cheek, capturing the few drops of glycerin pooling on her cheek.

'No way,' Hazel said. 'Drinking this early? I'll take a double. I sure could use it.'

Agnes waved her off.

'It's an antique,' Agnes explained. 'It's a tear catcher. It reminds me of what's important to me.'

'The things you cry over?'

'Something like that.'

'Well, then I'd have a few flasks full myself. I call dibs on that if you ever want to part with it.'

Agnes smiled and dried her eyes. She gathered some homeopathic supplies from her antique green vanity – oils and salves – and sat down next to Hazel on her crushed velvet antique chair.

'OK. So what is everyone saying?' Agnes asked, dressing Hazel's wounds, naturally and gently.

'Well, about half the school thinks you're nuts and the other half thinks you're making it up, that you like the attention.'

'So they're either judgmental or jealous? Seriously?'

'Who cares? They're all haters anyway,' Hazel responded. 'Ouch!'

'Sorry, I'm almost done,' Agnes said putting on the last of the salve. After she finished, she reached for Hazel's hand and took it in hers and led her to the corner of the bed. They sat down. Agnes stared directly into her friend's eyes.

'What do *you* think, Hazel?'

Hazel swallowed hard, flipped her hair behind her ears a few times and reached into her bag for a lip balm and ran it across her lips. She puckered a few times. Her batting eyes gave away her nervousness.

'Can't you see what I think?' Hazel said. 'I mean, look at me. Look what they did to me?'

'What happened to you?'

'A few girls in class jumped me after school in the bathroom.'

'Because of me?'

Hazel's tears flowed freely now as she nodded yes. Agnes began to cry as well.

'They were talking shit about you and I wasn't get let them get away with it.'

'Didn't you tell anyone?'

'I'm no snitch bitch. I can deal with my own problems.'

'I'm so sorry, Hazel. So very sorry.'

The two of them locked in an embrace on her bed for several minutes, crying and comforting one another.

'Kids have a lot of questions,' Hazel said through her tears, 'but I can handle it. I don't take any shit, you know that.'

'Yeah I can see,' Agnes said, getting a smile from Hazel.

'Whatever you do, don't go online. There's a lot of sick crap posted,' Hazel said, getting back to business. 'Trolls everywhere.'

'One nice thing about being away is that I really don't miss that stuff. I'm so done with it.'

'It's definitely an addiction. Maybe I should try getting a 5150 hold on me or something. I'm crazy.'

'Hazel,' Agnes said, reprimanding her in a playful way.

'Guess I'm just hoping now that you're back that maybe our lives will get back to normal?'

'This is the new normal for me, for as long as I'm here.'

'Agnes, please don't talk like that. It scares me.'

'Don't be afraid,' Agnes said, echoing Sebastian's words.

Hazel started shaking slightly. 'That's easy for you to say, Agnes. I'd take a bullet for you but I have to know it at least matters to you.'

Agnes thought of all the things she could have said but said the only thing that really mattered. 'You are such a good friend, Hazel. I'm so lucky to have you.'

'If you really mean that, just promise me you won't do anything stupid, OK?'

But Agnes couldn't promise no matter how much she wanted to and Hazel knew it. 'Whatever I do, it's what I need to do. You understand?'

Hazel stood and turned to look out of Agnes's bedroom window at the crowd. 'Honestly, I don't. You have a chance at a new start. All those people out on the street, they don't know you.'

'Did my mother ask you to come here?'

'No. I'm just freaked out for you. I'm petrified.'

The concern was showing on Agnes's face. Frey, she thought, would have only let her go for one reason and that was to kill her.

'It's OK. I'll be fine. No matter what happens. Peace in the eye of disaster. That's what I know now.'

'Oh, Agnes,' Hazel said. 'I do believe you. Believe in you.'

'I know,' Agnes said. 'I mean, look at you.'

The two laughed a little and hugged more.

'Have you heard from Cecilia or that guy Jesse?'

'Not since I left. I think we all need a little time away.'

'Maybe that's not such a bad thing.'

Cecilia noticed that everything in the room had an otherworldly glow – the walls, her vinyl records, even her skin. She looked at her arms and then her hands; she was so pale in the morning sunrise, almost dead-looking. She'd been working all night and lost total track of time.

Exhausted, emotional and exhilarated, she closed her eyes and listened back to the demos she'd recorded the night before. She could barely hear her cellphone ringing through the blare from her speakers, the melodic ringtone sounded like another part of her composition. It fit with her beat, at least for a few seconds.

She walked into her bedroom, removed it from the charger and held it up. The name on her touch screen left no doubt who was calling her. It didn't say Daniel. It didn't say Mr Less. It read Daniel Less. His full name, as if she would forget. She swiped the call answer bar and spoke.

'Hello,' she said softly.

'Is this a good time?' Less asked just as politely.

'Perfect,' she said, a small smile involuntarily crossing her lips. 'I've been working.'

'Really? I wouldn't have expected it so quickly.'

'You're in early,' she jibed.

'You're up late,' he retorted.

'I don't fuck around.'

'Apparently not,' he said.

'I want to play something for you. Not sure if you'll get it through the phone but . . .'

'I've been doing this a while, Cecilia, and my ears still work,' he said dryly.

'Sorry,' she said, momentarily forgetting who she was dealing with. 'They're really rough so if you don't like them I can keep working.'

'Just press play.'

Cecilia did as he asked. Bringing up the track in the music program she'd been working with. A squall of processed guitar feedback that sounded more like meat frying than music burst through the speakers, anchored by a synthetic, metallic snap of a virtual sneer drum. The track was harsh. Edgy. Unique.

Cecilia fiddled with her chaplet nervously. For the first time in a long time, she felt uncomfortable. Needy even. Wanting desperately for him to like what she'd done. She imagined him leaning back in his leather high-back office chair, eyes closed, drinking it in. Drinking her in. This was her shot at last. An opportunity to not just record her most heartfelt recordings or even perform them on stage, but to release them to a wide audience. It was what she'd been hoping for ever since Sebastian revealed her truth, but somehow, along with her anxiety, she was feeling hollowness inside. The events of Precious Blood, now six months behind her, suddenly seemed a long time ago.

She watched her laptop screen intently as each second of the track clicked by, her mind racing wildly over what he might say and how she might respond. The sonic storm faded gently away and she waited for his critique, but all he said, was . . .

'Next.'

She played the next demo for him, this one softer and spacier, and the next, a straight-forward power rocker. There was heart and blood and soul in all of it.

'I'm impressed. It's a brilliant start,' Less said with characteristic understatement. 'You are a true artist, Cecilia.'

She could barely keep herself from pogoing around the apartment, fists raised upwards in victory, smiling from ear to ear.

'Thanks,' she said flatly, not wanting to give herself away. 'I'm happy with them so far.'

'As am I,' he continued.

'That's not just music, that is communication.'

He gets me, she thought. Cecilia was barely able to contain herself but somehow managed.

'That's what I'm about, Mr Less.'

'Call me Daniel,' he asked flirtatiously.

'OK . . . Daniel.'

'Your fans will be happy and I'm a lock for a return on my investment.'

'Investment?' she whispered. 'Is that what I am?'

'No, Cecilia. You are more than that. Much more.'

There was an awkward silence between them. There was something incredibly intimate about what had just happened. She'd exposed her most vulnerable side to an almost total stranger, but one who now occupied an unexpectedly major part in her life.

'Something wrong?' he asked.

'No, I just thought you were about to ask me what I was wearing.'

'That's funny,' he said, 'I thought you were just about to tell me.'

11

Sutured

Jesse reached into his duffle bag and pulled out the small square plastic cartridge that Agnes had slipped him. He turned it around in his hand like an archeologist examining an artifact from a time long ago.

'Tape? Really?' he whispered to himself.

He opened his bedroom closet door and dug out an old player, dusted it off and plugged it in. It took him a second to find the connections in the back of his flat panel LED screen. It had been that long.

He sat and watched as the player warmed up and took the opportunity to go through the emails he'd missed in the Byte contacts box. Message after message popped up, most wishing him ill. No surprise, he thought. Some clever, some not so much.

> *Heard you were still alive. Proves the theory that it's impossible to kill cockroaches.*
> *Riddle me this, asshole: what's the difference between you and Lucy Ambrose? Lucy is dead. EMT response time is just a little too good. Who can I talk to about that?*
> *Can you spell KARMA? J-E-S-S-E.*

Jesse hardly reacted. He scrolled down and scanned the subjects of each email before opening them. They went from bad to worse. But there were a few good ones, supportive ones. Sympathetic ones sprinkled in. Mostly expressing condolences about Lucy, prayers for them both, wishing him a speedy recovery and the strength to forgive his enemies. Forgiveness, however, was the last thing on his mind.

The more digital correspondence he read, the more lost he became in them. The hate, the anger, the vitriol, the bitterness, the disgust that dripped from every comment. He could not stop thinking that he probably deserved it. And that he was still much too young to have pissed off so many people. But he had after all put a target on their backs. Ruined lives for spite and profit. For his own gain. And for Lucy. His eyes turned from the computer screen to the tape player.

Jesse pressed play and hoped for the best. He got his worst

nightmare. There was Lucy, sitting helpless, being interrogated by that man who called himself a priest. It could easily have been mistaken for a hostage video, but it was even worse than that because Jesse knew without watching that there would be no way Lucy would ever denounce herself, no matter how wrongheaded he thought she was being. She was too proud for a start. And too stubborn.

What did they need this for? Jesse kept asking himself. To embarrass her? Humiliate her? That was an area he was far too familiar with. He couldn't count the number of friends, and even former enemies, who'd landed in his digital crosshairs. Their digital crosshairs to be exact. Lucy was no shrinking violet when it came to the game. She played it expertly, right up to the end. She didn't give an inch. Not even to save her own life.

No, he figured. The reason for this recording was too invalidate her. That was Frey's big thing. To share with the world, like one of those secret sex tapes that he'd been offered by jealous ex-boyfriends. Most confessions are voluntary, heard by priests for the purpose of forgiveness, but this was anything but. He found himself wanting to reach through the screen to save her or just to hold her hand, to comfort her in her moment of agony.

Guilt overwhelmed him once again. For being so stupid. For going to Born Again. A place he had no business being alone. For trying to be a hero. Her hero. Now she was dead. As the tape continued to roll, he watched the questioning become more and more intense. There was a burst of white light, which blinded him even through the TV screen, and then the mood in the room seemed to change. A look of peace came across Lucy's face. He'd seen that self-satisfied smile of hers many times before, though under different circumstances. A frenemy taken down a peg, a nemesis's darkest secret exposed, an A-List party crashed and documented for the haters to see. As he pushed pause and studied the look on her face, he saw that there was a lot of the old Lucy in the new one. This smile he knew, though, was not for him, but for Sebastian.

Funny thing about video, he found himself considering, is that it often survives its subject. All that footage shot over the years, used in tribute clip packages of celebrities and politicians that are rerun ad nauseum upon their death. Old TV shows, old movies. They always seem so alive even though they've long since passed. Digital immortality. It was the same with this. It was the new stained-glass window. A visual meme, a shared reference point, that ensured immortality and inspired eternal devotion. He regretted not being able to do Lucy justice with a tribute of her own. But as usual, Lucy made sure that she was the star of the show – package or not. The clamouring for her, the whispers, the gossip was greater than ever, but mostly favourable. Even he couldn't have managed that on their best day together.

Then, finally, the sound of Cecilia and Agnes bursting in, of sirens, and of sacrifice.

He wanted to turn his head as Lucy pulled at her eyes and her blood flowed freely, a deluge of crimson tears, soaking her outfit and the floor beneath her. He watched her crawl, determined, out of the room towards the robed men. He seen her crawling on all fours before, after a particularly bad night at the club, but this time she wasn't worshipping the porcelain god. It was a much higher power she was in touch with.

He stopped the tape and pressed eject. The cartridge popped halfway out of the machine and sat there. Taunting him. He was conflicted. This was so inflammatory, so raw, so ugly and so beautiful. Judging from the messages he'd received, Lucy's followers knew what happened, how she died. But many did not. Seeing it would be even more powerful. More affecting. It needed to be seen.

'What should I do?' he asked himself out loud.

The answer suddenly came to him. He heard Agnes's words in his mind. *Lucy is dead*. But Jesse was alive. He grabbed a USB cable and connected to the port in his computer and snapped the other end into the player.

'Seeing is believing,' he said, echoing Lucy's favourite phrase.

Despite the guilt that buried him in an avalanche of regret, this was his chance to do something, to show the world who Lucy really was and who he believed her to be.

His chance to do something he had little experience doing.

The right thing.

* * *

'Are you sure you want to do this?' Hazel asked, handing Agnes a backpack and jacket.

'I'm sure,' Agnes said. 'I've got nothing to hide.'

'It's not going to be fun for you at school. Just sayin'.'

'Was it ever?'

The two girls walked slowly down the brownstone steps towards the small crowd gathered on the sidewalk. Agnes had on red lipstick, and her hair flowed freely over her mustard-yellow coat, bouncing slightly as she descended the stoop. Greetings and compliments filled the air. Hazel stood back a few steps behind, instinctively.

'Bless you, Agnes,' said one. 'Pray for me,' said another. 'So sorry about Lucy,' offered another. 'She's in a better place. With better people. Death is easy, life is hard,' she said trying to give Agnes strength.

They reached out respectfully for her, to touch her hand or her coat. Agnes smiled gently and reached back to them. Those who did touch her crossed themselves, as if they'd been in the presence of a holy person.

Agnes and Hazel continued down the tree-lined street. The leaves and flower buds were popping in the morning sun. They walked and talked, both Agnes and Hazel keeping one eye over their respective shoulders.

'You really don't have to do this. I'm sure our teachers would understand if you needed a few more days.'

'I'm OK, really,' Agnes insisted. 'And I don't want to spend any more time in that house with my mother than I have to.'

'I know but people can be so cruel, you know,' Hazel said, referencing her scars with a look. 'Sometimes worse.'

'Believe me, those kids are the least of my worries.' They reached the corner and crossed the street. A few houses down the block they were startled from their conversation by the sudden rev of a loud car engine starting up. An old beater that looked like it should have been scrapped long ago.

'Jesus!' Hazel shouted, covering her ears. 'Get a muffler.'

'That's a pretty tight spot,' Agnes frowned sympathetically. 'Not sure they can make it.'

'Yeah, alternate side of the street parking is a bitch.'

They kept walking. The loud squeak of a steering wheel turning tightly one direction and then the other, the thud of bumpers bumping and the dull rub of brakes against worn brake pads filled the quiet street. Freed eventually from its space, the car and driver began to roll slowly down the street towards the intersection.

Agnes and Hazel chatted obliviously waiting for the light to change from red to green. The right of way secured, they stepped into the crosswalk. The car that had been creeping down the block suddenly came to a complete stop. Hazel squinted and could just barely make out the driver through the glare. It was a girl, wearing shades, her long hair spilling out of an army-green ski cap, behind the wheel. Her face was familiar to Hazel, but not in a good way.

'Agnes, come on.'

Agnes kept staring, as if she were playing a game of chicken with the driver.

The engine revved, tyres spun and screeched, grabbing hold of the tarred road and peeled out, straight for them, like an arrow shot from a bow. For a moment, Hazel and Agnes were frozen in place.

'Look out!' Hazel screamed, tugging Agnes by the strap of her book bag and pulling her to the other side of the street as the car sped by, missing them by inches.

They tumbled to the ground and felt the draft and breathed in the smell of engine exhaust from the car as it breezed by them both. A shrill sound of laughter was audible through the growl of the engine.

'What the fuck?' Hazel screamed. 'She was trying to kill us!'

They both brushed at their scraped palms and knees and stood up slowly.

'Do you know her?'

'I'm pretty sure that was one of the girls that attacked me,' Hazel said soberly.

'You saved my life, Hazel.'

'Well, if I would have left it up to you we'd both be going to the morgue instead of school,' Hazel said, shaking her head. 'You know you're no match for a speeding car, right?'

There was both concern and anger in Hazel's tone.

'Are you OK?' a passerby asked nervously.

'I couldn't get the number plate,' another said apologetically.

'Don't move. I'll call an ambulance.'

'No please don't, we're fine,' she said. 'I've had enough of the hospital.'

'That was too close,' Hazel said, shaking.

'Yes, very close,' Agnes calmly agreed, steady as a rock.

'You sure you want to go to school today?'

Sister Dorothea exited the elevator at the top floor of Perpetual Help hospital, signed documents firmly in hand and readied for a fight. The receptionist smiled condescendingly as she approached. 'Can I help you?' she asked perfunctorily, knowing full well the reason for the nun's visit.

'Dr Frey.'

'I'm sorry, he isn't available.'

'Well, he'd better make himself available,' the sister said. 'Now.'

'Perhaps I can help you,' the charge nurse said, approaching the desk.

'I'm here for the boy. Jude.' The nun stated, waving an envelope. 'I have all the paperwork from the city agencies signed.'

She slid it through an opening in the glass and the nurse took it and opened it.

'Seems everything's in order.'

'Yes, except for the release documents which Dr Frey needs

to sign. And I'm not leaving here without them or Jude.'

'No need to get testy,' the nurse said, 'I have the discharge right here.'

The nurse reached into the outbox for a clipboard with a single sheet. She handed it back through the glass and the nun scanned it. To her surprise, Frey's signature was indeed at the bottom. After weeks of back and forth, she could barely believe it. It seemed too easy. Too good to be true.

'Jude?' the nurse called out.

The boy was seated, fully dressed, shoes tied, coat zipped up, halfway down the hallway. Sister Dorthea was so intent on getting him out she'd barely noticed him sitting there.

Jude stood and walked slowly towards her, keeping his eye on the nurse suspiciously as she pressed the unlock buzzer and opened the door. The nun got down on one need and hugged him tightly for a long time, then pulled away and looked him in the eye.

'Are you OK, son?'

Jude nodded *yes*.

They began to walk towards the elevator to leave and the nurse called out to her.

'Good luck, Jude. You're on your own now.'

'No, not on his own,' the nun replied, placing her arm gently around his shoulder before stepping in the car. 'Never on his own.'

Cecilia's Idyll

*I*t was like a dream.

Cecilia arrived and stepped from the limousine on the red carpet, lit by the flashes of photographers and video cameras. She never would have guessed she was at an exclusive Hamptons estate and not some swanky New York City club or party space. All she could think was that this was Lucy's domain, or once had been, not hers.

As she heard her name called out by one shutterbug after another, she was frightened and thrilled. The crystal spikes on her shoulder harness gleamed and the strobing lights reflected off them, bouncing away into the night sky mixing with the distant stars.

'Show us your hands,' they shouted.

She looked at them. They were scarred as always from the Iron Maiden's spikes in the lower chapel of Precious Blood that had pierced them, but clean and dry. She rubbed them on her skirt and did as they asked, holding them high, only somewhat reluctantly, in front of her.

'Money shot,' one shouted.

She suddenly understood the seductiveness of it, of fame, and recalled her first meeting with Lucy in the church and how nasty she'd been. She felt like crying even in the midst of this entire spectacle organized for her benefit. But if she had Sebastian to thank for Lucy, and for who she had become, then for this party, she only had Daniel Less to thank. How gracious was it she thought, for him to open up his home for her listening party.

She was escorted through the black velvet drapes that separated the media vultures from the main entrance to the house and stepped into a different world. Not exactly through the looking glass but it felt like it. All the noise and vying for attention faded into nothing and a bucolic paradise revealed itself. From the large black and white checkerboard marble tiled foyer she could see the cedar trees, the brush, the sand and the ocean through floor-to-ceiling windows, as the sunset seemed to set right on cue. Inscribed on the church-like lintel above them, a phrase:

Et in Arcadia Ego (Even in Arcadia, there I am).

Candles lined the banister of the long Victorian staircase and flickered from the vintage chandeliers above. If the arrivals carpet outside was all Lucy, inside was all Agnes. Pure romance. Cecilia found herself amazed at how much she had of each of them inside of

125

her. How similar they were in so many ways, despite their obvious differences. Was that what Sebastian saw? she wondered.

She waded uncomfortably into the Gatsby-esque excess, her music wafting from the surround sound system. A crush of servers dispersed through the crowd carrying hors d'oeuvres and crystal flutes of champagne on elaborate pewter trays. Was this a listening party she wondered, or a society wedding? Not that she'd ever attended one or even seen such an event outside of the pages of the glossies her mother had kept in the bathroom magazine rack.

This was it. The fantasy. She walked slowly into the party and everywhere she turned was a famous face. Movie stars, directors, fashion designers, multi-platinum record producers, rock stars, hipster restaurateurs. And executive and Wall Street types she didn't recognize but gave themselves away with their expensive suits and salon grooming. Ironically, she seemed to be the least well-known person in the room, judging from the fact that no one had even given her a second glance so far.

Standing towards the back of the dining room, surrounded by members in the ruling class and some recently signed artists intent on kissing ass, was Daniel Less. He spotted her immediately.

'Cecilia!' he shouted through the din, making a move towards her, reaching out his hand. She walked to him, unaccompanied, and took it.

Less turned to face the crowd and introduced her. The entire room went silent without his having to ask. Some girls, dressed in skintight outfits, pursed their lips and shot jealous looks at her like darts.

'Flavour of the month,' one whispered just loud enough for her to hear.

'Yeah, arsenic,' another chimed in.

'Ladies and gentlemen, our guest of honour, the reason we are gathered here and the next household name for Tritone Records: Cecilia Trent.'

A round of polite applause broke out. It was not the shrieks of excitement and looks of awe she was used to receiving from the street punks and fans that attended her gigs or even on the street these days. But then this was not just a random crowd. These were the top of the heap. Saints and sinners were met with equal indifference.

Cecilia acknowledged them with a smile and a nod and took Less's hand. He escorted her through the crowd to a dais at the back of the dining room.

'I can't believe you put this together so quickly,' Cecilia whispered.

'No time like the present,' Less responded.

'Thank you,' she said sincerely. 'It's what I always imagined it would be like.'

'I thought so,' he replied with a smile. 'Nothing less than the best for you.'

Cecilia smiled demurely at the pun. 'Somehow I think you've probably used that line before.'

'I always prefer to strike while the iron is hot, Cecilia, and you, my dear, are hot.'

She wasn't exactly sure if he was creeping on her or complimenting her. His flirtatiousness always seemed to have a subtext, if not an outright ulterior motive. Yet she didn't discourage him. Regardless, his cards and his money were on the table. He'd clearly made the investment in her and she was signed, sealed and delivered. They were past the courting stage in their professional relationship. This was the real deal. In a world of put up or shut up. They'd both definitely put up.

'I'm not sure everyone here agrees,' she laughed.

'But they're here, so who cares what they think?' Less parried.

'For you or for me?'

'Does that matter? The pictures will look the same in the newspapers either way.'

'I'm not really interested in the attention, Daniel.'

The uncertain smirk gave her away.

'Easy to say when you get so much of it,' Less answered, the smile leaving his face as he reached for the magnum of champagne nestled in the ice bucket before him and poured them each a glass.

'Without it I wouldn't be sitting here, would I?' she observed dryly. 'Wouldn't have this . . . opportunity.'

He raised the flute and the chime of crystal touching crystal as the rim of her glass met his rang out clearly like a bell even through the idle chitchat that had all but obscured her music.

'Cheers,' he said. 'To taking advantage of opportunities.'

They drank.

'Everybody thinks they're in this business for a different reason, but it's always the same reason, themselves.'

'Not everyone,' she said.

Less laughed out loud as the waiters continued to serve their table. 'You really ought to eat something,' he insisted.

'Trying to fatten me up for the kill?' she asked sarcastically.

'The only place you need to worry about killing is on stage, Cecilia.'

'Cheers to that,' she added, emptying her glass.

She set the flute down and looked around. Waiters scurried, setting and removing utensils and plates as each course was served. Filling glasses with water and with wine. Invisible almost to the partiers. It occurred to Cecilia that she probably had more in common with them then the people they were serving. In the bacchanalian commotion, as her music played, she suddenly found herself feeling dizzy. Maybe, she thought it was the champagne, or just her anxiety about the entire event and the pressure she'd now put on herself. To be a commodity and not just a messenger. Or maybe Daniel was right. She needed to eat something.

'Are you feeling all right?' he asked.

'I'm not sure,' she said, searching for the bread bowl. 'I think I need to put something in my stomach.'

'Of course,' Less waved his hand. Right on cue, a waiter approached bearing a large silver platter. It was covered. 'This is a special dish, prepared just for you.'

The closer the waiter drew to the table, the worse Cecilia felt. There was a growing tightness in her chest, rising upwards into her neck. Her throat tightened and her skin began to crawl. The platter approached and she could see her reflection. Two hands were at her throat, grabbing at her, but not from the outside, from the inside, moving under her skin, like a kicking baby trying to escape a uterus. She gasped but could not make a sound.

The platter was set down and the cover removed. It was a piece of meat but raw and bloody. More like an organ than a shoulder cut. She recognized it. It was a heart.

'Sebastian!' she rasped through the ever-tightening grip around her neck.

Her hands were throbbing and began to spurt blood over the tablecloth and her pricey outfit.

'Dig in,' Less ordered, followed by the sound of knives and forks being lifted from the table.

The guests attacked the tray, hacking away at it. She could do nothing but sit and watch, nearly paralyzed, as they seemed to transform into wild animals right in front of her. Their teeth sharpening and lengthening. Their eyes turning bloodshot, then black and dead and rolling over white like hungry sharks as they devoured the feast.

Less howled in laughter at the carnivorous scene as the hands around Cecilia's neck tightened like a noose, strangling her, stifling her screams. The hands grew thorns, cutting into her flesh.

She awoke screaming and ran from her bed into the bathroom and stared at herself in the mirror. Standing there, alone in her silk grey nightie, she turned on the cold-water faucet and ran it over her wrists to ease the panic and ground herself. A little trick she'd learned from her cocaine days.

Cecilia closed her eyes and exhaled slowly and began to relax.

She opened her eyes slowly and looked in the mirror again, and there he was.

Standing there. With no shirt, and bullet holes in his perfect chest.

'It was a dream,' he whispered, seductively. 'Come back to bed.'

She turned around and he was gone. She turned back around, hoping to see him in the mirror again, but he wasn't there. She put her hand on the mirror, right where he was standing and tried to feel for him. She lowered her head, letting it hang limply from her tightened shoulders.

'It was just a nightmare,' she said reassuring herself. She noticed a reddish-pink wash-off collecting at the bottom of the sink and turned her palms upwards.

They were bleeding.

✦

12

Hell is for Children

'Sister?' Agnes called out.

'Agnes!' the nun replied joyfully. 'So very happy to see you!'

Agnes stepped in and the nun stepped around her desk and took Agnes in a long and warm embrace.

'Glad to be seen, sort of,' Agnes said. 'At least somebody's happy to see me.'

'First day back would be difficult, I'm sure.'

'You have no idea. I almost didn't make it.'

'What happened?'

'Hazel and I were almost roadkill,' Agnes quipped.

'They need more crossing guards on these streets. I've

been complaining for years!'

'Well, I think they need more then crossing guards, Sister. The driver didn't need traffic school, she needed an exorcist.'

'It was intentional?'

'No doubt. And it didn't get any better once I got to school.'

'We never know for sure what the day will bring,' Sister Dorothea said.

'All I can tell you for sure is that there is a definitely a hell,' Agnes replied, wanly pointing over her shoulder towards the high-school hallway.

'Why do you even bother to come at this point?'

'What else would I do? Sit at home in a glass box like some piece of museum-quality jewellery awaiting visitors. That's coming anyway. We both know it.'

'Oh, Agnes! Don't say that.'

'I'm really not like Lucy and Cecilia. They had their goals and a lot of stuff they wanted to do. Which is great. I just wanted to be a normal girl. To be loved. That was my dream.'

'Which might just be the most ambitious dream of all, Agnes,' Sister Dorothea commented. 'And the most difficult to accomplish.'

'Yeah, well, I'm not ready to give it up. I guess all this, the good and the bad, is just a part of that dream. It's what I know. It's how I feel. For me it's about love even in the face of all the haters. If I'm going to be an example of anything, I want to it to be that.'

Sister Dorothea smiled proudly.

'A noble and universal cause, Agnes. Befitting a brave and thoughtful young woman.'

'I just wish it wasn't so hard.'

'Nobody said it would be easy.'

'And they were right,' Agnes concurred. 'Especially when the person you love most in the world is gone.'

'We're never gone, Agnes, as long as we are loved.'

The girl smiled. It wasn't just Sister Dorothea's words, but her very presence that comforted Agnes.

'Enough about me. How's Jude?'

'He's doing fine now. He's with us, at the convent.'

'Frey really let him go?'

'I'd like to think we forced his hand but I know better.'

'So we're all out now,' Agnes pondered. 'Easier to kill.'

'Don't say that! We should go to the police.'

'We tried that. Captain Murphy means well but Frey is so tied in to everything its impossible to know who you are really speaking to. I don't know how that record guy got Cecilia out.'

'Money talks.'

'I guess,' Agnes said.

'How is Lucy's friend? The boy that was attacked?'

'I don't know. I saw him when he was leaving the hospital and he seemed so frail. I check his website every day but there's nothing new.'

'After what he's been through, maybe he just needs some time to process things.'

'That will take more than time.' Agnes admitted. 'Well, I really need to get to class.'

'Take care of yourself, dear.'

'I'll try, Sister. Kiss Jude for me. Tell him I'll come by to see him soon.'

'He'd like that.'

Agnes smiled. 'Ever since I met him in the hospital I've felt very close to him. Like he's my little guardian angel or something.'

'He's a good boy. He understands many things.'

'I feel so bad for him. He's been through so much for such a young kid and now to be caught up in all this.'

'We don't always get to choose our path, Agnes. Sometimes it is chosen for us.'

Agnes nodded and hugged the nun.

'I know,' Agnes conceded. 'Pray for me, Sister?'

The nun smiled.

'Only if you pray for me.'

Jesse's phone rang. The buzzy, repetitive tone seemed to him to bounce off the walls of his apartment, assaulting him. He reached for his ears in a vain and childish attempt to shut it out. It had been days since he'd picked up. Days since he'd spoken to anyone in fact. There was too much and nothing at all to say, even to people who cared.

He checked the number and it was one that he vaguely recognized. Not his parents, nor an old friend or acquaintance, but a professional connection. He thought about it letting it go to voicemail, as he had hundreds of others, but this time he didn't. He answered the call.

'Jesse?'

Jesse listened to the voice but did not respond.

'Jesse. It's Tony. The bouncer.'

Once again he did not respond but exhaled loud enough to be heard.

'C'mon. It's Tony. Lucy's friend. You gonna talk or what?'

'You weren't her friend.'

'Maybe not like you, but I was there for her.'

'Listen, Tony. I don't know what you want from me, but if you're looking for some cash to drop a dime on some crackhead socialite you're shit outta luck.'

'I'm not calling about money or anyone.'

'Then what?' Jesse said disinterestedly.

'I called to see how you're doin'.'

'Now I've heard everything.'

'I mean it.'

If nothing else, Jesse knew that Tony was a straight shooter. 'To be totally honest with you, I don't know how I am.'

'We're all shaken up, man. But you got to keep it together. For her sake.'

'What sake? She's gone.'

'Not really. You know what I mean?'

'It's not that simple.

'Yeah, it is,' Tony replied.

Jesse admired Tony's ability to see things simply. He envied his certainty and wished he had more of it.

'OK, then I'll rephrase. She's not here. And it's because of me,' Jesse sulked. 'That's what I know.'

'Have you been to the shrine?'

'You mean the chapel? Yeah.'

Tony's voice started to break. Not from bad reception, but from pure emotion.

'Me too. I went. I don't get down on my fuckin' knees for anybody. Not even for Jesus. But I hit my knees for her. And I cried my heart out.'

Jesse believed him. He swallowed hard, desperately trying to keep his own raw feelings in check.

'She was special.'

'More than special,' Tony said, speaking for the throngs of followers who visited the chapel daily. 'She was a saint.'

'I don't know about all that.'

'Well I do. I believe it. And so do a lot of other people. And I know deep down, you do too.'

'I'm struggling, man.'

'We all struggle with the truth. It doesn't come wrapped up in a neat little package or a column item. But once you accept it, everything changes.'

'For a tough guy, you're startin' to sound a lot like a philosopher.'

Tony laughed and so did Jesse. For the first time he could remember.

'I grew up in this neighbourhood. With all the superstitions and stories of the cults, the saints, the curses, the malocchio, from the old country. It's not that hard to figure. It boils down to this. There is evil in this friggin' world. And there is good. And they are at war. Every day.'

'And what are we supposed to do about it? What are Lucy, Cecilia and Agnes supposed to do about it?'

'Again, simple. Wake people up out of the fuckin' coma they're in so they can see how much power they really have over their own lives. It's all mixed up now.'

Tony was coarse, but he was right. Jesse knew that. He felt the same way.

'I have this clip of what happened to Lucy. I'm thinking about posting it. For everyone to see what they did to her.'

'I heard rumours about that tape. If you do that, they'll come for you. You know that right?'

'Good.'

'What, did you get brain-damaged in the hospital? Lose a bunch of oxygen? You think you can do this alone? How'd that work out for you last time, Captain America?'

'They're coming for me anyway, Tony.'

'True. I have a few friends who been keeping an eye on that druggie house on the Gowanus where you almost got whacked. Lots of crime in the neighbourhood, all traces back to them but nobody can prove a thing. Maybe the cops or whatever are protecting them. In cahoots. Wouldn't be the first time.'

'It goes higher than that. Much higher.'

'Yeah, I heard that too.'

'You know what I want? How you can really help me?'

'Just say the word.'

'I want revenge. Not just for me. But for Lucy.'

'I'm down but that's gonna be dangerous you understand?'

'It's more dangerous this way. Especially for the other girls.'

'Time to crack a few heads then?'

'I don't know about drafting you into my fight.'

'You're not drafting me. I'm volunteering. I would have crawled over broken glass for Lucy.'

'You just might get a chance to prove that, Tony, if this goes down.'

'I'm ready. You gotta win the battles before you can raise the flag. Get me?'

'I'm gonna give it a little thought and I'll hit you back.'

'OK, you got my number. But don't think too long. Sometimes the best defence is a good offence.'

The last notes of Cecilia's completed audio opus faded into the ether. Into silence. Catherine remained still, with her eyes

139

closed, processing what she'd just heard.

'What do you think?' Cecilia asked.

'That was friggin' awesome!' Catherine said, shaking her head in disbelief as the final chord of Cecilia's last song faded from the speakers.

'No, what you did in that crazy crowd was awesome. I saw the news clip online,' CeCe said. 'You're brave, Cat.'

Cecilia gently brushed the hair away from Catherine's brow and gently ran her finger on the outline of the adhesive strip covering her stitches.

'That was nothing. Now this album. That is something.'

'You really think so?' Cecilia asked modestly. 'I tried to mix it up. Doesn't sound too much like hold music, does it?'

'You mean muzak? Like *the customer service representative will be with you shortly* sort of background stuff?' Catherine said, shaking her head.

'Yeah,' CeCe answered earnestly.

'Seriously? I couldn't do what you did if I had the best producers and writers in the world working with me.'

Cecilia smiled, both grateful and relieved that her friend had given her stamp of approval.

'You'll do your own thing. That's what matters.'

Catherine smiled at CeCe's generosity. 'Have you played it for anybody else?'

'Nope. Not the whole thing. You're the only one that's heard it. And Daniel.'

'Oh, it's *Daniel* now, huh?'

CeCe smiled sheepishly.

'Don't get any ideas, Cat!'

Catherine bounced up and ran her fingers along the edges of the expensive couch and coffee table that furnished Cecilia's new apartment.

'Well, he did get you out of the hospital and got your case dropped. You can't blame a girl for being curious.'

'Exactly. I'm an investment, not a girlfriend. He's been really encouraging. Pushing me to get this stuff recorded as quickly as possible. While I'm still hot.'

'Ha, while you're *hot*. Finally a little honesty!' Catherine laughed. 'Listen, he's rich and powerful. Who could blame you? I just thought you had a different goal in mind.'

'OK, enough sarcasm. It's not like that. I just think he wants this music out while there's still a lot of focus on me.'

'Still,' Catherine said, still wandering around the apartment and stopping in front of a beautiful floral terrarium near the window, 'you did check for hidden cameras right?'

'Of course,' CeCe said, bringing them both to tears with laughter.

'Well, just saying, he might have made the best bet of his career. That stuff is brilliant.'

'I'm happy with it. It's what I want to say. What I want out there.'

'I hope I get there some day.'

'You will, Cat. Just be yourself. Be honest and the rest will take care of itself. You have a deal, so that stress is off.'

'Since we're being honest. You know the whole Less thing,' Catherine asked. 'To be totally honest with you, I considered it.'

'You mean *being* with him?'

'Yeah. I know that is so wrong of me,' Catherine admitted. 'You were tempted too, weren't you?'

Cecilia exhaled.

'Tempted. Yes.'

'Then why not? Didn't you have any doubts?'

'There's no going back for me, you know? Maybe a year ago I might have. Probably would have done anything for a shot. I did much worse for a lot less.'

'Is it because of Sebastian?'

Cecilia didn't answer and Catherine knew not to press the issue.

'I'm so sorry I can't be at the show.'

'I'm not,' Cecilia said. 'You have your own gig that night, that's the best reason to miss mine.'

Catherine nodded appreciatively and dried her tears. 'But it's your big night.'

'And a big night for you, too. Do your thing, Catherine. No matter what anyone tells you or dangles in front of you.'

'I'm really scared for you, Cecilia,' Cat fretted. 'I saw those guys with the knives outside the hospital when you left. Looked them right in the eye. They're dead inside. Remorseless killers.'

'I know. Ever since Ricky we've been dealing with them. It's everywhere now.'

'People thought they were there to rob the crowd but maybe they were really there for you?'

'Probably were. Either way, they sent a message. Frey sent a message.'

'Once this album it out, your message will be the only one that counts.'

CeCe nodded weakly. She'd seemed more reflective, even melancholy, then usual and Cat felt like she was about to find out why.

'When you asked me before if I had doubts. I wasn't being honest.'

'No way, you hooked up with Less?'

'No. But when I watched your interview, saw what happened outside the hospital, I really started to wonder if following this calling was worth it.'

'Maybe it isn't?' Cat asked.

'I don't care if they come for me but I don't want anyone else getting hurt. Not on my account. One way or another it's got to stop.'

'It's just so surreal, with what happened to Lucy and everything. I don't know what I'd do if . . .'

Cecilia walked over to Catherine and hugged her tightly, as if she'd never let her go.

'You'll carry on, that's what you'll do,' Cecilia whispered. 'Promise me that. No matter what happens you'll always carry on.'

'Only if you promise me you won't let anything bad happen?'

'To you? Never,' Cecilia swore.

'You won't be mad if I steal one of these songs and do it in my show will you? I'm still your biggest fan, you know.'

Cecilia took Cat's hand in hers.

'What's mine is yours.'

Agnes's Expectation

*T*he red taper candle flickered and the intermittent hum of her sleeping laptop filled the otherwise quiet room like a sleep aid.

Agnes was left alone with her thoughts, trying to fall asleep. Twisting. Turning. Flipping her pillow over and over. A sense of foreboding overwhelmed her. She struggled with her down comforter too, kicking one leg out at first, then tossing it off completely. She stared upwards into the darkness, counting the floaters that danced above her and watching them appear and disappear like soap bubbles in a warm bath.

She felt her head about to explode. Was her restlessness from her anxiety, she wondered, from all the looking over her shoulder? From Lucy? From the Vandals that continued to stalk her? From Frey? She got up and walked over to her window and pulled the curtain back just a touch. There were a few die-hards still outside, as they had been every night since she got back from Perpetual Help.

Keeping watch. Where before they'd seemed a nuisance, she now found comfort in their presence. And a measure of safety. She flicked on her desk lamp, surrendering to her involuntary alertness.

She thought about calling out for her mother, to talk, and just as quickly decided that was probably a bad idea. What was there to say anyway? On some level, Martha felt that Agnes and the others had this coming to them. Their punishment for daring to believe in Sebastian and their own inner voice. In themselves.

She remembered seeing those cheesy coffee mugs in the corner store asking what would Jesus do, or if Jesus showed up today, would he be greeted as a saviour or a psychotic. Frey's verdict was definitely in and so, she suspected, was the verdict of a lot of other people. Sadly, she had to count her mother among them.

Agnes returned to bed. The only thought that would soothe her was of Sebastian. Many had claimed to have seen him, but whenever the reporters showed up it was always some wacko or fanatic. But she really had. He was there when Lucy died. A spirit. An angel. A saint. No matter how desperate she was feeling, in her bedroom or the psych ward, the very thought of him was enough to ease her mind. But not her restless heart. Thoughts of Sebastian only made her miss him more. She called out to him in the darkness. She closed her eyes. Repeating his name like a sacred mantra.

The desk light dimmed and shadows filled the room. Agnes could feel a presence. A living one not far from her. She opened her eyes.

'Sebastian,' she called out.

'Agnes,' came a gentle reply.

All fear left her and she smiled a satisfied smile, as if she'd conjured him through she force of will. Then, her lips began to quiver and tears filled her eyes at the sight of him.

'You came to me?'

'I'm never far from you, Agnes.'

She sat up in her bed, expectantly.

'There is so much I need to ask you. To tell you.'

'Ask,' he said.

'Is Lucy with you?'

'She is with all of us now. Everywhere.'

'I miss her. And you.' There was pain in Agnes's voice.

'Can I come closer,' he asked.

'Yes,' she said.

He smiled. 'I've come before.'

'Yes, but only in my dreams. Is this a dream?'

'No,' he assured, taking her hand in his.

It was solid and warm.

'My mother thinks none of this is real. That it's just a delusion. I'm sorry, I mean an illusion.'

'The difference between what is real and what is illusory is not as great as we think, Agnes. It is only matter of how much you want to believe in it. Have faith in it.'

'Like love?' she asked, drawing him closer into her arms.

'Like love,' he whispered quietly into her ear.

Agnes looked deeply into his eyes and their lips met. She felt her body rise to meet his as he pulled her close. Sebastian brushed

147

her hair away from her face and ran his hand along her neck and her shoulder and down her side, placing his palm on her stomach. Her body tightened, she threw her head back ecstatically and then relaxed in euphoric response. She was filled with a shuddering peace from head to toe by his touch. By anticipation. By their single kiss.

'I'm yours,' she said. 'From the moment we met.'

'Blessed are you,' Sebastian replied, lifting his hand from her belly. He stood and lingered above her, reaching again for her hand.

'What am I supposed to do now?'

'You will know when the time comes.'

'What does the future hold for us?'

'You are holding the future, Agnes.'

'I hope I can be as brave as you and as Lucy.'

He grasped her hand even more tightly, a sweet but melancholy expression crossing his face.

'Much has been given and much asked of you, Agnes,' Sebastian said.

Her eyes began to flutter and close as if the weight of the world had been lifted from them. Her hand fell from his, limply to her side.

'I'm so tired.'

'Sleep, Agnes. And dream.'

She felt him departing but didn't have the strength to open her eyes. 'Just one kiss to last me?'

He replied as if from a great distance. His words echoing in the room and in her mind before fading away into nothing. 'One kiss to last forever.'

13

iCONFESS

The chapel smelled of roses and incense. The room overflowed with fresh cut flowers, some just in the verge of blossoming, and large myrrh candles, surrounding Lucy and Sebastian. Not a petal out of place, not a random drop of wax running down the candelabras or pooling on the floor. The bone fixtures that survived the fire were carefully reconstructed. The place was cared for meticulously, lovingly, as he might have expected.

The fragrant aroma filled Jesse's nostrils as he sat quietly before Lucy's casket. It was a visit he was making regularly these days. The caretakers at Precious Blood knew him now and, for lack of a better word, he'd cut a deal with them that allowed him to visit after hours. Away from the prying eyes of the followers or anyone else. The church was not exactly guarded, but it was watched and Tony would often accompany him for safety's sake, usually preferring to wait outside to keep watch in case of any trouble. Usually, but not this evening.

Jesse hung his head, silently reflecting on their life together, as he had been doing each time he came to visit. The smoke and the dim, flickering candlelight began to affect him. It was so surreal. He could've sworn he was high if he didn't know better. If nothing else, the sensory overload had heightened his own self-awareness and feelings of guilt. He was almost embarrassed to look at her and seemed to be asking her permission to do whatever it was he felt needed doing, sitting like a disobedient child listening to a lecture from a disappointed parent.

After a while, he felt his solitude interrupted. As if he was no longer alone. His heart began to pound in excitement. He'd hoped for another visitation from Lucy. Like the one he'd had in the hospital. But that, he'd concluded, was just a dream or some sort of drug induced hallucination. He wasn't just looking for answers, but for proof of her continued existence. He didn't have a deep well of faith to draw upon like the priests and nuns or her followers. Jesse was a practical guy, not prone to magical thinking, but he'd seen too much to not consider the possibility. So far, however, that was what it remained. A possibility. Now perhaps, there would come an answer.

'Lucy?' he whispered.

He felt a hand on his shoulder but it didn't feel like her touch. Alarmed, he jumped up reflexively, fists clenched, ready to defend himself and her. He turned to face his attacker only to see it was not an attacker at all. But a child. It was Jude. Jesse relaxed but only a little bit.

'How'd you get in here, kid?'

Jude just stared at him, looking deep in Jesse's eyes, as if he could communicate directly with his mind. Without words.

'That's right, Tony isn't here,' Jesse reminded himself. 'It's late. Shouldn't you be home or something?'

Jude shook his head *no*.

Jesse looked around awkwardly, unsure of whether to be happy or freaked out at the boy's presence. He turned towards the glass casket with Lucy's body on display and became even more uncomfortable.

'Listen, I really don't know if this is the right place for you.'

Before he got his warning out, Jude walked past him to the display case and placed his hand upon it and closed his eyes, deep in thought.

'Hey,' Jesse said, reaching for Jude. 'It's OK.'

Jude turned towards him as if in a trance. The flames of the candles suddenly grew higher, throwing shadows across the boys face. Lucy's casket and Sebastian's urn seemed to glow, to become illuminated. Rosebuds opened, as if feeling the sunshine for the first time. Jesse backed away nervously.

'I think we need to get out of here,' he said.

Jude's eyes rolled over white, his head fell backwards and his body stiffened.

'Holy shit,' Jesse murmured, rubbing his hands together.

A cold chill descended upon the chapel. Jesse grabbed for his shoulders. His bones began to ache. Each of his injuries from Born Again pained him as if he'd only just received them. He shivered uncontrollably, both from the drop in temperature and the sound of his name echoing, emanating, as if from a great distance but actually coming from Jude.

'Jesse.'

Again he asked, 'Lucy?'

The voice grew louder and clearer and closer. It was deep and resonant. Not a girl's voice or the child's, but a voice he recognized.

'Jesse.'

'Sebastian?'

The boy pointed an accusing finger at him and spoke. 'Why are you here?'

Jesse was overwhelmed and not sure how to answer or even if he should answer. He shook his head to clear it his mind, unsure if he was hallucinating. The question hung in the frigid air and finally Jesse answered.

'I don't know.'

'You do.'

'To think. To talk. To be close to her.'

'No. That isn't why.'

'Then you tell me,' Jesse shouted anger and frustration. 'You tell *me*!'

'It's because you *believe*.'

Tears welled up in Jesse's eyes.

'Believe?' Jesse growled.

'Yes. In them and in their purpose.'

'Yeah, I do believe. I *believe* this is all your fault!'

Jesse pointed at Lucy's casket.

'Do not seek to blame, Jesse, what has happened has happened.'

Tears flowed freely now and he fell to his knees, pleading futilely.

'I want her to be *alive* again.'

'Then keep her alive.'

'So I can become a raging lunatic like you were?'

'So you can become yourself.'

'I have no idea who I am anymore.'

'Your life was spared once. Do you remember?'

'I do. She saved me. From you.'

'What will you do with the life you have been given?'

'That's the question I keep asking myself. I don't know.'

'You are needed, Jesse. Open your eyes and your heart.'

'For what?'

'As her reputation was entrusted to you in life, her legacy, our legacy is entrusted to you now.'

'I'm not that guy. There are a lot of other people around who will make sure of that. I don't even know where to start.'

'When the time comes you will know.'

Sebastian's voice faded into nothing and the candle flames receded. Jude collapsed to a heap on the floor and Jesse rushed to him. He lifted the boy up gently and cradled him in his arms. The blood gradually returned to the boy's face.

'Hey. Wake up, Jude.'

Jesse was startled by the sound of footsteps rushing down the staircase.

'Oh Jude,' the woman cried. 'Thank God you are here.'

'He's OK, Sister.'

'I've been looking everywhere for him.'

Jesse helped Jude to his feet and smiled at him. Jude appeared exhausted but returned it.

'You OK, kid?'

Jude nodded *yes*. The nun grabbed him in her arms and held him tightly.

'Oh Jude, all these terrible thoughts were going through my head. You nearly scared the life out of me.'

'Me too,' Jesse said.

Martha heard Agnes retching in the bathroom from down the hall. She walked to the door and listened for a second.

'Let me guess, you're not going to school again today.'

'I feel like hell. I can't seem to shake this flu.'

'Are you sure that's what it is, Agnes?'

Agnes flushed the toilet and opened the door just a crack. Martha could see she was pale and sunken eyed. Weak.

'What else would it be, Mother?'

'Oh, I don't know. I just hear you've been having a hard time at school. Not that you confide anything in me.'

'Still gossiping with your friends? If I didn't feel like such shit I might be pissed at you but I don't have the energy.'

She closed the door and turned on the faucet and brushed her teeth for the third time that morning.

'At this rate you'll never graduate,' Martha warned. 'All that money for tuition down the drain.'

'Wow,' Agnes spat as she left the bathroom. 'You really don't get it.

'Why don't you just go into school and make an announcement that all this nonsense has just been a terrible mistake. It's obviously ruining your health, physically and otherwise. Costing you your friends and your education. Why Dr Frey let you out I'll never know.'

'He wants to keep his hands clean, Mother, until he makes his move.'

'More conspiracy talk. You're just making my point, Agnes. I have never seen a persecution complex like yours.'

'Except for yours, you mean?'

'Have it your way, Agnes. It's not my future that's at stake.

There are enough waitressing jobs available, I'm sure you'll find one.'

'I'll be fine, Mother, don't worry.'

'Fine? You think those desperate vagrants outside care about you, Agnes? Their virgin queen? One wrong step and they'll turn on you. Believe me.'

Agnes slammed her bedroom door just as the front doorbell rang.

Exasperated, Martha trudged through the living room and toward the door. She peeked through the hole and huffed. The crowd had gotten noticeably larger suddenly and now she knew why. Martha opened the door and stood there like a security guard. Cool and unwelcoming, one hand on her hip, the other holding the door, as she greeted the visitor.

'You are not welcome here,' Martha groused. 'Please leave and take those people out there with you.'

'I'm here to see Agnes.'

Agnes heard a familiar voice from the hallway and noticed a friend in the door.

'Cecilia!' she shrieked, running for the door.

Martha stepped aside reluctantly and the two girls embraced.

CeCe stepped back and took a good look at her friend.

'You look like shit,' Cecilia said with a laugh.

'You can say that again,' Martha agreed, stomping off into the kitchen.

'Never mind me, how are you?' Agnes asked.

'I'm good. Life is good.'

'Come in.'

Agnes closed the door behind Cecilia and led her to her room.

'This is definitely your room,' Cecilia laughed, spying the boho spiritual décor, vintage clothing spilling from the closets and drawers and uber romantic bedding and plants and nature everywhere.

'It's my sanctuary, you could say,' Agnes smiled.

They sat on the floor just staring at each other for a while.

'You haven't called or returned my texts,' Cecilia said. 'I was worried about you.'

'I'm sorry. I've just been really sick the past few weeks.'

'That's no excuse,' Cecilia said flatly, shooting Agnes a knowing glace.

'I know. So tell me about your album and everything. Even kids at school were talking about it.'

'Daniel Less, the guy who got me out of Perpetual Help, is pretty happy, he set me up in the new place with all this equipment, a computer.'

'And a phone, I see,' Agnes joked.

'Yeah, I finally caved. It's always blowing up now though.'

'You're a popular girl.'

'We'll see. He's rushing the first single out, which is why I was texting. I'm doing a show and I need you to be there.'

'You really think that's a good idea? You know what happened last time.'

'It's not really an option. I signed a contract. It'll be fine,' Cecilia reassured her. 'He's providing security.'

'You seem pretty comfortable with it.'

'It's what I always wanted.'

'Used to want, I thought.'

'What better way to get the message out, Agnes? I really need you to understand.'

'OK, I'm with you.'

'Have you seen Jesse?'

'No, I tried calling and emailing but he doesn't answer. I'm going to go see him when I'm feeling better.'

'I heard he's in a bad way. If you see him please invite him to the show. I really want him to be there too.'

'I will.'

The look on Agnes's face said otherwise to Cecilia. In fact, she was starting to look terribly pale. As if she was about to be sick.

'I'm sorry,' Agnes said covering her mouth and bolting for the bathroom.

Cecilia could hear her heaving in the toilet. And after a few minutes she returned.

'That really is a bad bug you've got,' Cecilia said, rubbing her friend's back as she sat doubled over on her bed.

'I don't know,' Agnes said.

'What do you mean?'

'I've been dreaming a lot.'

'Me too,' Cecilia said, rolling her eyes upward.

'Of Lucy. And of Sebastian.'

'So have I,' Cecilia said quietly.

'He came to me. Right here in this room. It was so real.'

'Maybe it was? But you've been sick. Fevers can do strange things.'

'I don't have a fever.'

'You should see a doctor.'

'That's what my mother keeps saying but I've seen enough doctors to last me a lifetime.'

'I know what you mean,' Cecilia said. 'What do you think is going on then?'

Agnes paused for a second; unsure if she should say out loud the one thought that had been running through her head for days.

'I think I'm pregnant.'

14

Souled Out

Frey was pacing his office expectantly and grumbling under his breath just loud enough for the nurse at the desk outside his office to hear. She stepped in to ask if there was anything he needed.

'I'm sorry, Doctor, did you say something?'

'What? Oh no, just thinking out loud.'

He appeared unusually distracted to her. On edge. Not being a man who shared his thoughts or his problems openly, the nurse thought it best not to inquire any further.

'OK, then I'll just close your door if you don't mind.'

'That's fine, nurse. I'm expecting a call.'

'Yes, Dr Frey. You told me earlier.'

Frey nodded, recalling that in fact he had mentioned the call to her. Several times.

'Well, please just put it through as soon as it comes in,' he asked tersely.

'Yes, Doctor.'

Frey turned toward a his window and looked down. The lack of crowds gathered outside the hospital entrance below was glaring to him by their absence. As a matter of strategy he believed he'd done the right thing by letting Agnes, Jude and Jesse go, by spitefully making more problems for Less, if only to prove his own point, but that didn't mean he liked it. It wasn't so much the fact that it had been forced by the idiot idolaters that had gathered daily, or the predatory media looking for a story that bothered him so much. It was that a one-time colleague-turned-rival had undermined him that was most galling and that had sparked such resentment.

The nurse's voice blaring from his phone's speaker settled him down and cleared his throat.

'Your call, Dr Frey.'

He grabbed the receiver tightly from its cradle.

'Hello, Daniel.'

'Alan.'

'To what do I owe the pleasure?'

'Just calling for an update, you might say.'

'About?'

'Please don't be cagey, Doctor. It's insulting,' Daniel said antagonistically. 'I understand you've released the others?'

'Yes, that's true. Just taking your lead.'

'Are we playing chess here?'

'I'm not playing anything. Besides, aren't we on the same team, Alan?'

'I would've thought so.'

'I was persuaded, mostly by your efforts to get Cecilia discharged, that there was no use in keeping them here, so they were free to roam. Speaking of which, how is she? Still breathing, last I heard.'

'Everything is going according to plan.'

'Your plan?'

'Yes.'

'So signing her to a record deal and promoting an album release with a big concert is supposed to diminish her influence?'

'I'm giving her what she always wanted, Alan. And still wants. In the end, it will be her undoing. She's sold herself, so to speak. I can spin that when it's all over.'

'The corruption of St Cecilia,' Frey mused. 'Sounds like the title of a Renaissance poem.'

'Or a Greek tragedy.'

'That's quite clever, Daniel, but the first thing that comes to mind is Elvis, you remember him?'

'You mean about the lunatics that still see him at the

truck stop in Tuscaloosa or wherever?'

'Partly,' Frey replied.

'Elvis, Jesus, Joan of Arc, it's the same thing. We've had to deal with it for centuries now. '

'Death is not necessarily the end, Daniel. That's all I'm saying.'

'But it is more manageable. Life, as you have seen in your practice, is far more unpredictable.'

'It might be worth noting, though it should hardly be necessary to an old record man such as yourself, that Elvis sold far more records dead than alive.'

'Yes, but its just old songs. Repackaged. Nothing new. Without new, you are just Fat Elvis. Passé.'

'Images can be rehabilitated, Daniel,' Frey cautioned. 'She will be seen as a martyr. Exactly what she wants. What they all want.'

'I don't understand your obsession with invalidating them. I say, exterminate them and let the pieces fall where they may.'

'You mean like Lucy? Where people gather outside her shrine each day handing out flyers. You can kill people but an idea is a very different matter.'

'With the media machinery I have at my disposal, she will soon be seen as damaged goods, a fraud and a sell-out,' Less enthused. 'And best of all, she'll be dead.'

'You seemed to have it worked out.'

'Mostly. To be honest, I'm also calling to ask a favour.'

'What can I do for you?'

'I'm going to need some assistance from your minions at that halfway house.'

'Isn't that a bit down-market for you, Daniel? Consorting with animals, as you call them?'

'Well, I'm not unaccustomed to a little slumming,' Less admitted.

'So I've heard.'

'As the Bible says Alan, to everything there is a season. Even for homicidal junkies.'

'Recovering junkies,' Frey corrected snidely.

'Yes, whatever you say. Just make sure they turn up when I need them.'

'Leave the details with my secretary and I'll see to it.'

'The dream will be shattered in a million pieces.'

'Just remember the old gift shop warning, you break it, you buy it. And it may come with a hefty price tag.'

'I'm not worried, Alan. I can afford it.'

Jesse waited patiently as the file loaded. The videotape of Lucy's death was completely digitized, edited and ready for upload. It would be his first post to Byte since he'd got back from the hospital. And quite possibly, he was thinking, his last.

His intention was not to surprise or provoke but to memorialize in a way that only he could. If he wanted to shock, he would have just posted the raw footage, but that, he thought, was a snuff film, not a tribute. He added slates and type, quick cuts and slow-motion dissolves, whatever felt right, whatever put across her message. If Lucy was a guide, a light in the darkness, then this little piece would help her show the way. A sort of inspir-mercial-informercial for the directionless, the disillusioned, the despairing. Not a piece to tell you, but to show you. And one without an 800 number to call at the end.

The upload bar filled slowly with data, turning from white to blue. Jesse floated the cursor over the upload button imaging what would happen once he clicked it. Byte was linked to virtually every major social media site possible. It might take a second for it to be discovered since his blog had been inactive for a while, but once it was, he figured, it would travel fast. And then what?

Jesse decided it didn't matter. He clicked play. He watched his clip as if he'd never seen it before. Watched grey words float over the black slate:

See For Yourself

They meandered by like a cloud across a darkened sky. Hopeful, but ominous. Paparazzi photos of Lucy from her earliest debut on the scene and some from his own personal camera roll filled the screen. Images of her, alternately imperious and inviting, flashed one after another. At clubs, parties, openings, premieres, charity events and police precincts. Leaving Precious Blood after Sebastian's death with Cecilia and Agnes and disappearing into a cheering throng. Dancing on tables in banquets, surrounded by adoring crowds on Brooklyn street corners and bending to acknowledge a child. The whole of her short, controversial and complicated existence boiled down to a handful of now-iconic images. Suddenly, the soundtrack stopped and the clip went silent. Voices rise. Questions. Answers. Demands. Refusals. A puddle of blood, a burst of light and screaming. Lucy, blinded and crawling in her bloodstained clothes, struggling, Sebastian's heart clenched tightly in her arms. It was hard for Jesse to watch, but then, it was supposed to be. Then news reports of her death, of the outcry, the lamentation and the indifference, and editorials of its meaning.

There was no accusatory finger pointed. No sinister portrait of Dr Frey dropped in, devil horns photoshopped on his head. No manipulation. No CGI. This was not about blame for Jesse. It was about Lucy. It was about truth. Revenge was his obsession, but not hers.

And finally, a cut to a single candle from the chapel that widened out to row upon row of them. As the camera pulled back, she was revealed in her glory. Beautiful and still. Encased in glass. Protected. Regal. Like a saint. And then more words. A message.

Know Yourself.
Be Yourself.
Seeing is believing.

The typeface dissolved into nothing and the reel faded slowly to black. He knew from his club days a good response to a blind invitation was roughly five per cent. He was always good for ten per cent and if Lucy was involved, maybe even twenty. They'd built a business on it. Now he was trying to build a movement. The viewer counter on his home page tripped from zero to one and he smiled. Jesse stared at his computer screen. And waited.

15

Aura

Cecilia walked for a long time, distractedly, trying to clear her head, to process Agnes's news. She was overjoyed and also overanxious for her friend. She could feel deep in her heart that it was true. If there was ever a sign that what had happened, what they had been told by Sebastian was real, this was it. Immaculate conception 2.0. It was clarifying. A much-needed reminder. Suddenly her own ambitions seemed less pressing, less important to her.

She walked from Agnes's house in Park Slope toward Third Avenue and into the rapidly gentrifying Gowanus neighbourhood. So lost in thought was she that she'd almost forgotten an important appointment she'd made.

Ordinarily, walking alone creeped her out now. Walking so near to Born Again even more so. It was the beauty of Less's apartment set up for her in the East Village. She felt safe and relatively anonymous. Back on the streets of Brooklyn, she could feel eyes on her once again. Fleeting glances of recognition, knowing nods, admiring stares, and contemptuous ones. That much had not changed. Leers, but nothing dangerous so far. Cecilia squeezed her fingers into her palms and they were dry. Not even a drop of blood. Strangely enough, she found herself thinking, the only times her palms bled these days, were in her apartment.

Before long she found herself at her destination, an iron works shop. She looked up towards the roof at the oversized Sacred Heart of Jesus statue encased in glass at the precipice. The place was run by an old no-nonsense Italian guy named Jimmy. He was a real craftsman. The first choice in that neighbourhood for the sort of Victorian railings and fences that decorated every single brownstone in that part of Brooklyn. He could make anything, she'd heard, so she commissioned a very special piece from him. And it was ready.

She stepped in the door and the smell of paint thinner, propane and rustoleum was almost overwhelming. Dressed completely in black, rail thin, shoulders thrown back, she seemed to fit right in with the rows and rows of black metal bars leaning along the walls. She strolled toward the white-haired old man fascinated by the kind of wrought-iron platform he was welding together. It looked to her like nothing less than the stand for some ginormous fish tank some Brooklyn Heights stockbroker had ordered custom made for his parlour floor living room.

'Magnificent,' she said.

'Fit for a queen,' came the reply.

The gruff but warm tone of his voice peppered with the slightest Italian accent landed softly on her ear. Like music.

'Jimmy?'

'Yeah,' he said, turning off his blowtorch and raising his welder's visor.

She reached for his hand and he took it, gently. She felt the callouses on his skin, the thickness of his fingers and the arthritic twist of his overused and hard-working knuckles.

'I'm . . .'

'I know who you are,' he said tersely. 'C'mere.'

She followed him back to a small office with dirty and overstuffed accounts payable binders piled high on a single desk. Empty coffee cups littered the floor.

'How's business?' she asked randomly, ogling the beautiful artisanry that lay along the walls of the workshop.

'Menza menza,' he replied, pursing his lips and turning his hand to one side and the other.

Cecilia knew the gesture and she translated for herself. It meant 'so-so'. Judging from the amount of work he was doing, what it really meant was that business was good, but I'm not admitting that to you. She loved how cautious the old-timers were. Ever vigilant for a jealous competitor or even a bargain-hunting customer putting the evil eye on them. How proud yet modest about their talents and their achievements they were.

He stepped behind the desk and reached for a long, narrow black leather case. He swung it around and placed gently it on the piles of bills and correspondence. The weight of it was obvious to her as the paperwork below gave way under the case. He flicked a gold latch and opened the case. The interior was lined in red velvet. Nestled in its centre was what she'd come for. He lifted up the piece as if it was fragile or delicate, but it was neither. It was rock-solid. Iron through and though. Cecilia was speechless.

'Wow,' was all she could muster.

'It's a lost art,' he admitted, sadness in his rough voice.

He removed the masterpiece from the case – a gold, burning, sacred heart with thorns around it was the guitar body with a pair of eyes at the neck. The Milagros of Agnes and Lucy, right there, in guitar form. 'My guy did good,' he said. Then he lifted a slender rod from the case and handed it to her. It was an arrow, with a sharpened head, affixed to a resin bow, the sort a cellist might use. Sebastian's Milagro soldered into part of hers.

'And so did you. It's so beautiful, Jimmy,' she said, in shock at what she was seeing. 'Exactly what I had in mind for the show. I don't know what to say. Grazie.'

'Prego,' he replied.

She turned the arrow around in her hands, feeling its sturdiness. Its weight. It was not quite as heavy as it looked, thankfully, she thought, as she brought the tip close to her eye to examine it. It appeared razor-sharp. She pressed the tip of her finger against it to be sure and was not disappointed.

'It's like a St. Hubert's Key, but bigger,' Jimmy said.

'What's that?'

'A metal bar with a head that they once used to cauterize wounds and kill infections from all sorts of things. Rat bites, dog bites, rabies, whatever.'

'Like a brand.'

'It can cure what troubles you.'

Cecilia laughed. 'Wish I would have known about that sooner.'

'Never too late,' he said.

'What do I owe you?' she asked.

The old man took the arrow from her and placed it back in the case next to the guitar and closed it, shaking his head *no*.

'Jimmy, I can't,' she said looking deep in the man's eyes. 'This is incredible what you've done. It's your work.'

To her complete surprise, he got down slowly on his knees before her and offered the case up to her, like a supplicant. This tough old man kneeling at her feet like she was some sort of royalty. She was breathless at this gesture of kindness and faith.

'Yes,' he said. 'It's my work. This is what I can give.'

Cecilia got down on her knees as well and accepted it from him.

'Thank you,' Cecilia said smiling.

'Musica bella,' he whispered to her.

'You're a saint, Jimmy,' she said, tears welling in her eyes.

'I'm just an old man,' he answered. 'Make a beautiful noise with it tomorrow and when the time comes, use it well.'

'I will. I promise.'

Cecilia rose and left the man still kneeling. Praying. She let her hands run along the rods of cold metal gates lining the walls like a bubblegum card in a bicycle spoke. She stepped outside and found herself directly across the street from the venue. Her name in huge letters on the marquee. The first time she'd ever seen anything like that. It was an old meeting hall that had been recently refurbished. It was called The Temple now and hers would be the first gig in the renovated space. How appropo. She always thought of herself as the leader of some kind of service for her fans, her disciples, even before Sebastian. Daniel had thought of everything.

Her cellphone rang unexpectedly and Daniel's name popped up on the screen.

'Hi Daniel. Great timing,' she said casually. 'I'm just outside the venue.'

'Nerves?' he asked curiously. 'That's not like you.'

'No,' she said flatly, gripping the handle on her guitar case tightly. 'I'm ready.'

'Good. It's all there for you, Cecilia. Money, fame, everything you could imagine. Right there on that stage. Everything you've always wanted.'

'And the music?'

'That too,' he laughed. 'Do you know what you're planning to do?'

She felt her palms moisten, the handle slipping slightly in her grasp. The phone sliding a bit in the other. She looked around but there was no one. Her hands and her head hurt.

'I do. In fact, I think it's all just become very clear to me,' she said calmly. 'The album will be released before I hit the stage, right?'

'Yes, as promised.'

'Good.'

Any surprises in store?'

'I'm full of surprises, Daniel.'

'That's why I signed you,' he said making eyes at her. 'Like what? I promise not tell a soul.'

'Ah,' she fumbled, 'I'm thinking I might close the show with a body surf across the crowd, if security can take it.'

Droplets of blood gathered on the side of her hands and ran down along them, hanging, suspended, as if on the edge of a cliff, until each one dropped to the cracked concrete under her feet.

'Now that will be a moment to remember,' Less enthused. 'The crowd will love being so close to you. Getting to hold you. To touch you . . .'

'If security cooperates.'

'Don't worry. I've arranged for all that. You'll be perfectly safe, I guarantee it. Throw caution to the wind, Cecilia. Like it's the last thing you will ever do.'

Maybe it was the tone of his voice, or Agnes's news, or Jimmy or her dreams of Sebastian, but suddenly the air around her and her mood seemed to change. She felt anxious. Uneasy. The fog in her mind began to lift. She stammered a bit, trying to regain her composure.

'Yes, I'll save that for the encore.'

'This is it, Cecilia. Your future is at stake tomorrow night. Life or death. For your career, I mean.'

'Worried about your investment, Daniel?'

'Just a little encouragement,' Less explained with some irritation.

'Thanks for the pep talk but I don't need it. I've seen the future, Daniel,' Cecilia answered firmly, thoughts of Agnes filling her with emotion. 'The crowd will carry me all the way to the back, right to you.'

'I'll be waiting.'

'I know you will.'

'I want you to go out there and kill, Cecilia.'

'That's exactly what I intend to do.'

16

Starf*cker

Jesse arrived back at his apartment, arms loaded with groceries. He was hungry, for the first time in a while. He was feeling stronger, even the weight of the bags as he climbed the stairs to his floor didn't bother him. Maybe it was the relief of finally posting the video. That was the real weight he'd been feeling since coming home. And now, it'd been lifted. As he ascended to the landing just below his apartment, the text notification on his phone rang. He balanced the bags against the banister and read it.

'Playing tonight at The Temple. I need you to come. Please.'

Jesse didn't like the sound of it, but what else could he do but go.

'Ok,' he typed.

'Great job with the video. Lucy would be proud of you. I'm going to use it in my show. You're not gonna charge me a licensing fee are you?'

Jesse smiled and picked up the bags, headed up the final flight of stairs and into his hallway. The smile quickly left his face as he looked ahead at his apartment door. It was ajar. Definitely not the way he'd left it. He put the supermarket bags down and yanked out a wooden spoke from the old banister, raised it like a club and approached the apartment slowly. Quietly.

His first instinct was to call the cops. Call Detective Murphy. But he didn't. Nothing good had come of it so far and he had no reason to think this would be any different. His second instinct was to leave. Call his parents and ask to stay for a while. But he didn't do that either. Too many questions he didn't want to answer, he thought. Instead, he walked closer, listening carefully for any sound coming from behind the door. He opened the camera app on his phone, switched it to video and began to record. It was this instinct that guided him now. The reporter's instinct.

He pressed his outstretched fingers against the door and pushed it. There was no resistance. He reached for the light switch just inside the doorjamb and flicked it. To his surprise, the ceiling light came on. He could hardly believe what he was seeing. The room was a shambles. Drawers emptied, furniture overturned, computers smashed to bits.

'Son of a bitch!' Jesse stepped in slowly and shook his head. He shuffled through mounds of broken glass, papers, files, folders and photos. His refrigerator had been emptied and its contents dumped all over the floors, carpeting and couch. He peeked into his bedroom and the mattress had been overturned, the white sheets stamped with boot prints. On the wall above his bed were mangled 8 x 10 pictures of Lucy, with her eyes cut out, Cecilia, ripped in half beneath her neck and Agnes with a hole in her chest. He'd seen this before. At the old lady's house after the murder. The work of vandals with a capital V. At whose bidding he had absolutely no doubt. His film, he thought, must be making an impact. He stood for a while, taking the carnage in. Let himself feel the anger inside of him building to a volcanic pitch. He scrolled his contact list and dialled for help.

'Tony?'

'Yo.'

'You were right.'

'About what?'

'Somebody didn't like my video.'

'You OK?'

'Yeah, but my place, not so much. It's bent.'

'It's a warning.'

'I know,' Jesse agreed. 'That's why I'm calling.'

'What d'you need?'

'I'm gonna need you and a few of your friends to be at The Temple tonight.'

Martha was beside herself. She paced her parlour floor living room, debating whether or not to make the call. She peered anxiously out the front window from behind the curtains at the small gathering and began wringing her hands, on the verge, suddenly, of a full-blown panic attack. She picked up the phone.

'This is Martha Fremont. I need to speak with Dr Frey.'

'I'm sorry but Dr Frey is unavailable, can I have him return your call?'

'No!' Martha shouted. 'He needs to make himself available. Tell him it's urgent.'

'If it's an emergency you should call 911, Mrs Fremont.'

'Don't patronize me! This is all his goddamned fault. Get him on the phone. Now!'

'Hold on,' the nurse said politely.

'Dr Frey?'

'Yes, Mrs Fremont?'

'Thank God you took my call.'

'Well, I've instructed the staff not to put through any outside calls. Many of them are from gossip columnists looking for information about your daughter and Cecilia. The screening process is for your privacy and protection, you understand.'

Martha was barely listening. 'I'm worried sick about Agnes.'

'Well, I'm sorry to hear that, but as you know she's been discharged and no longer in my care.'

'That's right and I still can't figure out why. She's delusional!'

'Slow down, Mrs Fremont. What exactly is the matter?'

Martha paused, unsure of exactly how to phrase it, but if there was anyone who would understand, she thought, it was Frey. 'Agnes hasn't been feeling well lately. At first I thought it was just an excuse to get out of school. That she'd been being harassed or something.'

'That wouldn't be unusual,' Frey replied, his voice taking on a casual, analytical tone.

'Then I overheard something, when that Cecilia came over to visit that I could not believe.'

The doctor sat up in his office chair, suddenly quite a bit more interested in what the woman had to say. 'What did you hear, Mrs Fremont?'

'It's so ridiculous I don't think I could tell anyone but you without being dragged off to the mental ward myself.'

'I'm listening.'

'She said she was . . . pregnant.'

Frey was silent for a long while. 'How do you know she isn't?'

'Don't be ridiculous. She's a virgin, for God's sake. There hasn't been a boy around here since Finn.'

'Why are you calling me? You should make an appointment for her to see an obstetrician.'

'You don't understand. She thinks it's . . . Sebastian's!'

Martha broke down in tears.

'And you believe this?' Frey asked.

'No, but she has been showing all the signs. Nausea, weight gain around the middle. I just don't know what to think.'

Frey remained calm in his demeanour but inside he was anything but.

'If what you say is true, it seems to be a classic case of pseudocyesis.'

'I'm sorry, what?'

'False pregnancy. Agnes is prone to delusion and fantasy, we know that,' Frey expounded. 'Her obsession not just with the boy but with the idea of idealized love, that brought her here in the first place, make her a perfect candidate, I'd say.'

Now it was Martha's turn to stay silent. 'Then I do need a psychiatrist.'

'Perhaps, but not me.'

'Why not? You know her case. Her history. I'll be laughed out of another doctor's office.'

'We've been down this road, Mrs Fremont. She doesn't trust me. She's refused treatment. Worse then that, she believes I intend to harm her and her friends. There is no way I could help her under those circumstances.'

'Dr Frey, you don't understand. It's not just Agnes's mental state that concerns me. If word gets out that she might be pregnant, those lunatics outside my door, the ones that follow her around, worshipping their virgin saint, will turn on her in a heartbeat. God knows what they'll do to her.'

'Yes, only God knows. Perhaps you should call the police?'

'You must be joking. I can't even get them to send a squad car down here to clear the street anymore. You think they're going to provide a police escort because a girl is having a hysterical pregnancy?'

'I see your point.'

'I'm begging you,' Martha pleaded through tears. 'Please help me. Help Agnes.'

'I'm truly sorry, Mrs Fremont, but there is nothing more I can do. You'll have to find someone else. Goodbye.'

The doctor leaned back in his chair and rubbed at his eyes. Martha's news had hit him hard. It was news he'd feared right from the start. A pregnancy. A continuation of their line writ in DNA. How much greater would be their fame, how much greater the sympathy, the adoration with the birth of a child. The media would eat it up.

'Nurse, can you please get that reporter from Page Six on the phone?'

17

Blood Moon

The Temple was gleaming, its marquee lighting up the entire block of the industrial neighbourhood. Cecilia arrived early, in the limo provided by Daniel Less. There was a cross and a four-leaf clover dangling from the driver's rear-view mirror and Cecilia watched it swing like a pendulum as the car approached its destination.

'Backstage entrance?' the driver asked.

'Yeah, but can you circle around the front first?'

'Yes, Miss,' he answered.

They pulled around the front of the venue and Cecilia asked him to stop for a second. She stared at her name in big bold letters and bright lights. Fans were already lining up, tickets in hand.

'You must be very proud,' he opined in a lilting Irish accent.

'Just what I always wanted.'

'You're lucky,' he said. 'Not everyone gets to see their name in lights.'

'Yeah,' she said quietly. 'Lucky.'

He pulled around the back of The Temple and she sat there for a minute.

'This is your stop,' he called back to her. 'Put on a good show.'

'I will if it's the last thing I ever do.'

She thanked him and handed him a hundred-dollar bill.

'Drinks on me,' she said.

'Oh I can't, I'm driving you home.'

'Don't worry about that,' she said. 'Have one for me.'

'I'll toast your future, lassy.'

'May you get to heaven half an hour before the devil knows you're dead,' she laughed, mimicking an Irish brogue.

'I was thinking something more like "May your neighbours respect you, trouble neglect you, the angels protect you and heaven accept you".'

'I like yours better.'

'You Irish?' he asked.

'No, Italian and Slovak. Trento. My grandfather had to shorten it to get work when he came here.'

'Well, that's OK. I'll give you a pass.'

'Sorry to disappoint.'

The driver flashed a warm smile and winked at her. Cecilia teared up. The man reminded her of one of the two men she cared about most in the world. Bill. As if his soul was reaching out to her through him. Comforting her.

'Oh, don't be crying. This ain't a night for tears.'

'You just remind me of someone I've been missing, that's all,' she said. 'Happy tears.'

'Well, I hope you are reunited soon.'

'Me too,' Cecilia said.

She grabbed her guitar and iron cello bow and exited. A loud cheer went up from a few longtime Apostles who'd been waiting for her to arrive. Security made way for her. She looked around at the smiling faces. The anticipation of something special about to go down. Thought about the driver and Vinnie the ironworker. There were still some good people in the world, she mused. Worth saving. Worth the sacrifice. Something worth remembering. It wasn't all Ciphers and vandals. Not yet. Not if she could do something about it.

Cecilia stepped through the door to the backstage area as if she were entering a cathedral, a sacred space, which any club, no matter how seedy, had always felt to her. She approached the security guard outside her dressing room and nodded. He was big and burly but there was a sweetness in his eyes that she locked on to. He opened the door for her, gently.

He reached out his hand, offering to take her guitar and

bow and garment bag but she declined. 'I'm cool,' she said.

'You are,' he replied in a deep, resonant voice that rang clearly even above the pounding bass of the DJ opening act. 'No visitors?'

'Oh, I'm expecting some friends. You can let them in,' Cecilia instructed, handing him a short, crumpled handwritten list on notepaper.

The security guard nodded and closed the door.

She took the alone time to reflect. Mostly on her upcoming performance. What she would do. How the crowd would react. She visualized the entire show. The beginning. The middle. The end.

She flipped her laptop open and searched for her new album. Less had promised it would be released in time for her show, but she couldn't find it on any of the sites. No streams, no downloads.

A few taps at the door broke her concentration and then it opened, letting sounds of the backstage chatter in along with Agnes and Jesse.

Cecilia beamed at both of them. Happy.

'I'm so glad you came. I'm so glad you remembered.'

'Are you kidding,' Agnes said, running into her arms.

Cecilia hugged her tight and then pulled back, looking deeply into her friend's eyes, and brushed her hands through her curls.

'You look beautiful.'

'You look ready,' Agnes replied.

'Better be,' Jesse grumbled under his breath. 'People out there paid good money.'

'Hey,' Cecilia said, holding out her open arms. 'Come here.'

Jesse was far less demonstrative than Agnes and shuffled slowly towards Cecilia. His head down. They embraced.

'You sure this is a good idea?'

'I'm sure.'

'Jesse's apartment got ransacked,' Agnes added. 'I don't think they liked his film.'

'Well, then they're really not gonna like my show. I'm using it.'

'Jesus, Cecilia. You remember what happened the last time. Why provoke these terrorists?'

'I could ask you the same thing, Jesse,' Cecilia countered.

Another knock at the dressing-room door ended the discussion for the moment.

'Mr Less to see you?'

'Let him in.'

Less strutted in sporting a big smile and made a beeline for his protégé.

'Hello darling,' he gushed, planting kisses on both her cheeks. 'The big night is finally here.'

'It is,' Cecilia agreed.

'Have you worked out the end of your show?'

'Yes. It will be unforgettable, I promise.'

187

Less grinned and turned politely towards Agnes and Jesse to greet them.

'How rude of me. I'm Daniel Less.'

'Agnes,' she said, taking his outstretched hand.

'Jesse.'

'Oh, you are that infamous blogger we hear so much about. Good to see you here.'

'Good to be seen,' Jesse snarked.

'Yes, the papers said it was touch and go there for a while, but you are looking quite well.'

'Looks can be deceiving, sir,' Jesse replied, clearly unimpressed with the executive's smarmy small talk.

'Very true, young man,' Less concurred somewhat uncomfortably. 'Well, I hope you will support our budding superstar. Help us get the word out.'

'I'm not really in the gossip game anymore, but I'll do anything to help Cecilia.'

'Then we'll count on your support, Jesse. I'll be off now. Back of the room, my usual spot.'

He blew a kiss towards Cecilia and prepared to depart.

'Daniel, can I talk to you for a second?' Cecilia approached him in the doorway, like a suspicious retail clerk might approach a shoplifter.

'I thought you said my album would be live in time for the show?' she whispered.

'Oh, it's just a technical glitch. I have the IT team in the office working on it as we speak.'

Cecilia nodded. 'OK,' she said quietly.

'Don't worry about anything, Cecilia. You have a job to do tonight. Do it.'

'I know my job tonight,' she assured him.

'See you at the end.'

Less stepped out and the door closed behind him.

'I know that guy helped you get out of the mental ward but he gives me the creeps,' Jesse admitted.

'He kind of reminds me of Frey,' Agnes added.

'From what I hear, they aren't friends, to put it lightly,' Jesse said. 'Because of you.'

'I thought you were out of the gossip game, Jesse,' Cecilia joked. 'Frey. Less. All the same shit. Doesn't matter anyway.'

'It wasn't your apartment that was turned upside down,' Jesse reminded. 'It should matter. Which brings me back to my original point. This is way too dangerous for you.'

'I know what I'm doing.'

'Well, I'm not taking any chances. Tony and some of his guys will be out there.'

Cecilia smiled. 'Don't be afraid, Jesse.'

There was an uncomfortable silence.

'Well, we should probably let you have some alone time,' Agnes suggested. 'Get your armour on in private.'

Cecilia knelt down before Agnes and kissed her stomach softly.

'What the hell?' Jesse blurted.

Cecilia stood and Agnes hugged for a long time. 'Take care of yourself,' CeCe said. 'Both of you.'

'I love you,' Agnes whispered, her emotions overwhelming her as she stepped into the hallway.

'Be careful,' Jesse warned.

Cecilia reached into her backpack and produced a thumb drive which she handed over to him. The title of the album, 'Save Yourself' was handwritten in magic marker.

'Everything is on here. My album. Lyrics. Everything. Make sure it gets out there.'

Jesse was confused. 'It's about to be released? They've spent a fortune on you.'

'It won't, Jesse. Please do this for me. When you're done with it, give it to my friend Catherine. Her address is in a file on there.'

'OK.'

She kissed his cheek as he was leaving. 'Thank you. And if anything happens out there, make sure Agnes is protected no matter what.'

'Listen, you're freaking me out a little bit now.'

'Jesse,' she said firmly. 'No. Matter. What.'

18

Rid of Me

Daniel Less stood uncomfortably in the rear of the venue, back against the wall, watching the swelling crowd growing wilder and wilder with anticipation for Cecilia to hit the stage. He surveyed the crowd but saw no sign of Frey's minions. Just a sea of black-clad rockers, Goths, punks, hipsters, metal heads and ravers. A typical gathering at any Brooklyn musical happening except for the sprinkling of neighbourhood types, a little older and out of place, but nevertheless looking happy to be there. All waiting, just like him, but for completely different things. Less was not used to waiting.

An enviable cross-genre collection of trendsetters, he might have thought under other circumstances, but in this case it was alarming and the primary cause of his distress. These girls had made an impact. This was proof enough. He began wondering if it was already too late to stop or even contain, arguing with himself much as he had argued with Dr Frey at their clandestine meeting in the shadow of Lucy's enormous billboard. As show time approached, his anxiety grew along with the crowd's energy.

He stepped into the only semi-quiet space he could find, under the mezzanine staircase next to the bar and hit speed dial.

'Hello?'

'Alan, where are your men?'

'Aren't they there?'

'No and Cecilia is about to hit the fucking stage!'

The music executive was livid and more than a little annoyed with the doctor's nonchalance.

'Calm down, Daniel. I told them—'

'I don't care what you told them, Alan,' Less sniped contemptuously. 'They aren't here.'

'They're there, believe me.'

'Don't fuck with me, Doctor,' Less growled. 'Whatever your problems with me, this is a much bigger problem.'

'They're there under doctor's orders,' Frey said.

'What the hell is that supposed to mean?' Less asked.

'Sometimes you have to take matters into your own hands.' Frey said, smugly. 'I instructed them to deliver Cecilia to you.'

'But . . .'

'Alive,' Frey said as the line went dead.

'Fuck,' Less shouted, throwing his phone into the audience before him. He was suddenly distracted, noticing Jesse and Agnes being guided to the side of the stage by a security guard with a flashlight. Cecilia stopped to put on her shoes. Dolce and Gabanna reliquary heels made from glass with silver ornamentation surrounding openings. She opened the first heel and placed a piece of Lucy's blonde hair inside. She closed it tight with the intricate silver handle. She opened the second heel and placed a chip of Sebastian's bone. She closed the opening. She was ready.

The lights in The Temple went down. A heart-pounding bass loop was triggered from the sound board and began to reverberate throughout the venue, shaking walls and even bodies, forcing some fans to clutch their chests in fear of passing out. It was literally breathtaking. Smoke billowed from fog machines at either end of the stage, heralding Cecilia's arrival. It was beyond dramatic.

The blood-red curtain rose and she appeared, alone, like a vision in the clouds, sacred heart guitar slung around her shoulder and cello bow in hand. There was a laptop and tiny keyboard next to the mic stand. Lasers exploded like the Big Bang, thrusting outwards, shining all around her like stars forming, in empty space, over and around her head and shoulders, through her thigh gap, and into the crowd. The sheer snow-white chiffon mini-dress, emblazoned with music notes, that hung mid-thigh, was illuminated, glistening in the spotlight. The beams danced and caressed her in a rainbow wash of colour, like a hologram. No band, just her.

'Hello, Brooklyn!' she shouted and another roar, even bigger than the first went up.

For a moment, even Daniel Less was lost in the spectacle, enjoying a certain pride in authorship. This was truly a superstar, he mused from the shadows. The kind that comes along only rarely. He witnessed first-hand the intense connection and a rawness of talent that he'd only heard about until now. He was struck by her presentation. It was majestic both in hue and in purpose. Jet-black hair streaked with purple. Raccoon mascara to match. A headpiece of metal and crystal spikes, entwined with lavender roses, armour plates fit like dinner gloves along her arms and hands, leaving her fingers uncovered. Part Joan of Arc. Part virgin bride.

A warrior. A messenger. A queen.

Then the spotlight was put on her guitar. Agnes was speechless. The crowd screamed at the sight of all of their Milagros.

Cecilia strummed it in a way that was apropos, representing each of them – Agnes got a ballad, slow strum. Lucy got a pop strum. Sebastian got a sexy, rockabilly strum. And Cecilia, she gave herself a deafening, powerful strum and then ripped into a blistering and seamless set of covers from her earliest days on the indie club scene to originals from her new album. Punk, rock, metal, EDM, even folk and icy cool No Wave Teutonic ballad *Janitor of Lunacy* – she touched all the bases. The new songs were deeply personal but catchy and sat comfortably next to the more familiar versions of The Cure, The Damned, Eno, Johnny Cash, The Velvet Underground and more, inspiring singalongs from the crowd to songs that they never heard.

Midway through her set, she parked the guitar on its stand and settled in over the keyboard affixed to the laptop stand. In an intense evening of theatrical moments, this was to be the most dramatic.

'This is not a love song,' she shouted into the mic and began.

The sound of a harmonium filled the room. A neoclassical and ominous atonal tone of repeated phrases. Images of saints and sinners filled the screen behind her. Scenes of desire, tenderness, and violence. The music and pictures accompanied Cecilia as she sang:

> *Janitor of lunacy*
> *Paralyze my infancy*
> *Petrify the empty cradle*
> *Bring hope to them and me*
>
> *Janitor of tyranny*
> *Testify my vanity*

Mortalize my memory
Deceive the devil's deed

The crowd was rapt. Swaying in time. Feeling her every word. The song, which was rarely heard outside of hardcore critics' circles and lovers of musical obscurities, was delivered with uncompromising passion. Like a rock standard.

Tolerate my jealousy
Recognize the desperate need

Janitor of lunacy
Identify my destiny
Revive the living dream
Forgive their begging scream

Seal the giving of their seed
Disease the breathing grief

The choice of Nico to cover was lost on most of the Apostles, but not on Less. Like that great, haunting, self-destructive beauty of Warhol Factory legend, that infamous Chelsea Girl, Cecilia was pouring out her innermost feelings in an echo-fx voice filled with fire and ice. She made this version her own, definitive, right on the spot. She inhabited each biting and despairing verse as if she'd written it. And, true to her nature, there was a message in it. The message, Less had instantly concluded, was for him.

Only him.

'You OK?' Jesse practically shouted in Agnes's ear.

'I need to sit down for a second. Can we go back to the dressing room?'

'Sure,' Jesse said, a little confused. He tapped the security guard in front of him and pointed to Agnes and to the backstage exit. The guard nodded and led them out of the sweaty venue and into the cool dressing room. She sat down awkwardly, which Jesse noted.

A closed circuit broadcast of Cecilia's performance was playing and they both looked up to watch. The sound was tinny and thin, nothing like the wall of noise Cecilia was bringing just beyond the soundproof walls. Nevertheless, Agnes was grateful for the diversion. She could sense a million questions running around in Jesse's mind and she really didn't feel like talking about it.

'That's better,' she exhaled, taking off her coat and wiping some sweat from her face.

'Really? Cause you look awful.'

'How sweet,' Agnes replied, mildly irritated. 'I'm not one of those plastic girls you write about, Jesse.'

'Used to write about, Agnes,' the irritation now evident in his voice as well. 'What the hell is going on with you?'

'Nothing. I'm just tired of crowds, that's all.'

'Bullshit. If you aren't honest with me, I can't help you.'

'I'm not asking for help, Jesse. Besides, no one could help me even if I wanted it.'

'Give it a try.'

'I'm pregnant, OK,' Agnes raged, grabbing his shirt and pulling his face to hers. 'I'm pregnant,' she repeated softly.

Jesse was stunned but the gossip blogger in him instantly understood the gravity and the urgency.

'Whose is it?'

'I don't want to talk about it. You wouldn't believe me anyway.'

'OK, so you tell me you're pregnant and now you don't want to talk about it . . .'

'You won't believe me.'

'That's not really the point, Agnes. Pregnancy isn't something you can keep secret. Believe me, I know. And once those people that follow you around find out their virgin queen is knocked up it isn't going to sit well. You understand?'

'That's what my mother said,' Agnes offered tearfully. 'She thinks it's like an hysterical pregnancy anyway. Like I'm insane or something.'

'Why would she think that?' Jesse prodded, almost afraid to hear her response. 'Whose is it?'

Agnes took a deep breath. Gathered herself. And opened her eyes wide.

'Sebastian's.'

Jesse's face reddened and he threw his arms up in the air. He was apoplectic. 'I think she's right. You are batshit crazy!'

'I don't care if you believe me. If anyone believes me, Jesse.'

'C'mon Agnes. Getting pregnant by a dead dude? That's a stretch even in this fucked-up nightmare we're living.'

'It's real. I'm having it, Jesse.'

Jesse rubbed at his forehead and paced the dressing room, running scenarios through his head like a military strategist or a crisis public relations manager, none of which had a good result as far as he could figure.

'So this is why Cecilia was more concerned about you than about herself,' he mumbled. 'You need to leave here, Agnes. I'll have Tony send some of his guys with you.'

'I'm not leaving Cecilia.'

'Frey is going to find out. He might already know, Agnes.'

'I'm staying until the end for her, Jesse.'

Jesse reluctantly relented. 'OK. Let's go.'

As they left the dressing room he texted Tony.

'MEET ME NEAR THE STAGE. IF ANYTHING GOES DOWN GET AGNES OUT OF HERE. SAFE.'

Tony replied, 'WHAT ABOUT CECILIA?'

Jesse didn't reply.

19

Crucifixation

Sweat poured down Cecilia's face, purple and black streaks of mascara trailing along her cheeks to her chin. She was working hard. Giving her all for the crowd and for herself. She closed with blistering versions of Public Image Limited's *Flowers of Romance*, a bitter mainstay from her first shows, and the title track from her album, *Save Yourself*.

She placed her guitar down on the stand and left the stage to cheers and the loudest applause she'd ever heard. It was almost deafening. She noticed Jesse and Agnes standing in the wings applauding her and she smiled at them. Shouts for an encore filled the room.

Less watched it all from the back, nervously.

Cecilia leaned against a backstage wall in the wings, overwhelmed, and began to sob.

The house manager ran up to comfort her, gushing with breathless praise.

'If no one's ever seen you before, or never sees you again, they saw you. Out there. Tonight. One for the ages, baby. Legend. Know what I mean.'

She composed herself.

'Thanks,' she whispered, putting her trembling hand on his shoulder. 'Listen, I'm going to go out in the crowd during the encore. When I do, I want you to turn the lights off, OK?'

'That's really against club policy, I mean, there are fire laws and . . .'

'Just promise me, OK?'

He couldn't refuse, not after what he'd just seen. 'You got it.'

Cecilia returned to the stage and acknowledged the raucous reaction of her fans, their smartphones raised, snapping pictures and videos. She waved to them, a melancholy smile on her face. She strapped on her guitar and took a moment to address the audience. She was feeling emotional but kept it together to say what she needed to say.

'When I first came to this city, I thought I knew who I was, what I wanted, what I was meant to do.'

Scattered cheers of encouragement and whistles of appreciation rose up from the quieted crowd. Less gave her a wink from the back.

'But I didn't.'

The room fell almost completely silent. This was not the gracious stage patter of a rising rock star but something more.

'If there's anything I can leave you with tonight, any thought, any message, it's only this. Know yourself. Not the person you see in the mirror. The person you see inside. Once you know that, you know everything. Once you know that, you'll know who you are, accept who you are, and be who you truly are, do what you were meant to do. With clarity. Without judgment. Without fucking fear.'

She hit the space bar on her laptop and triggered a video. Jesse's video of Lucy. Smoke poured once again from the fog machines and the lasers beamed.

'This is for a boy I miss.'

Cecilia bowed her head for a moment and stepped to the mic, a hypnotic beat and washes of atmospheric synthesizers began to play. She strummed the first chords of her favourite song, *Hurt* by Nine Inch Nails, and began to sing.

The crowd joined in on the chorus, quietly at first, then full throated, with abandon.

She started singing from her soul, looking towards the back, towards Less. '*I will make you hurt*,' she wailed.

Cecilia picked up the iron cello bow and drew it across the strings of her guitar as she continued, turning it into some sort of space-age-sounding cello. Fans could see blood running from her palms down to her arms and on to the bow and the guitar.

She raised the bow in her hand and pointed it upwards. As she did, she rose off the stage, floating a foot or two above it, and turned in the air to face the video playing behind her.

Gasps at the miraculous occurrence filled the room. Less, too, was shocked. 'What the fuck is she doing?' he whispered.

She struck the guitar strings several times with the bow, forcing an ear-shattering clang that sounded like nothing less then the tolling of a cathedral bell.

'I have a bad feeling, Jesse,' Agnes admitted. 'Very, very bad.'

Agnes felt her insides tighten and reached for her abdomen. Jesse grabbed Agnes by the arm.

Cecilia's eyes turned towards Agnes and she blew her a kiss. As her feet touched the floor again, Cecilia dropped her guitar into its stand, still clanging in time to the beat. She turned her back to the audience. Stretched her arms out wide, closed her eyes, and fell backwards into the faceless crowd. Just as she did, the lights went out. Agnes dropped to her knees, chanting something over and over: *Sanctus Fortis**

Cecilia was body surfing, face up, arms out to her sides, like a cross. The first few rows of fans that passed her over their heads towards the back. She was singing. It was like a revival. A baptism. Fans reaching up to touch her, crying, kissing their

* *Holy and Strong.*

fingers once she'd passed over them. There were so many reaching for her. So many hands. Boys, girls. Indistinguishable. Less was confident he could do the deed in anonymity. In the dark. The way all Ciphers did things.

Cecilia's eyes were fixed on the video of Lucy behind her as she surfed the crowd. Watching her beautiful friend in a moment of terrible sacrifice. Drawing strength and consolation from her.

'This ain't part of the show,' Tony yelled in Jesse's ear as she surfed to the back. 'I gotta get to her.'

'Don't move,' Jesse barked. 'We can't leave Agnes.'

Jesse's heart was pounding along with everyone else's but for a different reason when, without warning, the lights in the venue went out completely. Cecilia was nearly at the back, close to Daniel Less. Tony started to run towards the floor, towards Cecilia, but Jesse grabbed his arm, holding him back.

'Come to me, Cecilia,' he said.

She sang even louder as the clang of the guitar began to wane. Now, repeatedly being stabbed until she fell, delivered, to Less standing in the back. She looked at him knowingly, and he stared back like a deer in headlights. In the throng, Less grabbed at her chin in the darkness and pulled it back, exposing her throat. She raised the iron bow in both her hands and as she felt the slice of Less's switchblade against her skin, she thrust the bow towards him and through him, impaling him into the wall behind. There were loud screams, not of joy but of sheer terror. Agnes fell to her knees in torment, wailing Cecilia's name.

The lights came up and there was a shower of crimson pouring from Cecilia's wounds, her white dress was now red. Blood was spurting from her neck on to the few that had remained with her, that did not run. Christening them in her blood. Cecilia went limp and fell to the floor as the crowd, realizing what had happened, stampeded for the exits.

She muttered the last of the song, gurgling on her own blood. The show and Cecilia were finished.

She felt a hand take each of hers and in her dying moment smiled at the faces of Sebastian and Lucy on either side of her. She felt herself lifted, floating above her self, watching from above. Singing until she could sing no more.

'You stopped me. I could have helped her!' Tony screamed, grabbing Jesse by both arms. 'Do you know what you just did?'

Jesse was silent. In shock.

Agnes looked up at the doorman and spoke for him through her tears.

'He knows, Tony. He knows.'

The Word According to Cecilia

I don't have a soul to sell,
It's already gone for cheap.
So there's nothing to feel sorry for,
Don't pretend to weep.
God save the queen,
He's already in me.
I can't seem to fill the hole,
I'm digging within thee.
Sacrifice and pain,
Love you care not know.
Self-respect and shame,
The fastest way to go.
Crank it up louder,
So you cannot hear,
The beating of my heart,
The blinding sound of fear.
Only the good die young,
That is what they say,
It's better to burn out,
Than it is to fade away.

Cecilia, pray for us.

20

Metanoia

Jude sat quietly in his room staring out the window into the
dark night. He could see the upper floors of the brownstones
where families were settling down for bed. Mothers and fathers
kissing their children, helping them brush their teeth, reading
to them and tucking them in. An experience which he had
never truly had. For Jude, it was like watching a Disney movie
or a family sitcom, an idealized version of life. Still, he didn't
feel sorry for himself or the least bit envious. It looked like a
movie and that's how he processed it. Like a movie. A fantasy
version of reality, most especially his.

He was grateful, despite the turmoil. Grateful to the nuns
who sheltered and fed him. Grateful for Sebastian, who'd

brought him together with Agnes. It was he that first understood Jude, what was special about him, not just different. He'd been charged with a lot of responsibility and he hadn't shirked from it. He continued to watch out the window at the scenes of domestic normality and a sudden chill went through his body. The sound of sirens – police, fire and EMT – filled the air. He lifted the window and stuck his head out, looking from side to side for signs of the emergency vehicles and smelling for smoke. But there was neither a sign nor a smell. Just the distant cry of sirens and horns echoing down the blocks.

He returned to his chair and closed his eyes, envisioning what he dared not see. The horrible present and, potentially, an even more horrible future. He stood and ran to his bed, banging on it. Jude scratched at his eyes and his throat mercilessly, drawing blood, which trickled from his brow and his neck, lodging under his fingernails. He slammed the walls with his fists in anger and anguish, throwing whatever he could find. The late-night racket woke sister Dorothea, who ran down the hallway to his room. She knocked but he didn't answer. Instead the room became suddenly quiet.

'Jude?' she called out to him, turning at the knob. 'Are you all right? Please unlock the door so I know you're OK.'

He did not come.

She ran back to her room and grabbed the master key. Her hands were shaking as she tried to fit it into the lock. It slipped in and she turned, opening the door. The bedroom was in tatters but Jude, his face a mask of blood, was sitting calmly and quietly sobbing in his chair by the window.

'Oh, Jude!' she said, relieved, running in to hug him. 'I was so worried. What's wrong, son?'

He looked up at her, the mute boy's eyes bloody and swollen from tears. She wiped at his face and dried them and asked again, in sign language.

'Is something wrong?'

He shook his head up and down fervently.

'Is it the girls?'

Once again he nodded *yes*.

'Jude it's so late. We can go see Agnes tomorrow. That will make you feel better, won't it?'

'Take me back!' he said, clearly, demonstratively.

The nun was stunned. This time she was the speechless one. The boy had spoken for the first time in her presence.

'Take you back where?'

'To the hospital. To Dr Frey.'

Cat was pacing back and forth in the tiny dressing room, shaking out the nerves, mumbling to herself. Motivational slogans, pithy self-help maxims, 'fuck yeah!'s and anything else upbeat she could think of to make the wait until showtime bearable. But as usual, doubt began to creep in to the conversation she was having with herself. Her thoughts turned negative, berating herself, criticizing herself, both for not being good enough and for not being where she really wanted to be – by Cecilia's side. She'd had a bad feeling, which didn't bode well for a great show.

Hearing Cecilia's music was inspirational for her, but also a little intimidating, a sonic reminder of how far she had to go. Unlike CeCe, she wasn't a natural. Not the most charismatic girl at the party, the quickest wit with the best turns of phrase. She had been a fan after all, a follower and, despite Cecilia's confidence in her, she had yet to muster much in herself. She wasn't as tough, as thick-skinned or as fearless, creatively or otherwise as her mentor. And the fact that Less seemed to be spending all his time and effort on Cecilia's album and show wasn't helping. At least she'd booked in the late show, so a few stragglers might turn up once Cecilia was done, that is if they had any energy left once that show was over.

Regardless of how she was feeling about herself just then, she could hear the sound of the arriving crowd bleeding through the peeling plaster walls of the Crown Heights dive bar turned hot spot and there was some satisfaction in that, or so she tried to convince herself. The promoter wandered by and smiled, which was a good sign. They never smiled unless they were making money, she figured, which meant the room was going to be full. The downside was that if she flopped it would not go unnoticed. All she could hope was that most reviewers and bloggers would be at Cecilia's show in Gowanus.

'Stop it. This is your night,' she reminded herself. 'Be here now. In the moment.'

She stepped back into the cubbyhole that served as a dressing room and eyed her guitar as she might a hot guy. Longingly. Lovingly. Besides Cecilia, the six string was her best friend. It had seen her through the hardest times, the worst decisions, and the poorest judgment. She picked it up and began to strum, closing her eyes, doing a vocal exercise. The din from inside the club was actually comforting, a sort of white noise background for the meditative state she was falling into. Less comforting were the sudden pings from her cellphone. The sound of social media alerts. Trolls she figured, hating on her before the show, or glowing posts from Cecilia's gig. Cat wasn't sure which was worse. Either way, she didn't look. Cat held down the off button until the power off bar came up and she swiped. The spectre of Cecilia hung so completely over her, she just needed some space from it, no matter how happy she was for her friend.

Cat returned to her guitar but just as she was about to reach her most relaxed state, something changed. A chill ran through her body and she forgot the words of the song she was rehearsing. Maybe, she thought, a sudden bit of stage fright, but this felt different. Her hands became clammy and she began to involuntarily run one hand obsessively along the length of the steel strings from the saddle to the head, clutching the neck tightly, like a capo, with the other. Cat couldn't stop.

It was as if her mind and body were beyond her control. She was in a full-blown panic and there was nothing she could do about it.

A pall of silence fell over the boisterous crowd and then a few shrieks and a collective gasp went up. A short, sharp knock at the door startled her.

'Come in,' Cat said in a shaky voice, still rubbing her guitar.

It was the promoter. The happy expression on his face from moments before replaced with a grim one.

'What's going on out there?'

He rubbed at his brow and looked away from her, clearly uncomfortable with making eye contact and with what he had to say.

'Have you heard?'

"Heard what? Is there some problem with the sound? Someone sick in the crowd?'

The promoter stepped inside and closed the door.

'It's Cecilia.'

Cat stopped her obsessive rubbing of the guitar strings and felt a warmth in her palms. She checked them for moisture, nervous at the news she suspected was coming, but still dreaded to hear. But when she looked down, it wasn't droplets of water, but drops of blood.

'What about Cecilia?' Cat asked calmly.

'She's dead. Less too.'

Cat placed the blood-smeared guitar down and leaned it

against the wall. Her pulse quickened, her chest heaved and she got an odd metallic taste in her mouth, as if she'd rinsed with rusty nails.

'What happened?'

'No one really knows. It's insane over there. She went out into the crowd. One tweet even said it might have been Less that did it. I think she killed him too. Can you believe that?'

Cat didn't answer. She could barely even speak, she was so horrified and ashamed. All of a sudden everything started to make sense. It was all planned. A brilliant set-up by Less, with Frey as the head fake. Daniel had used her to get to Cecilia with a promise of fame and fortune. The oldest trick in the Devil's bag and she'd fallen for it. Freeing Cecilia, getting her case dropped, fast-tracking her album and stage-managing every aspect of her show, it was all a smokescreen for murder. The one thing he couldn't have expected was the twist ending Cecilia provided. An iron rod twisted right in his fucking guts. Leave it to Cecilia to finish it.

'The room is still packed, Cat. Nobody's leaving. I think they want to hear from you.'

'What do they expect me to say?' she asked.

'Listen, I understand if you don't want to go out there,' the promoter offered sympathetically. 'I'll make an announcement from the stage. We'll refund the tickets and take the blame for the cancellation. They'll understand, believe me.'

Cat turned her palms upwards and noticed that the

long slits across them continued to fill with blood. As she clenched her hands tightly to stop the bleeding she heard a chant building in the venue. Getting louder and louder. They were chanting her name. Summoning her in this moment of group sorrow.

'Cat. Cat. Cat Cat CAt CAt.CAT!' they cried out desperately.

Catherine reached over for her guitar and picked it up, holding it by the neck like a battleaxe, the blood from her palms dripping down it and from it.

'I'm going out there.'

The promoter swallowed hard.

'I don't know if you should, Cat. I really can't guarantee your safety after what happened. Every cop in town is in Gowanus.'

'I'm not afraid,' Cat said, looking him dead in the eye.

'OK,' he said reaching into his pocket.

Cat thought he might be pulling out some sort of last-minute insurance waiver for her to sign but instead he just texted the sound and light engineers. The room went dark, except for a single spotlight onstage. Catherine walked out on to the dark floorboards and stepped into the light. The place was silent except for the sound of sobs that emanated from every corner. Cat also couldn't keep from weeping.

'My heart, our hearts, are broken,' Catherine said through bitter tears. 'I don't know how to describe a loss like this, where to begin.'

Shouts of support and commiseration filled the venue. They could tell this was hard for her.

'We love you, Cat!'

'Cecilia was my friend. My mentor. My sister.'

Cat could barely get the words out, even with all their encouragement.

'I wouldn't be here, or anywhere, without her. And neither would any of you. She brought us together. And that's how we'll get through this. We'll honour her as she would have wanted. Together.'

Catherine slung her guitar over her shoulder and strummed a single chord and looked upward toward the ceiling. To Heaven. A few handclaps and whistles of approval quickly grew into a thunderous wave of applause, rocking the club from back to front. This was what Cecilia would have wanted. What she promised to do. To carry on.

Cat ripped into her set, blood, sweat and tears dripping from her on to the stage. She played a few of her own and a few of Cecilia's, even one of the new ones, and some songs they both loved. The show was like an exorcism, driving the demons of doubt and pain and suffering out from the among them. Cathartic and celebratory.

Ecstatic fans sang along, danced and twirled to her music. There were no jaded junior label execs with hands in pockets leaning against back walls tonight, no cooler-than-thou Brooklyn hipsters judging them, no radio and media types hanging at the bar abusing the company credit card. It was a fan's show, a memorial, with Catherine as their pied piper, leading them.

Cat was exhausted but satisfied. She'd given it her all, left it all on stage, just as she'd seen Cecilia do so many nights before. But with the last song came also a sense of finality, not only for the show but for Cecilia.

'Cecilia wasn't the first and she won't be the last,' Cat began, channelling into a message much larger than she had intended. 'I don't want you to be bitter. Cecilia wouldn't want that. Nor do I want you to be naïve. She wouldn't want that either. Be vigilant. There is evil in the world. All around us. All the time. The only thing that protects us from it are our choices. The more of us, the more good, the less of them.'

The audience was rapt. Cat began her final song. *Take Me To Church*. A melancholy and mournful ode about death and rebirth through love. It worked just as well for friends as lovers. She turned up the amp and pressed down on the effects pedal at her feet, fuzzing up the tone on her guitar until it fed back through the PA and the onstage monitors. It was a wall of melodic but ear-piercing noise. Pretty and painful. A perfect tribute to her martyred mentor.

My lover's got humour
She's the giggle at a funeral
Knows everybody's disapproval

I should've worshipped her sooner

Cat's vocal was fervent, strong and clear. She wanted every word to pierce their souls and rise up to Heaven's ear where Cecilia might hear them.

> *If the heavens ever did speak*
> *She's the last true mouthpiece*
> *Every Sunday's getting more bleak*
> *A fresh poison each week*

> *Take me to church*
> *I'll worship like a dog at the shrine of your lies*
> *I'll tell you my sins and you can sharpen your knife*
> *Offer me that deathless death*
> *Good God, let me give you my life*

She sang. For them. For herself. For Cecilia. Eyes shut tight. Blood and tears flying from her on to the crowd in a sort of baptism, as she smote the guitar like a blacksmith might a piece of molten metal on an anvil, fashioning her future.

In the madness and soil of that sad earthly scene

> *Only then I am Human*
> *Only then I am Clean*
> *Amen.*

Amen.

Amen.

The music stopped and Cat looked out over the crowd and whispered a final time and the crowd joined her in unison:

'*Amen.*'

The song was over. She thanked them and left them with a final thought.

'Never forget, she did it all for us. Be worthy of the sacrifice,' Cat said, her lips trembling. 'My Sweet St. Cecilia. Pray for us.'

21

Gospel Girl

The procession for Cecilia began at St. Cecilia's church in Williamsburg and wound through the thick crowds along Park Avenue through Fort Greene and Downtown Brooklyn into Cobble Hill toward her final resting place at Precious Blood. Headlines blared from every newsstand, following her every step of the way. The investigation into the deaths had barely begun and she was being interred on no less an authority than the personal request of the Pope himself.

TEMPLE SACRIFICE!
SUBWAY SAINT IN DOUBLE MURDER
SHADOWY WORLD OF MEDIA MAVEN REVEALED

219

Jesse, Agnes and Catherine followed right behind the casket, which was dripping with blue orchids, dark irises and black beauty roses. Tears of mourning flowed freely from the eyes of her followers and fans. With Cecilia gone, they were now apostles in the truest sense, left to carry on her legacy. They carried pictures of her, poster-sized, and raised high in the air. Jesse did as she'd asked, as he promised. He uploaded her album and now her music blared from speakers in cars, from apartment windows, from cellphones and bodegas.

As the procession arrived at Precious Blood, Captain Murphy stepped from the crowd and approached Jesse. 'Mr Arens?'

Jesse looked at the detective and ignored him.

'Jesse. Listen, I'm sorry about Cecilia.'

'This really isn't a good time, you know? What do you want, Captain?'

'I want to talk.'

'Not now. Not ever, to be honest with you.'

'I can make you talk but you don't want me to drag you down to the station, do you?'

Jesse was unimpressed. 'Nice turnout from the precinct, Captain. Shame you couldn't find a few men to place in the club the other night.'

'I warned them but I'm not a fortuneteller, kid. Know what I mean?'

'You didn't need to be. I warned *you* a long time ago what was going on.'

'Frey was nowhere near that club and neither was any of the Born Again residents. I already checked.'

'Check again, Captain. There's still one girl left. You know what *I* mean.'

'We're still investigating. What can you tell me about Less?'

'Nothing you don't already know.'

'He gave her a deal. He sprang her from the hospital. His lawyers got her case dropped. Why would she want to kill him?'

'Correction. He killed her. Self-defence.'

'You know what I'm asking you.'

'No, I don't.'

'Was there anything between them? An affair that went wrong maybe?'

'You need to turn her, all of them, into whores now? Is that it? Would you be doing this if they were dudes?'

'First, I don't need any lectures in ruining people's lives from you. Second, I'm not the one destroying reputations, and I'm certainly not sexist,' Murphy said, pulling a newspaper from his jacket pocket. 'Have you seen this?'

Jesse scanned the banner item on the top of the city's most-read gossip column. It was titled 'Immaculate Deception' and it was a story about Agnes being pregnant. Jesse's expression spoke volumes to Murphy. They both understood what it meant.

'This is crap,' Jesse replied, crumpling the tabloid and

tossing it to the street. 'People won't believe it.'

'People believe all kinds of crazy shit, Jesse. Perception is reality, buddy. Now you've got three saints that turned out to be a suicide, a murderer and a tramp. Frauds.'

Murphy's attempt to provoke Jesse was nearly successful. 'If you weren't a cop I'd punch you in your face.'

'Tell me what you know and I'll forget I heard that. As I recall, you don't do too well in jail.'

'I'm going into the church now, Captain, to bury my friend. If you want to know about Less, dig a little deeper, and maybe you'll find what you're looking for.'

'A connection to the doctor?'

'You're the detective. You figure it out. Until then, I'll do what I have to do. This isn't going to stop.'

'Don't be a hero, kid. I'll assign some men to Agnes's house and to the church for a while until things calm down.'

'Better late than never right?'

Jesse turned away from the cop and entered Precious Blood. He saw Agnes in the front pew alone and walked towards her.

'What did Murphy want?' Agnes whispered.

'We can talk about it later,' Jesse demurred.

Cecilia's funeral mass was just beginning. It was a sombre affair and an uncomfortable one. Emotions were running high and, just as the crowds of followers had grown larger, the divide between those who believed and those who didn't was growing wider. The Pope had said Lucy's mass, but this time, it was just a parish priest. While the investigation was going on, and the actual circumstances of her death so unclear, the Archbishop wasn't going to get anywhere near Cecilia's funeral. Politics, Jesse surmised.

The investigation into Cecilia's death wasn't the only scandal rearing its ugly head in the cathedral. As Jesse approached Agnes he picked up on the icy stares from parishioners, not towards him but for her. The news was obviously travelling fast and it was clear to him that she was beginning to notice. She might as well have been wearing a scarlet letter.

'The mass is ended, let us go in peace,' the priest concluded.

The parishioners blessed themselves and filed out from the pews and into the throng of media that had gathered outside. Some stopped to be interviewed by the local reporters, expressing their sorrow or consternation at the events of the past few days. They talked of miracles and of murder. The presence of something either holy or horrid in their midst.

Jesse and Agnes remained inside, alone with the priest, pallbearers and Cecilia. They accompanied the casket down to the chapel for a final blessing and interment. The old man from the ironworks across the street was waiting inside, standing beside an ornate, black wrought-iron frame that would be the permanent stand for Cecilia's bier. Agnes and Jesse both noted the unique carvings that matched the ones on Cecilia's bow. He nodded respectfully at them and placed one hand gently on the glassket.

'It's beautiful,' Agnes said. 'Thank you.'

He smiled sadly. Cecilia's encasement was guided carefully on to the platform where it sat perfectly, opposite Lucy, like a piece of art.

'It was an honour,' he said and left the room followed by the pallbearers.

The priest began the Rites of Committal and Commendation.

'Receive her, we pray, into the mansions of the saints.
As we make ready our sister's resting place,
look also with favour on those who mourn
and comfort them in their loss.'

The words rolled solemnly and sweetly off the priest's tongue and echoed in the small chamber.

'Saints of God, come to her aid!
Hasten to meet her, angels of the Lord!
Receive her soul and present her to God the Most High.'

The priest's eyes and his voice rose as he sang in supplication.

'To you, O Lord, we commend the soul of Cecilia your servant; in the sight of this world she is now dead; in your sight may she live for ever. Forgive whatever sins she committed through human weakness and in your goodness grant her everlasting peace.'

Jesse knew that these ancient prayers for the dead were common, but the thought that Cecilia needed forgiving, from God or anyone, was irritating, even in this peaceful moment. Incense was lit and holy water was sprinkled on Cecilia's casket as the prayers of pardon were offered. The familiar scent filled the chapel and Agnes was comforted by it. She stared at the chaplet on the stilled arms of Lucy and Cecilia and at the one dangling from her own. Then at the statue of St. Sebastian standing between them. Jesse took her hand and squeezed it gently, sharing together the moment of grief.

The priest concluded: '*Eternal rest grant unto her, O Lord.*'

'*And let perpetual light shine upon her,*' Agnes replied.

'*May she rest in peace.*'

'*Amen.*'

'*May her soul and the souls of all the faithful departed, through the mercy of God, rest in peace.*'

'*Amen.*'

The priest extended his hand to each of them as the church bells rang out. 'I'm sorry for your loss. And for ours. All of ours.'

Sister Dorothea squeezed Jude's hand tightly as they rode the elevator up to the pych ward at Perpetual Help. Jude was incredibly serene, not the least bit agitated as he might normally be for an appointment with Frey. She, on the other hand, was beside herself, unsure if she was doing the right thing. They stepped out into reception and approached the desk nurse, who was genuinely surprised to see them.

'Too much for you, Sister, caring for the boy?' the nurse queried snidely. 'We're not the dead-letter office here you know.'

'Nor am I delivering a package,' Sister Dorothea sniped, showing uncharacteristic venom. 'Do your job and tell Dr Frey we are here to see him.'

The nurse buzzed the doctor. He responded immediately.

'Bring him in,' Dr Frey asked.

The boy stood in the doctor's office doorway, the nun directly behind.

'Hello, Doctor,' the woman said coolly.

'Hello, Sister. How nice to see you both.'

'We are not here for a social visit as I'm sure you have guessed.'

'I wouldn't have thought so, Sister. What exactly does bring you here?'

The nun paused and touched the boy's shoulder. 'He asked to come.'

'He asked, you say?'

'Yes. In his own words.'

The doctor got up from his desk and walked around it, to get closer to Jude.

'Is this true, Jude?'

The boy said nothing.

'He had an episode the other night. The night that Cecilia was killed,' the nun said.

Frey got down on one knee, at eye level with the boy, and studied his face with utmost curiosity, especially the bruising and scabs around his eyes and his throat. Jude did not make eye contact with him. He examined the boy's fingertips, noting the traces of dried blood still beneath his fingernails.

'Yes, an episode at least,' Frey concluded. 'Perhaps he shouldn't be watching the local news, Sister. It's not surprising that he would be so troubled and act out over it. He has a history of impulsivity and outbursts as you know.'

'This happened before we knew anything about it, Doctor.'

Frey was intrigued. Very intrigued, and the intensity of his interest was plain to both Jude and the nun.

'You did the right thing bringing him here.'

'I did as he asked. That he is here is his will and God's.'

'Yes, well, whatever suits you, Sister. With your approval, we will examine him and keep him under observation to see if there are any other recurrences of these episodes, as you call them, and to make sure he is not a danger to himself.

'Are you *sure* you want to stay here, Jude?'

The boy nodded yes.

'Don't worry. We won't keep him any longer than is necessary,' Frey assured her.

'Necessary' was one of those vague words with loose definitions that the disciplined and fastidious nun despised.

She was leaving the boy for now at her own discretion, she thought. Not Frey's.

'Yes, well, I'll make sure of that, Doctor. God bless you, son. I'll be in to check on you,' she said.

Jude smiled slightly, as if to reassure her. She gave him a kiss on the cheek and turned to leave but suddenly stopped in her tracks.

'Oh, Doctor, I understand that Daniel Less was a colleague of yours, wasn't he?'

'Not a colleague exactly, Sister. But we have been known to travel in the same circles.'

'Which circles are those?' she asked. 'The ones in Hell?'

22

Teenage Riot

Agnes arrived at home to find a squad car parked outside with two uniformed officers inside it but no one else. Not a sign of the small crowd that had been gathered for months now. She was both relieved and dismayed. There was an odd sort of comfort in seeing them day after day. If anything, it had made her feel she wasn't crazy. In fact their presence was more than comforting, it was needed. More now that Lucy and Cecilia were gone.

She trudged up the steps and walked into the house.

'It was a beautiful service, Mother,' Agnes called out.

Martha didn't reply.

Agnes called out to her again and walked to Martha's

room only to find Martha running around frantically, suitcases open.

'What are you doing?'

'Packing and so are you.'

'Why?'

'Why? Have you seen the papers?'

'Mother what are you talking about. I've been at church. You know that. What happened to everyone outside? Did the cops make them leave?'

'No, Agnes, they left before the squad car arrived,' Martha said tersely. 'No surprise.'

'I don't know what you're trying to tell me, Mother, but why don't you just spit it out!' Agnes shouted.

Martha walked to the coffee table and picked up the morning paper which she had open to the gossip page. 'This is what I'm trying to tell you, Agnes!'

Agnes took the paper and scanned the headline, bringing her hand to her mouth in surprise. 'Oh my God.'

'Have you been bragging, Agnes?' Martha fumed.

'No,' Agnes said, letting the paper drop to the parquet floor. 'Have you?'

'Don't be ridiculous. Do you know how embarrassing it is for me to have that scandal printed in black and white?'

'Is that what this is about? Your phony friends?'

'No, Agnes, this is about your deluded friends. Former friends, I should say.'

Martha continued emptying drawers into suitcases, pulling coats and dresses from the hall closet.

'What the hell is going on with you?' Agnes screamed.

'I'm not going to stay here and wait for someone to throw rocks at our windows, Agnes, or burn a cross in our front yard or worse. You understand?'

'No, I don't.'

'You've ruined our lives, Agnes.'

'For being who I am?'

'Who you are? A saint who is destined to show us the path to true love? What matters is who those people think you are. You played along. Encouraged them. Don't you see?'

'Some people have more faith than others, Mother.'

'You have been revealed, Agnes. Their virgin saint has turned out to be a whore. A pregnant one at that. The joke of it is that it's all a lie. But then it's been a lie the whole time.'

'It's not a lie, Mother. I'm sorry this has come out but it's not a lie and I'm not ashamed!'

'Have it your way. Just get packing, we're leaving today.'

'I'm not going anywhere.'

'Don't worry. Even the Virgin Mary took off on a donkey, Agnes,' Martha sniped. 'It's not safe here.'

'I'm not afraid.'

'You are sick, Agnes. First you deluded yourself with the whole romantic love thing that put you in the hospital, then you let that crazy boy and those girls delude you into believing something that is impossible. And look where it got them.'

'Heaven?'

Martha was unrelenting and not in any mood for sarcasm.

'You let those silly desperate people outside worship you and now they're gone. You know why? Because the worst feeling in the world is to be disappointed. When they fully realize what you've done, you won't have to worry about being hunted by some nefarious force or shadowy villains, Agnes. They'll come for you like some kind of medieval witch that's been outed.'

'You are the sick one, Mother!'

Agnes was beginning to shake. Not just from anger.

'You are like one of those reality show charlatans that claim to speak to ghosts, except you go one better. You got pregnant by one.'

'How dare you mock me!'

'Mark my words, Agnes. And now even the one man who was willing to help you, who could have helped you, made you well, wants nothing to do with you.'

Agnes was bristling. The veins in her neck bulging. The source not only of her distress but also the gossip item was standing before her.

'Dr Frey? Have you spoken with Dr Frey? Did you tell him about me?'

'Yes. Yes I did! I would do anything to help you.'

'What have you done!' Agnes felt faint. She began hyperventilating.

'Agnes, what's wrong?' the maternal tone in her voice suddenly returning.

'I don't know, I'm not feeling well,' Agnes said quietly reaching for her stomach.

'Take the stupid overcoat off. You're overheating for nothing. Hiding nothing.'

'It's not that,' Agnes insisted.

'Agnes, you are not pregnant!'

Martha's attempt to drum some sense into her daughter fell on deaf ears. She could see that Agnes was pale and weak and in distress. Agnes moaned loudly and Martha ran to her. She grabbed her daughter under one arm and steadied her with the other hand over her abdomen. What she felt nearly knocked her backward. Her eyes widened and her mouth dropped.

'Mother, what is it? You're scaring me.'

Martha replied in a barely audible murmur.

'It's a baby. It's kicking.'

It was late. For most people, but not for Jesse. He was a night owl by trade, or had been until recently. Barely leaving his apartment before midnight for any reason. The streets of Cobble Hill were thin with people by now. Just a few workaholics arriving home from their offices and horny couples heading back to their love shacks after a few too many drinks.

A few blocks further up to the Gowanus and it was a ghost town. Which was the perfect environment for what he was planning. Few witnesses, no collateral damage.

He turned the corner at Bond and DeGraw and saw Tony and his guys leaning up against a shuttered deli. In this neighbourhood, at this time of night, they fit right in.

'Hey,' Jesse said, fist bumping Tony and the rest.

'Ready to do this?' Tony asked.

'Ready. When you got a wasp problem, you go right for the nest.'

'There's more of these pricks around, you know that right?'

'I know,' Jesse agreed. 'But just because you can't do 'em all, doesn't mean you don't do what you can.'

Tony nodded. 'Let's send a message.'

'Special delivery to Dr Frey. He's done,' Jesse added, tossing the bottle in his hand. 'I just wish I could stick around to see their junkie killer faces when their world blows up around them.'

'This is serious shit, Jesse. You sure you want to do this?'

'I'm so sure.'

They pulled their hoodies over their heads and walked the few blocks to Born Again. Tony shimmied up the lampposts on either side of the house, put a towel over the glass lampshades to muffle any sound and smashed each of them, plunging the sidewalk and the entire front of Born Again in total darkness.

'Looks like a haunted house,' Tony observed wryly.

'It is,' Jesse said flatly.

'OK, when I whistle, it's go time.'

Tony put on his gloves and handed Jesse and his men bottles filled with kerosene, a wick made from shoelace jutting from the top of each one. Tony directed each man silently around the facility. Within a few second they had the place surrounded. Tony reached into his sweatshirt pocket and pulled out his lighter, lit his cigarette and then brought the flame to the wick. He inhaled deeply, took the cigarette from his mouth and whistled loudly. Jesse and the guys lit their wicks and threw the Molotov cocktails through the windows of Born Again.

'Burn in hell, bitches!' Jesse cursed as he heaved his firebomb.

It was an old-fashioned torch job. Half the buildings in this area had been lit up for insurance money, but Jesse was looking for a different kind of payoff. Revenge first among them.

Born Again was up in flames in seconds. Fire spread quickly from the lower floors to the upper ones and shouts from the residents were heard from inside. Jesse and Tony waited just long enough to make sure the job was done and ran off in separate directions like teenagers on Mischief Night, minus the rotten eggs and toilet paper. Police sirens and fire horns filled the night within seconds. By the time the first units arrived, Jesse was long gone. He got home, cleared a place on his couch and turned on the news.

The fire at Born Again was the lead story, breaking news. Crews were already dispatched and on the way. He watched the reporting intently, waiting to see their faces.

'Watch your ass, Dr Frey.'

23
The Girl Who Has Everything

Agnes left home for school and the first thing she was greeted with as she closed her front door was the sound of silence. At the bottom of the brownstone steps, where once crowds of adoring faithful had gathered, was no one – just a squad car and some wilting flowers. The sort you might see at a gravesite several days after the holiday visits were over. They were beginning to stink. The metaphor was not lost on Agnes. It was all beginning to stink. A wretched noxious stench of confusion, betrayal and death.

'Hazel, wait up,' Agnes called out. The two girls hugged. Agnes was ready to be bombarded with questions.

'It must have been awful for you,' Hazel said. 'Cecilia and

everything. I'm so sorry.'

'I know it happened, but it doesn't seem real yet, you know? I'm numb.'

Agnes reflexively reached for her stomach and Hazel swallowed hard.

'Agnes, I swear I didn't say anything,' Hazel said tearfully. 'I would never.'

'I know,' Agnes reassured her.

'Who then?'

'My mother.'

'No way!'

'She all but admitted it.'

'And one of those gossipy bitches called the newspaper?'

'No, it was nothing like that.'

'Then what?'

'Hazel, there's a lot I can't tell you.'

'I know, you still haven't even told me who the father is. I thought we were best friends.'

The hurt in Hazel's voice was real. These weren't the curious questions asked by just anyone.

'I'm not trying to keep secrets. It's for your own good,' Agnes insisted. 'You just have to trust me, OK?'

Hazel sniffled, and then laughed. 'It's not a teacher, is it? That's, like, epidemic right now.'

'No.'

'OK 'cause I thought it might be our science teacher

Mr Monastero. I mean no harm, no foul if it is. He's hot. I'd do him.'

Agnes just shook her head and laughed.

'No, Hazel, but at least I know your type now.'

'Silver fox? Yes please.'

'Got daddy issues much?' Agnes teased.

'Don't we all?'

With all that had happened, it felt good to have a light, silly moment, even it couldn't last very long. The door of the school building came in site and she stopped. There were already stares and whispers building like a thundercloud.

'I'm OK,' Agnes repeated, steeling herself.

'You sure?'

'Yeah.'

'Jealous bitches,' Hazel snarked. 'They only wish people would talk about them.'

'Yeah, jealous. If you say so,' Agnes smiled, resigned to what she knew was to come.

Hazel took Agnes's hand in hers. 'Seriously, would you trade places with any of them?'

It was a much bigger question than Hazel could have imagined, but it inspired Agnes, the way that only a true friend, even unknowingly, sometimes can. They waited until the very last minute. Until the morning bell sounded and hurried up the steps.

'Let's go to school,' Agnes said.

The mocking she expected didn't take long, arriving right on cue just as she and Hazel entered the hallway. A wall of students had formed to block their path.

'Slut,' one girl growled through her pretend cough.

'Hypocrite,' another taunted.

Agnes kept her head up and her hand over her stomach, protecting it, walking towards her locker.

'That's all you got, bitches?' Hazel shouted, getting up in their faces.

Agnes took her arm to hold her back. The hall monitor felt a fight about to break out and intervened.

'That's enough,' he said sternly. 'Class. Now!'

Agnes and Hazel passed through the crowd, trading icy stares and bumping cold shoulders with the intimidating gaggle of girls that had attempted to intimidate them.

'I'm surprised they didn't throw stones,' Hazel said.

'I'm sure they thought about it,' Agnes replied.

Her locker quickly came into view and so did a much welcome visitor waiting there for her.

'Hello dear,' Sister Dorothea said, reaching out warmly for a hug.

'So happy to see a friendly face,' Agnes replied.

'Hey,' Hazel said, elbowing her friend in the arm.

Agnes smiled back at her. 'You know what I mean, Hazel. I don't have to tell you how much I love you, do I?'

'Yes, you do,' Hazel quipped.

'All right, I love you.'

Agnes kissed Hazel on the cheek as they parted.

'You're in good hands,' Hazel observed. 'See you at lunch.'

'That's a good friend you have there,' the nun observed.

'I know,' Agnes agreed. 'One of the few left.'

'I can't imagine how hard this is for you Agnes, but the others simply do not understand. It might be asking too much considering the world we live in.'

'I don't blame them, sister, it just hurts.'

'There is always suffering for people that are different, Agnes. And you are different in ways that no doctor or scientist could ever explain.'

'Diagnosis, martyr.'

The nun smiled at the subtly and profundity of Agnes's joke.

'In some ways, it is an affliction,' Sister Dorothea mused. 'But difficult as this may be to process, all this is not about you, but about the example you set. About how you live with the cross you have to bear.'

'It's hard not to take it personally, when I've got classmates kicking me out here in the hallways and a baby kicking from inside my belly.'

'True, and yet you are here. Willing to accept the torment as those who came before you. The slings and arrows, as Shakespeare once wrote. It speaks well of you, Agnes, and of your lineage.'

'My mother thinks we should leave.'

'She may be right. It is not safe for you or the child you carry.'

'Not safe for Jude either then,' Agnes wondered.

'That is what I came to tell you. I thought you should know that he is back in Dr Frey's care.'

'What? Why would you allow that?'

'It is what he wanted.'

'What possible purpose could that serve? What good can come from that?'

'Only Jude and God know.'

Martha, wearing a black lace veil and beige trench coat, approached the church slowly. Its majestic towers and stonework making it appear like nothing less then a fortress, which was fitting, considering the treasure it was believed by many to contain. The patrolman outside only reinforced for her the sense that there was something precious within, something worth guarding. Worth protecting.

She walked the steps up to the church doors and was greeted by a parishioner who'd clearly been stationed out there. It was someone she'd recognized. One of the people who'd congregated outside her home. She approached the man sheepishly. 'I'm Agnes's mother.'

'I know who you are,' he answered.

'I'd like to visit the chapel.'

'You are welcome here. He opened the door for her and

stepped aside. She entered and, as the door was closing behind her, she turned to him.

'I'm sorry for how I treated you and the others. I was afraid for my daughter,' Martha apologized.

'I understand. You are a mother. I would expect no less.'

'Thank you,' Martha said sincerely.

'You cannot be too careful these days, Mrs Fremont. Not everyone is well intentioned.'

'So it seems.'

'The chapel is toward the back and downstairs. There, they rest.'

Martha continued in through the vestibule and into the church and blessed herself with holy water in the stoup at the entrance of the massive nave. She was struck immediately by the silence. How loud it was. Beyond the stands of candles, she saw the door to the chapel and walked slowly toward it, taking in the awesome stillness of the space. She entered the old refurbished sacristy, charred in places and still smelling of burnt wood, and headed down the stone staircase. It was a holy place, she knew, but she was afraid.

However still it was in the church above, the stillness was magnified exponentially the further she descended. As if each step downwards was a step upwards, her anxiety replaced by understanding. Martha entered the chapel and was immediately struck by the heady mixture of roses and incense. The cool space, decorated with dry, bleached bones and lit by burning

243

candles, was the most peaceful place she'd ever been and whatever anxiety remained within her quickly abated. She walker over to the glass casements displaying Cecilia and Lucy flanking the statue of St. Sebastian. She admired their beauty, their serenity. Like paintings. Sculptures. Pieces of fine art frozen in time and space. Like Icons. Relics.

She couldn't help but notice that there was room for one more casement directly in front of the statue and was overcome with emotion. At first, with anger. 'Why?' she asked. 'They're so young.' She wept. 'Not my child too, Goddamnit! You can't have my child!'

Her harsh words rang out in the old chapel without reply.

She read the text on the wall inscribed behind them out loud:

Et pax Dei, quæ exuperat omnem sensum, custodiat corda vestra, et intelligentias vestras*

As a churchgoing woman, she knew the phrase, she knew the passage from St Paul's letters to the Philippians, extoling those who had stood fast against their enemies and sacrificed for their faith. She never imagined these words read from the pulpit on Sunday could ever have such personal meaning to her. Martha felt almost as if those words had been put there for her.

'I'm sorry,' she cried, bringing her hands to her face in grief.

---

* And so shall the peace of God that surpasses all understanding guard your hearts and your minds.

'I misjudged you all. Please, please, forgive me.' She dropped to her knees between Lucy and Cecilia, one hand resting on each of them. 'Please, I beg you. Forgive me. Please.'

The candle flames flickered with each heaving gasp. Martha went and sat in the front pew and prayed silently for a long while.

She felt at peace.

She felt forgiven.

Dr Frey arrived at the station on time. He thought the meeting unusual, but it was clear to him that Murphy's suspicions had been raised and that he'd best cooperate. The local police photographers gathered on the stoop in front of the station house and raised their eyebrows as he approached, snapping a few photos of the local celebrity for the record. Murphy was waiting at the desk to welcome him into the dingy facility.

'Good morning, Doctor.'

'Good morning, detective,' Frey said politely.

'If you'll follow me please,' Murphy requested.

The two men walked down a dark hallway lined by walls of chipping green paint and scuffed, water-stained hard wood flooring. It felt very nineteenth century to the doctor, musty and old. The sound of typewriters pinging, a sound which he hadn't heard for more than a decade, only reinforced his first impression.

245

'Not a very up-to-date facility is it, Captain? I could help with that. Push for some funding from the Mayor.'

Even Frey's quips were pregnant with meaning, reminding the detective of his wealth, power and influence without losing stride.

'We do just fine, thank you, Doctor.'

'This might be the perfect environment, if you were looking for Jack The Ripper,' Frey chided.

'How do you know I'm not?' Murphy retorted.

Frey cracked a slight smile.

Murphy escorted the doctor into the main interrogation room, the same one that Lucy, Cecilia and Agnes had found themselves in several months earlier.

'Surely this is a matter we could have addressed in my office, with greater discretion.'

'This is a police matter, and I prefer to conduct police business on these premises,' Murphy explained in no uncertain terms.

'If I didn't know better, I'd think you were trying to intimidate me.'

'I'm only trying to seek out facts, Doctor, and follow them wherever they may lead.'

'Yes, of course, the facts. Well, given the reports of rampant corruption in the department, perhaps you should start here,' Frey said. 'I was talking to the Chief of Police and other of your superiors about that very thing the other day.'

'My superiors? Are you sure you aren't the one trying to intimidate me, Doctor?'

'Never crossed my mind, Detective. Now what can I do for you? I have patients to see.'

'Yes, you are a busy man. Very busy. So I'll proceed.'

'Please do.'

Frey sat bolt upright, hands folded on the table, almost refusing to get comfortable. The detective noted his body language as defensive posture in his notebook and began.

'As you know, we have a number of open and ongoing investigations since the events at Precious Blood. And they all seem to have one thing in common.'

'And what is that, Detective?'

'You.'

'That sounds like an accusation, Captain. Perhaps I should have brought my attorney.'

'It's just an observation, Dr Frey. A fact.'

'Well, given that Sebastian, patient zero, as I call him, is at the bottom of this, and he was my patient, that should be unsurprising. And while we are talking commonalities, Captain, he was killed by your men. That is also a fact.'

Murphy let the dig roll off his back for the time being.

'Yes, and both Agnes Fremont and Cecilia Trent were under your care at some point.'

'That's right. The Fremont girl was brought in on a gurney as I recall and has been back since. Attempted suicide. The other was remanded for observation pending trial for murder. Both released. Not the most stable bunch, but in need of care.'

'Well, I imagine you see a lot of that, Doctor, in your line of work.'

'Sadly, yes.'

'It's Cecilia Trent I'm most interested in right now, Doctor. Daniel Less and his attorneys arranged for her release right?'

'Yes, that's right. Over my objection.'

'Less was a friend of yours, isn't that right? Wouldn't he trust your professional opinion, even if he did stand to make some financial gain off of the girl? He hardly needed the money.'

'Well, I'd tell you to ask him, Captain, but that would be impossible.'

'Yes, which brings me to my next question. Why would she want to kill him?'

'Who knows? She was under suspicion of the murder of Finn, whoever he was to begin with. A belligerent, rebellious, self-centred girl, as most artists are, with a borderline psychopathic personality, if you want my diagnosis. I warned Daniel. She should have never been released. You see the result for yourself.'

'I'm asking because a review of phone records indicate that the last call Less made was to you. From Cecilia Trent's concert that night. And for the record, Finn whoever was also a patient of yours, correct?'

'Correct. Where are you going with this, Captain?'

'Just trying to keep the facts straight, Doctor. So about that phone call?'

'If you must know, he was concerned about her mental stability. Not to speak ill of the dead, but he should have thought of that sooner.'

'Clearly. The weapon used to cut her throat was clean. No prints. And in the dark, no witnesses, even though she was surrounded by a crowd of people.'

'Most unfortunate. I guess we'll never know. If there's nothing else?'

'Just one more thing, Doctor. The fire at Born Again? What can you tell me about that?'

'Nothing, although I do have my suspicions.'

'Don't hold back. You're the psychiatrist.'

'Who would have a reason to burn the place to the ground?'

'Sure you want to go there? It's not the most popular place in the neighbourhood.'

'I'm not talking about the stroller patrol that's invading, Captain, or those delusional followers of the supposed saints. I'm talking about someone who had motive, who wanted revenge.'

'You mean the Arens kid?'

'Exactly.'

'Who could blame him after what was done to him, right, Doctor?'

'One bad apple doesn't turn the whole barrel rotten. You

249

can find one anywhere. At Born Again. In business. In your own department.'

'At Perpetual Help?'

Frey did not take kindly to the insinuation.

'I'll be speaking to him,' the captain informed. And for the record he doesn't like you either.'

'No doubt, but I'll put my reputation against that two-bit jailbird gossipmonger anytime.'

'No love lost, I take it?'

'If you are looking for a nexus, Captain. He's your prime suspect.'

24
The Boy with the Thorn in his Side

Agnes endured the uncomfortable probing and scanning by the obstetrician and waited on pins and needles for the result. What she'd heard was a routine procedure now seemed anything but, as nurse followed nurse, physician's assistant preceded physician's assistant into the room to examine her and to administer additional sonograms. None of them said a word as they took their measurements of the baby onscreen and registered her vital signs. She was petrified. Hazel took her hand to comfort her.

'Something's wrong,' Agnes moaned. 'I should have come here much sooner.'

'Stop worrying, Agnes,' Hazel whispered, her anxious

expression giving away her own concerns.

It seemed like forever to the two girls, but finally Dr Patrick entered the exam room, her expression not quite as grim as they were expecting.

'So the good news is that the baby is healthy. You are twenty-eight weeks pregnant.'

Hazel tightened her grip on Agnes's hand and both girls squealed with joy and relief. The doctor, however, did not smile.

'And the bad news?' Agnes asked.

'The bad news is that there are complications,' Dr Patrick explained. 'Your blood pressure is high and we notice some unusual swelling around your eyes and in your legs.'

'She's pregnant, that's not that crazy to be fat is it?' Hazel asked nervously. 'I mean if there's ever an OK time to put on a few pounds, this is it.'

Agnes shushed her friend.

'Along with the bouts of vomiting and abdominal pain you've been experiencing, it leads us to believe that you have a condition called preeclampsia.'

'What?' Agnes asked, barely able to even pronounce the diagnosis.

'It happens sometimes in first-time pregnancies, especially in teenagers and younger mothers.'

'But the baby is fine, right?' Agnes asked.

'Yes, but I don't want to mislead you. It can be a

'life-threatening condition for you.'

'Is there anything she can do?' Hazel asked as reality smacked her square in the face.

'We'll keep a close eye on it from now on. Most importantly, eliminate as much stress as you possibly can.'

'Are there any other options?'

'Termination is always an option whenever the life of the mother is at stake,' Dr Patrick advised. 'Yours is the definition of a high-risk pregnancy, Agnes.'

Dr Patrick left the room, her words hanging ominously in the air. Agnes couldn't help but think this pregnancy was high-risk in more ways than one.

'Agnes,' Hazel stammered. 'I know how important this is to you but I'm telling you as a friend that loves you, I think you need to keep all your options open.'

'I have no options.'

The fiery attack on Born Again had left the house in a shambles and Frey's murderous minions temporarily scattered. It would be difficult to regroup them. Jesse had bought Agnes some time, to his credit, Frey acknowledged, he'd achieved that much. The heat was on in other ways as well. Despite his best efforts to influence the top brass and pin the arson on Jesse, the investigation was slowed down at every turn by Captain Murphy, while the investigation into Cecilia's death only seemed to pick up speed.

The longer and deeper it went, the more it appeared clear to him that Murphy was looking to connect him to it through Daniel Less. Discrediting Agnes might have helped him put a few points on the board in the short term but it was the future, which she carried inside her, that troubled him most. She was protected now, and the same eyes on her were watching him as well. But neither concern with Murphy or with Jesse was most pressing. His most pressing problem was the problem of Jude. The boy was back, of his own volition. There was a reason and Frey was determined to find out why.

The boy was waiting outside Dr Frey's office door as he had for the past several weeks since returning to Perpetual Help. Their sessions were brief and so far, uneventful, much to the doctor's dismay. Perhaps it was the additional scrutiny he'd been under, but Frey was uncharacteristically anxious and impatient.

'Send Jude in, nurse.'

Jude ambled through the door in hospital scrubs he'd been given by the psych ward staff, for his own protection. There was not a sneaker lace or hard sole or belt to be found on him. He was clothed pretty much in white paper, which gave the towheaded boy the appearance of an angel. He sat down.

The doctor studied him carefully, evaluating his mood, levels of alertness, eye contact, skin pallor, steadiness all in a few casual glances such was his expertise. Jude for his part remained impassive, indifferent to Frey's appraisal.

'You're looking well, son,' Frey said offhandedly, not a shred of concern in his voice. 'Being here must suit you?'

It was a leading question and Jude did not respond, not even a blink. The doctor circled the boy and returned the chair behind his desk.

'Surely, you must be getting tired of these sessions, Jude. I don't see you as a danger to yourself or others. Is there something you want to tell me?'

The boy tensed up and began to shudder slightly, then more violently. His head flew back and his eyes rolled white. The veins in his neck were popping as his hands grasped the chair like a frightened child on a rollercoaster. Frey half-stood with alarm, his instinct to help a patient in distress at war with his curiosity over what might come next. He waited and watched.

For a moment, the boy seemed to be seizing and then in a mild trance-like state the doctor had seen many times before in other patients before returning to a semblance of clarity. After a few moments, the boy spoke for the first time in his presence, as he had hoped. The words he'd chosen, however, were not the response the doctor was expecting.

'I'm not a danger to myself or to anyone else, except you.'

Frey leaned in closer to the boy across his desk.

'Is that so, Jude? How are you a danger to me?'

'I have knowledge that you covet.'

The use of the word covet in that context seemed a bit

arcane to the doctor's ear, especially for a child. Biblical, even.

'I'm not talking to Jude, am I . . . Sebastian?'

'You are talking to one who knows, Doctor.'

'Oh Sebastian, do you seek to impress me by invading the body of child? Even in death you are a fool.'

'The seeds have been planted.'

'Yes, the seeds of destruction. The same delusions that led to your own death have brought down Lucy and Cecilia. And Agnes too before long.'

'They are alive. Always. As you know. As you fear. As you believe.'

'They are dead! Because of you,' Frey shouted, banging his fist and then catching himself. 'Why do I argue with a ghost?'

'Because we are not ghosts, Doctor. We live in hearts and minds. Places you cannot touch.'

Frey gathered himself.

'You were always a stubborn boy, Sebastian. I told you none of this needed to happen. If you would have been more compliant, remained in treatment, you and your friends would be alive now. Enjoying your youth. Living.'

'With you there is nothing but death. For the body *and* the soul. What I did, I was compelled to do for the good of all.'

'Yes, you've set a wonderful example for others to follow. A legacy of blood, insanity and death.'

'Of sacrifice. Of faith.'

Jude shuddered once again and then relaxed. The mystical

moment had passed with the boy barely understanding what had happened to him.

'A most interesting session, Jude.'

Jude was weak, barely lucid.

'We'll talk again tomorrow. About Agnes.'

The Revelation of Martha

*M*artha could not sleep.

She twisted and turned in her bed, exhausted mentally and physically; yet unable to slip into the peaceful slumber she so desperately needed to quiet her troubled mind. She opened her eyes in hope of escaping the visions of Lucy, Cecilia and most of all Agnes. But they continued to haunt her like a waking dream. Her daughter's predicament and her fate weighed heavily on her. Seeking some solace. Some meaning to it all.

Martha closed her eyes again and unexpectedly found herself drifting off. Not into dreamland exactly, but somewhere she'd never been, witness to something she'd never seen. An ancient scene. Two men in a jail. One dressed regally. The other modestly. One an emperor. The other a priest. One an accuser. The other a prisoner. She was frozen. Unable to move or to do anything but watch and listen to the events unfold as guards stood by, swords at the ready.

The noxious smell of burning coals, human waste, stagnant water and decaying flesh filled her nostrils.

'What is your name?' the ruler demanded in a most authoritative tone.

'I am called Valentinus. Some call me Valentine.'

'I am Claudius Gothicus,' the tall man said, stretching his arm out from his white linen robe to reveal his emperor's ring.

'I know who you are. The whole world knows.'

The emperor eyed Valentine suspiciously as he had the enemies he had engaged and vanquished in mortal combat throughout the Roman world.

'You are accused of many things, Valentinus, not the least of which is marrying off men who would otherwise be sent to fight. Yet you have no authority recognized by the state to do so.'

'I have all the authority I need from a power much greater than yours,' Valentinus replied.

'You speak treason. What power greater than mine is there in the world?'

'The authority I claim is not of this world, Gothicus.'

The Emperor let out a loud impatient sigh.

'You realize that I have forbidden the worship of any other gods but the gods of Rome? On pain of death.'

'I do.'

'Yet you persist in this rebelliousness! The roads in and out of the city are lined with the severed heads and crucified corpses of those like you,' Gothicus spat angrily, pointing a long accusatory finger in Valentius's face. 'Don't test me. It will cost you your life. I swear it.'

'If that was your message, could not an underling have brought it to me?' Valentinus asked calmly. 'Yet the mighty Claudius Gothicus has come to this jail full of death and disease and despair himself to interrogate me. Why?'

Gothicus glared menacingly at the insolent prisoner and then threw his head back and laughed.

'You are a fool, but a brave fool, Valentinus. I like you,' Gothicus said. 'You are an idealist. A romantic. Dispense with these silly notions of yours, swear loyalty to me and I will spare you.'

'Never.'

The emperor was clearly displeased and began to pace before the jail cell, stroking his chin, deep in thought.

'It is said that you are a healer.'

'Not any longer, Caesar. Your soldiers destroyed my salves and medicines when they arrested me and brought me here.'

'On whose authority do you claim to do such magic?'

'It is not magic.'

'Then what?'

'Faith,' Valentinus declared.

'Liar! These are deceptions. Tricks!'

'If they are just harmless tricks, why am I here, Gothicus, other than in your employ entertaining your guests?' Valentinus queried. 'What do you fear from me?'

The red-faced ruler regained his composure and removed a

handwritten note from beneath his vestment and handed it to Valentinus through the prison bars. The accused took the tattered piece of rag paper and examined it in the dusty torchlight of his confines. It read simply 'From Your Valentine'.

'Is this your signature?'

'It is.'

'Are you in the habit of sending love notes to young women?'

'No I am in the habit of showing appreciation to those who are kind to me, those whom I cherish and love.'

'Even your jailer's daughter? The blind girl?'

'She was brought to me by her own father,' Valentinus acknowledged. 'Unable to see from birth. I treated her. I taught her. I prayed with her.'

'You healed her. Is that your claim?'

'Her faith has healed her.'

'And your faith condemns you,' Gothicus proclaimed. 'This note shall be your last.'

'It will be the first of many, Gothicus.'

The Emperor was handed a piece of parchment and he laid it on a small wooden table before him.

'This, my dear Valentine, is my signature.'

Gothicus dipped his ring in a small vat of hot wax and drove his seal on to the bottom of the writ of execution.

'I order on this fourteenth day of the second month that you be beaten with clubs until you are dead.'

'It is a sacrifice I make gladly.'

261

'Your only legacy will be one of wasted sacrifice. A lesson for all eternity.'

The emperor handed the document over and turned to leave. The prisoner called out to him.

'No,' Valentius smiled. 'That will not be my legacy.'

'What then?' Gothicus asked, indifferently.

'Love,' Valentinus replied. 'It will be love.'

The bars of the cell faded away before Martha's eyes, the sky opened and the prisoner priest's modest robes transformed from sackcloth into finest silk and linen of red, purple and gold. He cast his glance off in the distance. Approaching him were two figures. A boy and a girl.

'Agnes,' she gasped.

The girl was adorned by a floral headdress and flowing gown of blinding white. The boy in soldier's armour, a bow slung around his chest and a leather quiver hanging from his back. The couple stopped before the priest and joined hands. Valentinus blessed them and spoke.

'Who gives this woman, Agnes, to be married to this man, Sebastian?'

Martha burst out into tears. She did not respond.

Agnes and Sebastian turned to face Martha.

'No, please,' Martha begged.

Agnes smiled at Sebastian and then at her mother, and as she did her heart was suddenly visible through her chest.

'I . . .' Martha began, barely able to speak.

Agnes's heart burst into flame, the fire of eternal, sacred love.

'I do,' Martha said at the sight.

The fumes of the prison disappeared from Martha's nose along with the vision. Her body relaxed. She was able to breathe once again and as she exhaled she felt as if she'd received the answer she'd been seeking. She received it with both joy and terror. Martha looked down at her hand and found she was holding on to a white rose from Agnes's headpiece.

✦

25

Never Give All The Heart

Jesse opened the app for his favourite online radio station and out from his speakers poured one of Cecilia's songs. The label might have put the project on indefinite hold due to the shadowy circumstances surrounding the release, but despite cease and desist orders and pending copyright infringement suits being drawn up by label lawyers there was no stopping it now. Club DJs, radio jocks and streaming services had the material, thanks to him, and whatever their motives, were playing the hell out of it. Lucy's video had gone viral and was chalking up millions of views. Jesse smiled, despite his regrets. If he couldn't save their lives, he thought, he had at least preserved their legacies, their message, the thing that ultimately they'd lived and died for. For the longest time he'd been trying to figure out where he fit in all this but it had suddenly become clear. His mission now was Agnes.

Smoking out the vandals housed at Born Again and tightening the noose on Frey had bought him some time but it was clear to him that Agnes and her baby were at the top of Frey's agenda. There was a sharp knock at Jesse's door. He looked through the peephole.

'Mr Arens,' the detective said.

'Come to arrest me, Captain?'

'No, should I be?'

'Nice try.'

Jesse opened the door and let the captain in.

'I just came to give you a head's up.'

'Oh, well, that's mighty considerate of you. About?'

'I'm removing the police detail from the Fremont house.'

Jesse seethed. 'Why? You guaranteed she'd be protected.'

'Listen, these men are police officers, not crossing guards. They aren't on the force to walk Agnes to school. Besides, there hasn't been anything of concern there for weeks. No sign of trouble or of anyone, for that matter.'

'Yeah, not yet,' Jesse grumbled.

'It was an order from downtown,' the detective shot back. 'I don't run the department.'

'No that's true. You don't.'

'What are you getting at?'

265

'Agnes is pregnant. And she's in danger. Without protection, she won't make it.'

'You mean from those Born Again junkies?'

Jesse didn't know how to begin without sounding like a loon who'd be sent right to Frey's psych ward. 'I've been telling you for months now.'

'Your story is that there is some supernatural war between good and evil going on in the streets of Brooklyn and that Alan Frey is at the centre of it?'

'I know it's hard to fathom, Captain, but that is it.'

Murphy took a seat on Jesse's couch and turned suddenly pensive, debating with himself about how much he should tell Jesse. He was still, after all, a suspect.

'Daniel Less' phone records show that the last call he made was to Dr Frey.'

'Excuse me if I don't sound surprised.'

'The thing is, there was no love lost between them. Frey was bitter about losing Cecilia to his custody.'

'The enemy of my enemy is my friend. Ever heard that one?'

'You think Less is part of the whole thing?'

'I know it. And Cecilia knew it,' Jesse said. 'He got her out, gave her what he thought she wanted, what she thought she wanted, built some trust, to catch her off guard.'

'It squares with the facts, kid, but . . .'

'But nothing, Captain. What are you going to do about it?'

'You got to prove it, Jesse. You can't just throw charges around with a guy like Frey. This isn't a blog kid, this is real life.'

'I know, believe me,' Jesse said, holding his hands up. 'I've got the real-life scars. That's my proof.'

Murphy paused again and spoke quietly, as if he were thinking out loud more than speaking to Jesse.

'I also did a little digging into the doctor's past and it turns out he knew the Papal Nuncio also, from way back.'

'That connects him to Lucy and Cecilia's deaths, Captain, what else do you need?'

'He needs to show himself.'

'By the time he shows himself, Agnes will be dead. Don't you get it? These guys, 'Ciphers' Sebastian called them, operate behind-the-scenes, Captain. That's their whole thing. You're not supposed to see any of it. That's how it works,' Jesse ranted in frustration.

Murphy continued to play Devil's advocate, keeping his sceptical detective's hat on tight, testing Jesse.

'Sounds like another wild-eyed conspiracy theory,' Murphy challenged. 'Illuminati, Freemasons, New World Order, Bilderberg Group, Ciphers, Fight Club.'

'Maybe they're just different names for the same thing, Captain.'

'Maybe,' Murphy agreed.

'I'm not chasing a fantasy, Captain. I know what I know. I

have faith in Lucy and Cecilia. They died for a reason and someday people will understand – whether you do or not is irrelevant. Agnes is my priority now.'

It was the first time Jesse had made such an admission, such an unerring statement of faith. He surprised even himself.

'Somehow I don't picture you as a knight in shining armour on a quest for the Holy Grail.'

'Listen, I'm busy,' Jesse said. 'Is there anything else you came to tell me, 'cause if not I need to get back to work.' Jesse walked to the door and held it open, silently inviting the police captain to leave. Murphy took a deep breath and looked Jesse straight in the eye. He reached into his jacket pocket and pulled out a .38 special revolver, its grip taped over, and handed it over to Jesse.

'Yeah, there is. I came to tell you I believe you.'

Day after day Jude arrived at Doctor's Frey's office for his therapy session, with Frey trying to coax a reaction, or Sebastian, out of him. Yet the boy remained stoic, wilfully so, the doctor thought. The focus of Frey's curiosity was Agnes and her baby and Jude's lack of cooperation only intensified his curiosity. The boy knew something, he was sure of it. He pressed, both urgency and the volume of his voice increasing. Jude sensed his anxiety but was unmoved.

The session began as it always had.

'Is there something you want to tell me?'

Jude did not answer.

'I want to know about Agnes.'

Once again there was no reply.

'There is a reason why you've come back here. You have something to tell me, or Sebastian does.'

Jude raised his eyes to make contact, acknowledging his question, if not answering it.

'Your eye contact is much improved, Jude. And some said it couldn't be done.'

Jude averted his eyes once again. Frey was becoming increasingly agitated. He hung on Jude's every breath, every movement for a sign. A slight smile flashing across Jude's lips sent the doctor into a fit.

'Are you here to mock me, boy?'

Frey slammed his clenched fist on the table and walked around his desk, approaching within a few inches of the boy. He grabbed him by the shoulders and picked Jude up like a doll, shaking him. Jude remained limp and did not resist, angering the doctor even more.

'Tell me what I want to know. Sebastian told you didn't he? Told you everything before he escaped. Tell me about Agnes!'

Jude closed his eyes and prayed silently. He was hurting but there were no tears, no fear in him. Frey released him, dropping him to the chair, and offered him a deal.

'I have the power to release you, Jude. You can return to the

269

convent with the nuns. Return to school. Live your life.'

Jude shook his head *no*.

'This act of yours has become tiresome. Speak!'

Frey returned to his desk and sat, regaining his vaunted composure, but only to issue more threats.

'If you continue to play this game with me, Jude, I can make it very unpleasant here for you,' he swore through clenched teeth. 'I will break you.'

The air in the room changed, becoming charged in a way that was noticeable to the doctor. The hair on his arms stood on end and his hands began to shake. Jude dropped his head and began to speak, quietly at first. The words were Latin and the doctor knew them well. A prayer to St Michael seeking his help. A prayer of exorcism.

'*Sáncte Míchael Archángele, defénde nos in proélio . . .*'*

Frey sought to interrupt the boy's supplication, talk over it, neutralize in any way he could.

'Tell me what I want to know or you will never leave this place, Jude.'

'*Cóntra nequítiam et insídias diáboli ésto præsídium. Ímperet ílli Déus, súpplices deprecámur . . .*'**

'You will grow old and die here. Mark my words!' Frey shouted.

---

* *Saint Michael the Archangel, defend us in battle.*
** *Be our protection against the wickedness and snares of the devil. May God rebuke him, we humbly pray.*

'Tuque, prínceps milítiæ cæléstis, Sátanam aliósque spíritus malígnos . . .'*

'Go ahead! Call upon all the saints in your Fool's Paradise. None of them will be able to save you.'

There was fear in the doctor's eyes. And desperation.

'Not Lucy, not Cecilia. Not Agnes. Not the nun. Not Jesse.'

'Qui ad perditiónem animárum pervagántur in múndo, divína virtúte . . .'**

'Not Sebastian!'

'In inférnum detrúde.'***

'Not even God himself!' Dr Frey roared.

Jude raised his head and paused, staring directly into the doctor's eyes. 'Amen.'

* and do Thou, O Prince of the Heavenly Host
** by the Divine Power of God, cast Satan and all the evil spirits who roam throughout the world seeking the ruin of souls
*** Thrust to hell.

26

Keep Your Head

As the nun approached Agnes's home, she saw there were a few Valentines scattered about, little glitter and sequin hearts and a few flowers left for Agnes on the stoop. Not nearly what the nun had expected to see. She looked up and saw that there were no admirers across the street. It was empty. A notable difference from the reports she'd seen on the news and from local parishioners dedicated to Agnes.

She hadn't seen Agnes for a while and was becoming concerned, especially after the school nurse advised that she might not be returning for the rest of the school year. They were not exactly friends, but confidantes, in the unique way that only likeminded people can be. Sister Dorothea empathized with Agnes's joy and her terror at the sacrifice she was making, not so much at being pregnant, which was a condition she'd vowed sacredly never to experience, but with the experience of giving yourself over to a calling, to a power greater than yourself.

She rang the bell and waited. Mrs Fremont opened the door slowly. 'Hello Sister. Thank you so much for coming.'

'I was quite concerned, Mrs Fremont. How is Agnes?'

'She's not very well,' Martha explained, eyes reddened with worry. 'The doctor said she needs to remain as stress-free as possible and, under the circumstances, school isn't the best place for her right now. She could go into labour at any time.'

'I understand,' the nun said. 'Surely there is much less stress at home for her.'

It was not so much an observation as a question for Martha.

'Yes, there is now, Sister. I believe her.'

The nun knew the history between the two of them and smiled, shedding a few tears of her own. 'There is nothing like a mother's love, Mrs Fremont, to comfort and uphold us in our most difficult times.'

'I am here for her, Sister.'

The women embraced and Martha led the nun to Agnes's bedroom. At the sight of the nun, her eyes lit up. She walked to Agnes and hugged and kissed the girl, in the most comfortable of surroundings, lying uncomfortably in her bed.

'We miss you, dear,' Sister said sweetly.

'I'm not sure everyone misses me, but thank you. It's so good to see you.'

Agnes did indeed look unwell to the nun's eye. Swollen around her eyes and joints. Pale and obviously in some pain.

'Can I get you anything, Sister? Tea, coffee?' Martha asked.

'No, thank you, Mrs Fremont.'

'All right, I'll leave you two alone.'

'Thank you, Mother.' Agnes smiled.

As Martha departed, the nun praised the woman. 'It much be such a relief to you to have your mother on your side.'

'Miracles do happen, I guess,' Agnes laughed, reaching for her side to soothe a sudden stitch from stomach cramping.

'Is there anything I can do for you, dear?'

'No, just you being here means the world to me.'

'It is what you mean for the world, Agnes, that is important.'

It was a concept that Agnes still had a hard time getting her head around.

'How's Jude?'

'He is still at Perpetual Help.'

'By his choice?'

'Yes,' the nun confirmed. 'It is taking its toll on him but he refuses to leave and of course Dr Frey is in no rush to see him go either. In my visits and consultations with him, he seems obsessed with Jude.'

'I'm so worried for him.'

'He is only a boy, but he is special. Right now, you must be concerned only with yourself and your child.'

'I know I don't have to explain this to you, Sister, but my concern for Jude is part of my concern for myself and my child. I feel that he is there because of me.'

'I have faith in him and in his reasons. There is no need for you to carry any bigger weight then you are already.'

Agnes nodded. There was little she could do about it anyway. Trusting in Jude was part of the process of giving herself over. Sebastian had, Lucy had and so had Cecilia. She would do no less.

'Have you made your plans? Your mother says the baby could come soon.'

'I have. Don't worry, my mother is with me now. And Hazel and Jesse. I'm not afraid.'

'You are brave, Agnes.'

The nun began to cry, her own tears running down the side of the container.

'Oh, please don't cry, Sister.'

'You wept for your friends, and a boy, Agnes, and for what might have been. I weep for what might be, and for all of us.'

Jesse eyed the gun sitting on his coffee table. He'd never fired one before. Never even thought about it, but everything was different now. If ever there was a reason to use a weapon in self-defence, this was it. Murphy knew it, and presenting the gun to him was an unusual act, of both trust and illegality, on the policeman's part. Frey's Vandals would come packing heavy this time, leaving nothing to chance. No margin for error. He was sure of that.

He was heartened by Murphy's newfound support but it changed little. The threat from Frey was ever present, despite the setbacks he'd engineered and the police would be virtually useless against him. Oddly, there'd been an eerie sense of calm since Born Again and Jesse was increasingly suspicious. The retaliation he and Tony expected hadn't come yet and Jesse wondered more and more whether Frey was keeping his powder dry for a more auspicious purpose, namely Agnes. She was the big variable now and until she was ready, everything seemed to be on hold.

Jesse flipped open the chamber, noted that it was filled with bullets and began to plan, running different scenarios through his mind. How to keep her safe. Hospitals were no guarantee. In fact, it was probably easiest for Frey to reach her there. Home was little better. Without police protection, or even the watchful eyes of her fickle followers, she was vulnerable. Wherever Fate, and her baby led them, he knew it would be time to take a stand. Tony and his men were on call. He could count on them but that was about it. Murphy would really only be helpful after the fact. The police weren't in the business of anticipating crime. But there was Jude.

He was Jesse's trump card. Their first line of defence. As filled with fear as he was for Jude's wellbeing he couldn't help but laugh to himself at the fits the boy must be giving the doctor. From what Agnes had told him of her conversation with Sister Dorothea, Frey was hanging on the boy's every word, trying to read him like tea leaves. The boy was brave and selfless, he thought, to endure that kind of daily bombardment and if he wasn't crazy when he was readmitted, he would be a PTSD candidate by now for sure.

This waiting game was just another way for Frey to inflict suffering on them, he supposed. Sebastian, Lucy and Cecilia's deaths were clearly not enough. Discrediting them at every turn, leaving him mangled at Born Again, torturing a child under the guise of therapy, betraying even Daniel Less, his own colleague. He wouldn't stop until Agnes and her baby were dead and the threat to his agenda nullified. Frey was the conductor on this night train, punching tickets, collecting fares with a handshake and a smile, all the while making sure that none of the passengers reached their destination. It was actually admirable to Jesse in some ways in its pure, cold, calculated, uber-efficient and clandestine brutality.

Jesse pondered the immediate future that was revealing itself when a group text buzzed him back to reality. It was to him and Hazel, from Agnes.

PLS COME. NOW!

Jesse texted Tony and put him on stand-by, threw on his

jacket, holstered the gun, and hailed a gypsy cab outside his apartment.

He glanced down at his phone and read a second text from Agnes:

IT'S TIME.

The Prophecy of Jude

It is not by words
But by deeds
That a better world is born
One by One
That darkness recedes
That Light shines
This is faith
This is knowledge
Have Insight to see

Have Courage to change
Have Love to accept
Your True Self
And you will be forever Blessed
Sebastian, Pray for US
Lucy, Pray for US
Cecilia, Pray for US
Agnes, Pray for US

27

Vapour of Phantoms

The doctor was conducting the latest in a series of late night sessions designed to break Jude's will, to elicit from him whatever secret Frey imagined he possessed. This was now a matter of utmost urgency for him. His rivalry with Less had been a dangerous diversion and waiting for the music man to metaphorically hang himself had used up precious time. Less was gone now, as was the challenge to his authority from within, but in the wake of Cecilia's dramatic death the followers had grown far beyond a cult or even the protesting mob that had spurred Jude, Cecilia and Agnes' release from Perpetual Help. It was a citywide movement now, and beginning to catch on nationally.

Sightings of Sebastian, miracles and healings attributed to Lucy and Cecilia were on the rise. Thanks to increasingly rabid media reporting, their fame began to rival that of the biggest film and rock stars. Lines outside the Precious Blood chapel stretched for nearly a mile now and space within it was packed shoulder to shoulder with young and old alike. Sunday mass in the cathedral above also overflowed with new parishoners and was more like a pop concert than a religious service. And Frey was determined to put an end to it. For him, Agnes was the answer and Jude was the key.

The boy was dragged out of bed and brought to Dr Frey's office by two of the psych ward orderlies for questioning.

'Hello, Jude,' Frey said snidely. 'I'm sorry to wake you at this hour but it's been such a busy day and I know how much you look forward to our visits.'

The boy was groggy but wiggled himself into an upright position in the uncomfortable chair and faced the doctor.

'Is there something you'd like to tell me? About Agnes? About her child? Something that Sister Dorothea has confided in you?'

Jude shook his head *no* as he had many times before.

'I understand that Agnes is unwell. That she could give birth at any time. You know when it will be, don't you, and where?'

The doctor's frustration was evident. He sensed that time was short. He stood and thrust his hands in the pockets of his sports slacks and paced slowly behind his desk. Frey began to mumble, more to himself than the boy, thinking and fretting out loud.

'You certainly have kept me busy. Jude.'

The boy did not respond but his eyes moved involuntarily from side to side, which the doctor duly noted. He stopped pacing and brought his hand to his chin, pondering his own words as a moment of clarity struck him.

'You've kept me *busy*,' he repeated. 'That's it, isn't it?'

The boy swallowed hard, nervously.

'The reason you came back.'

Frey sat down and folded his hands, like a principal preparing to scold a naughty student.

'You are a very clever boy, Jude. Psyching out the psychiatrist. I've underestimated you.'

Jude did not react.

'And I'm a fool,' the doctor said, chastising himself. 'Playing a game of wits with a mute.'

The doctor picked up the phone and buzzed the night nurse.

'Nurse, please check with the ER and with Ob-Gyn department, ask if they've been notified of any imminent arrivals,' he requested, a definite urgency in his voice. 'Yes, the name is Fremont. Please check with the other ERs in the area as well. A pregnancy. Likely a C-Section.'

He summoned the orderlies to come and get the young patient.

'I'll deal with you after Agnes, and more importantly her baby, is dead, Jude.'

The orderlies arrived in seconds and took hold of the young patient.

'Take him away.'

Jesse ran up the steps to Agnes's house two at a time and pushed the doorbell. He waited anxiously looking over both shoulders and started knocking furiously until Mrs Fremont answered. Agnes was sitting on the living-room couch, in a cold sweat and breathing heavily.

'I told her I wanted to call the EMT but she wanted to wait for you.'

'I got here as fast as I could,' Jesse said.

He walked over to Agnes and knelt down, taking her hand. She looked relieved but in obvious distress.

'How are you?' he asked gently.

'Not good,' she moaned.

'Agnes, we need to call now.'

'No, I don't want to call. I don't want to be in an ambulance.'

'Please this is not the time, Agnes. It's the closest hospital to us. You need a doctor now,' Martha insisted.

'Will you go if I take you, Agnes?'

She nodded yes reluctantly.

Jesse looked up at Mrs Fremont reassuringly.

'I have a car waiting outside. I'll take her.'

'I don't know,' Martha fretted.

'Mother, it will be fine. Maybe you can get some clothes together for me and meet me at the hospital.'

Agnes reached up to her mom for a hug and the two embraced.

'I love you, Agnes,' Martha cried, worried for her daughter more then she could or would say. 'With all my heart.'

'I know Mother. And I love you. Always.'

Agnes was concerned not only about her health, but also her safety. And her child's. Who knew how long it would take for Frey to figure it all out. Not long, she assumed. A birth was not exactly something you could keep secret.

'Let's go,' Jesse said hurriedly.

He helped Agnes on with her coat and took her by the arm, helping her out the door and down the steps.

'You're not taking me there, Jesse.'

'I just promised your mom, Agnes.'

'It's not safe for the baby,' she insisted.

Jesse opened the door to the backseat, pondering the best alterative. She got slowly into the car, leaning on him almost entirely for support and suddenly doubled over, clutching her belly in pain. Martha was right, Jesse thought. She needed a doctor right then and there was no time to waste getting to another hospital further away. Jesse yelled to the driver.

'Perpetual Help!'

The car sped off, down the quiet, tree-lined Park Slope side streets.

'No, Jesse,' Agnes pleaded. 'I don't want to go there.'

'Agnes, I'm not going to lie to you. You look terrible. You need help now. I'll deal with Frey. Tony and his guys can meet us there. I'll call Murphy too. Your mom will be there in a few minutes.'

'No,' she said softly. 'I want to have this baby where I was born.'

Jesse looked quizzically at the girl. He was alarmed, wondering if she was delirious, losing it.

'What?'

'I want to go to Precious Blood.'

Martha rummaged frantically through Agnes's room, doing her best to stay focused and pack the things the girl would need the most: several changes of clothing, underwear, bathrobe, slippers, toiletries and a few photos of friends and family to place on the hospital nightstand. She double-checked the room, satisfied she hadn't forgotten anything important and as she reached for the light switch, she turned to take in Agnes room. The décor, the lighting, the furniture, the carpets and bedding, all of it screamed how wonderful and unique and creative her teenage daughter was. How romantic.

Mrs Fremont allowed herself a moment as she was totally overcome with emotion. She sat on Agnes's bed, recalling every intimate conversation they'd ever had, every moment of her daughter's childhood, the good and the bad, and sobbed. Martha stood and took a few steps towards Agnes' desk and pulled a drawer open. She saw the tear catcher and also a torn piece of vellum. The page of St Sebastian Agnes had removed from the Legenda at Precious Blood. She read the page and dropped her head in her hands.

'Help us,' she prayed. 'Please help us, Sebastian.'

The text alert bell rang on Martha's phone, interrupting her meditation. Her car was outside. She reached for the bag she'd loaded, zipped it up, grabbed her coat and headed outside.

'Where to?'

'Perpetual Help Hospital.'

The driver eyed his obviously distraught passenger in the rearview mirror.

'Nothing serious I hope, ma'am?'

Martha stared back at the kindly gaze reflected in the mirror.

'Yes, I'm afraid it is.'

Without speaking another word between them, the driver sped to the location.

'What do I owe you?' Martha asked as they arrived, fumbling distractedly in her purse for her wallet.'

'Nothing,' the driver said.

'Thank you,' she replied. 'You're an angel.'

'I'm happy to help,' he replied.

Martha rushed through the ER doors at Perpetual Help with

Agnes's overnight bag full to bursting in her hand. She ran to the front desk. 'I'm here to see my daughter.'

'Name?'

'Agnes Fremont.'

The desk clerk searched his list but found nothing.

'No, sorry.'

'What do you mean? She should have arrived here by now.'

Martha was petrified. The clerk checked his list again and made a few brief calls back to the ER and the OB floor as Martha waited on pins and needles.

'I'm sorry, there is no record of any Agnes Fremont being admitted here tonight.'

Martha stepped away from the desk, clearly distraught and dialled Agnes's cell. It rang into voicemail. She texted urgent messages to Agnes and Jesse. The elevator doors opened in the lobby and Alan Frey walked out.

'Hello Mrs Fremont. Such a surprise to see you,' Frey said, offering his hand. 'How is Agnes?'

Martha took a step back, as if she'd seen a ghost. Or a monster.

'Is there something wrong?' Frey asked, knowingly.

'No,' she stammered. 'I was just visiting.'

'Visiting whom?'

'Agnes,' Martha admitted reluctantly.

'I had no idea she was back with us?'

Martha was too distracted to be clever with the doctor. 'She's not.'

'I'm sorry. I don't understand.'

The message alert on Martha's phone pinged and she looked at the smartphone screen in shock, unwittingly repeating the message loud enough for Frey to hear.

'Precious Blood?' she read.

28

Gratia Plena

Tony and his men were already at the church when Agnes and Jesse arrived. He took her arm and helped her from the car and up the steps, Jesse took the other arm. Tony raised his lighter and guided them through the dark church and toward the chapel.

'I can walk,' Agnes insisted, seeming to draw some strength from her surroundings.

They walked downstairs and entered the chapel. Agnes immediately fell into the first pew, closest to Cecilia, Sebastian and Lucy. She was sweating, her curls matting around her face.

'Agnes, I think this is a really bad idea,' Jesse said.

'You need to be in a hospital,' Tony agreed 'We're not doctors. You're not safe here.'

Agnes looked up at the bodyguard and reached for his hand.

'No, Tony, I feel safest here.'

Agnes let out a loud moan and grabbed at her stomach as her waters broke. A puddle of fluid stained her dress and dripped from the pew on to the marble floor. Jesse and Tony both looked at each other, panicked.

'Agnes, I don't know what to do. We have to get help,' Jesse implored. 'Please, Agnes. For the baby's sake.'

She caressed her swollen belly and looked up at Jesse and over at the casements.

'OK,' she whispered weakly.

Jesse called 911 and texted Captain Murphy. Tony took off his jacket and Jesse did the same, laid them on the floor and helped Agnes lie on top of them. The sound of footsteps from above broke the silence.

'Agnes!' a shrill cry echoed through the catacomb.

'Mother!' Agnes called back as loudly as she could.

Martha rushed to her daughter's side and kneeled beside her, stroking her face.

'I came right from the hospital.'

'From the hospital?' Tony asked. 'Did you tell anyone where you were going?'

'I don't know. I was also confused when they couldn't

find Agnes's name,' Martha explained. 'Maybe the desk nurse or Dr Frey.'

'Frey?' Tony asked nervously.

Jesse locked eyes with the bodyguard. They both knew what that meant. It would only be a matter of time now before the Vandals arrived. They could only hope Murphy's men arrived before Frey's. 'You need to get out of here, Agnes, to where they can help you,' Martha begged, frantic.

'I'm not leaving here, Mother.'

The tone of Agnes's voice was not defiant, but resigned. The statement, Jesse thought, was as pregnant with meaning as Agnes herself.

'No way she can move in her condition. The EMTs are on the way. And the police,' Jesse informed.

'The police? Why?' Martha asked.

Before he could get his answer out, the sound of footsteps could once again be heard above. Even from the cellar chapel he could tell it was more than just one person. Loud shouts told Jesse this was not the EMT or the police.

'I'll check it out,' Tony said, heading towards the steps. 'Don't move.'

Jesse fingered the gun in his waistband and nodded.

As the sound of the ruckus above grew nearer, the situation in the chapel grew more desperate as well.

'Push, Agnes!' Martha shouted.

Agnes wailed in pain, using every ounce of the strength she

had left to push. Tony rushed back through the door to warn them.

'They're here.'

Jesse knew from the look on his face that it was not good. He drew his weapon as the sound of sirens began to fill the air. The cops would be there soon, he figured, but probably not soon enough. Agnes was straining and weakening fast. He bent down and whispered to her.

'Don't be afraid.'

The words were more powerful then any others he could have spoken to her. She found the strength to continue. Martha felt her stomach for signs of contraction and told her when to push. She grasped her mother's hands tightly and bore down once again. Agnes strained and began to bleed.

'It's coming,' Martha cried. 'The baby is coming!'

Jesse reached over near Cecilia's case and grabbed the iron bow she'd used to kill Daniel Less. He tossed it to Tony, who stepped outside the door and closed it tight behind him. He faced the four Vandals who were now at the top of the stone staircase, approaching him fast, like hellhounds, like barbarians at his gate. He had been a doorman, after all. The best in the city and he knew how to keep an exclusive space tightly guarded. 'C'mon you sons of bitches! I'm standing here.'

They rushed him at once and he let out a terrifying war cry, and swung the bar, like a designated hitter, for the fences. Psalms, which his grandfather had taught him as a young boy for protection against the local bullies, spilled from his mouth. Words he had not spoken since childhood came to him as if he'd only learned them yesterday. It was as if the martyred souls of the chapel rose up within him. Empowering him.

'*Eripe me de inimicis meis, Deus, et ab insurgentibus in me libera me.*'*

The bow struck the first Vandal, smashing his face to pieces like an overripe watermelon. As the first dropped to the floor, the second approached. Tony brought the bow over his head and slammed it down, splitting the enemy's skull; pieces of bone and brain sprayed him. He thrust the rod through the Vandal's chest for good measure but before he could withdraw it, the last two were upon him.

'*Avertet mala inimicis meis; in veritate tua disperde illos.*'**

He barely felt the first knife tear through his skin. Or the second. Blood poured from his chest and out his mouth as the Vandals stabbed him over and over. He grabbed them each by the throat, smashing the backs of their heads against the stone walls and choking them with all his might, keeping them at bay until he heard the sound he'd been waiting for before he expired. The cries of a newborn.

The sound of life in the chapel contrasted to the life draining from his own body and the Vandals as Tony crushed their

* *Deliver me from my enemies, O my God; and defend me from them that rise up against me.*
** *Turn back the evils upon my enemies; and cut them off in thy truth.*

windpipes in a last heroic act. He laughed a bloody laugh at the loud cries of Agnes's baby, released his grip on the dead men and slumped to the floor with a loud thud. Jesse knew the sudden silence beyond the door could mean only one thing.

'God bless you, Tony,' Jesse whispered sadly, speaking his friend's name with gratitude and respect.

Inside the chapel, the candle flames rose high and Sebastian's reliquary and the bodies of Cecilia and Lucy appeared to glow with joy. There was peace and life in contrast to the mayhem and death occurring just outside the shuttered door and well beyond. The sirens were getting ever closer.

'She's beautiful,' Martha cried, placing the baby girl on Agnes's chest.

Jesse too was overwhelmed but kept his composure and his aim squarely on the door. Agnes stroked the child's face gently. 'Hello baby, I'm your mama.' She was breathing even more heavily now and blood began pooling beneath her. 'You were born from love. You are love.'

The Vandals broke in and Jesse fired, emptying his barrel. Bullets struck one in the chest, groin and finally in the head, dropping him dead. He kept pulling the trigger, but there were no bullets left. He was unarmed.

The final Vandal stood at the door smiling.

'What are you doing here?' Martha shouted.

'Doctor's orders,' the marauder smiled.

Martha screamed and ran for the killer like a banshee herself and was quickly swatted back by the iron bow, which knocked her backwards and nearly unconscious. Agnes did not have even the strength to cry out to her.

Before approaching Jesse and Agnes, the Vandal pulled out his phone and held the screen towards them. The screen filled with Dr Frey's face.

'Hello, Jesse.'

'You will burn in hell for this!'

'Yes,' Frey acknowledged. 'There probably is a special place in Hell for me, which pleases me to no end. Since, however, you will be arriving before me, please do save a spot for me, won't you?'

'The police will be here any minute.'

'Yes, in exactly two minutes as the dispatcher assured me.'

As usual, Frey was a few steps ahead and flaunting his connections, which ran deep into the very heart of the city's services and agencies.

'You can't stop us,' Jesse warned.

'But I can. And I must. This is a place of death, Jesse. Full of bones and corpses and relics and a dead vision for the future. It is only fitting that you die here as well.'

'You evil bastard!' Jesse shouted, rushing the Vandal.

Jesse too was swatted away easily with a hard jab to his abdomen, which dropped him to his knees.

'Forget about him for now,' Frey instructed. 'Kill the girl and the child. I want to see it for myself.'

The Vandal approached Agnes and raised the iron bow over her, preparing to thrust it downwards. Agnes could not speak.

'The price of love, dear Agnes,' Frey mocked, 'can be very high indeed.'

The Vandal looked down, setting his aim squarely for her chest and the child that sat innocently unaware upon it. Suddenly, without warning, Agnes's hair began to grow, surrounding the mother and child, covering them, like birds in a nest. Strands of Agnes locks began to climb up the Vandal's legs, tying them together at the ankles, wrapping tightly around his neck and binding his hands. He struggled against her tresses, which only tightened the more he fought. No matter how hard he tried, he could not strike them.

'What is happening?' Frey shouted impatiently. 'Do it. Kill them.'

At the doctor's command, the killer managed to free his hands at last as Agnes continued to weaken. He raised the bow to deliver the deathblow.

Jesse shouted, 'Agnes!'

A burst of light shone from Sebastian's reliquary, blinding the Vandal. A gunshot rang out, striking the Vandal in the head, killing him. Jesse grabbed his ears and looked in the doorway but could only make out a shadow in the glaring light. It was Murphy.

'Are you OK?'

'Don't worry about me,' Jesse said, pointing to Agnes.

Murphy waved the EMTs in behind him and they rushed for the girl and then for Martha. Jesse reached for the phone, which was still connected to the call.

'Dr Frey,' Jesse said, still barely able to catch his breath. 'There is someone here who wants to speak to you.'

He handed the phone over to the captain and the line went dead.

'I'll pay him a visit later,' Murphy said. 'You all right, kid?'

Jesse dodged the question, his focus entirely on Agnes.

'Will she be OK?' Jesse asked the emergency tech.

He shook his head *no*.

'I'm sorry,' Murphy said, put a comforting hand on Jesse's shoulder and stepped away.

Jesse's gut reaction was to rage that it was too late for apologies, but in that moment, his heart was filled with nothing but forgiveness and with sorrow.

Agnes was trying to speak. Jesse brought his head close to her, holding back tears. She was reciting. Praying. In Latin. Jesse didn't know how to pray or Latin but somehow he understood. Every word. As she spoke, the candle flames rose and the words appeared on the walls of the chapel, as if they'd been carved there, burned there, her speech turned to fire.

et si habuero prophetiam et noverim mysteria omnia et omnem scientiam et habuero omnem fidem ita ut montes transferam caritatem autem non habuero nihil sum

et si distribuero in cibos pauperum omnes facultates meas et si

tradidero corpus meum ut ardeam caritatem autem non habuero nihil mihi prodest

caritas patiens est benigna est caritas non aemulatur non agit perperam non inflat

*non est ambitiosa non quaerit quae sua sunt non inritatur non cogitat malum**

These were not the words spoken at a funeral or as a requiem, but at a wedding. A joyous occasion where the nature and endurance and maturation of love is defined and celebrated.

*cum essem parvulus loquebar ut parvulus sapiebam ut parvulus cogitabam ut parvulus quando factus sum vir evacuavi quae erant parvuli***

Even in his pain, Jesse smiled. He could not help but feel this was a message spoken not just for the ages, but for him especially. From this moment forward, he would no longer be a boy, but a man.

videmus nunc per speculum in enigmate tunc autem facie ad faciem nunc cognosco ex parte tunc autem cognoscam sicut et cognitus sum nunc autem manet fides spes caritas tria haec maior

---

* And if I should have prophecy and should know all mysteries and all knowledge, and if I should have all faith, so that I could remove mountains, and have not charity, I am nothing.

If I give away all my possessions, and if I hand over my body so that I may boast, but do not have love, I gain nothing.

Love is patient; love is kind; love is not envious or boastful or arrogant or rude. It does not insist on its own way; it is not irritable or resentful; it does not rejoice in wrongdoing.

** When I was a child, I spoke like a child, I thought like a child, I reasoned like a child; when I became an adult, I put an end to childish ways.

*autem his est caritas**

She recited the last line in English, for emphasis. It was who she was, what she believed, what she had lived for.

'The greatest of these is love.'

Agnes squeezed Jesse's hand, turned her face towards his and opened her eyes wide, connecting with him, looking straight into his anguished soul.

'Take care of her, Jesse,' Agnes whispered, stroking her child's face.

'What's her name?' Jesse asked.

'Faith,' Agnes said.

Jesse nodded and took the child, bringing her face to Agnes's lips for a single kiss. Agnes then repeated a final phrase over and over again, like a prayerful chant, as if to imprint it on the infant's brain and on her soul.

*caritas numquam excidit***

As Agnes uttered her last words, she let out a heavy sigh and a great sense of peace came over her. Before her, she saw Lucy and Cecilia and then, then she saw Sebastian, standing at her feet, smiling. Sebastian walked over to her and held her hand and he gently kissed his daughter's head. Jesse saw it, too. And Martha, who had just regained consciousness and

* *We see now through a glass in a dark manner: but then we will see face to face. Now I know only in part; then I will know fully, even as I have been fully known.*

And now faith, hope, and love abide, these three; and the greatest of these is love.
** *Love never dies.*

crawled to her daughter and grandaughter's side, did as well.

Agnes's spirit now freed from her body, the saints stood together, shoulder-to-shoulder, visions of strength and beauty, and smiled at them. A smile of gratitude and farewell, transforming the bone chapel into a chapel of eternal love. Jesse closed his eyes, for the briefest of moments, and his mind was filled at last with understanding. When he opened them, they were gone. Frey had it totally wrong. This was not a place of death. It was a place of life. Agnes made it so.

'My baby!' Martha wailed inconsolably, stroking Agnes's hair and lifeless cheeks.

Jesse lifted the child from Agnes's arms and cradled her in his own.

Even the hardened police captain's eyes filled with tears. He clasped his hands together respectfully.

The crush of emergency service personnel and police filled the tiny chapel. Jesse sat in the pew grieving quietly amidst the chaos, protecting the child from the havoc all around them, his teardrops falling on to Faith's head one by one. A kind of baptism. He thought about the sacrifice that Agnes had made to bring the child into the world, the sacrifice they'd each made. She would have lived if she went to the hospital, she knew that, he thought. But her baby would be in their hands.

Gurneys from the medical examiner's office arrived quickly and so did the crime scene photographers. He could see these hardboiled men trying desperately to keep the tears in their eyes from ruining the focus. Tony and the four Vandals' bodies were wheeled out and taken away. The investigation had already begun. The captain stood over Jesse and put his hand gently on Jesse's shoulder.

'Who is the father?' Murphy asked, quietly.

'What?' Jesse said, still very much distracted.

'Whose child is this?' Murphy asked again.

'Mine,' Jesse said. 'Faith is mine.'

Police units had already surrounded Perpetual Help, leaving Dr Frey no exit. No escape. He could see the roof of their cruisers flashing red-and-white lights from the windows of his penthouse office. Lights from the vans of local TV news crews were already setting up and blaring into the night sky. With little recourse left, he sat in his chair and waited for the inevitable.

In short order, uniformed officers burst from the elevators, guns drawn, and headed for his office. At the sound of the commotion, patients began waking up and lining the hallways, not sure if what they were seeing was some sort of psychotic dream or drug-induced hallucination. The police entered and found Frey there, casually reviewing some paperwork.

'Can I help you?' he said snidely.

The sea of blue parted and Murphy stepped forward.

'Dr Frey, you are under arrest.'

He approached the psychiatrist, pulled his arms behind his back forcibly, and cuffed him.

'What is the charge, Captain?'

'Pick one,' Murphy said smugly.

The captain pushed the doctor forwards towards the office doorway like a common criminal and out into the hall where the patients were waiting for him like a jury. His humiliation was complete. He passed them silently, looking downwards, until he came upon the last of them. It was Jude.

'Seems the shoe is on the other foot,' Frey observed. 'At least for now, Jude.'

The boy stood there and met the doctor's gaze, unflinchingly.

'Not for now,' the boy said clearly. 'Forever.'

Frey smiled and continued towards the elevator, surrounded by officers.

'You won't be able to hold me for long, you know that don't you, Captain?'

'It's over, Doctor,' Murphy said.

Frey turned and looked toward Jude, resignation in his eyes.

'No, Captain. It's just begun.'

The last of the mourners expressed their condolences and said their goodbyes to Martha. The brownstone was empty of people but filled with silence. She glanced over towards the hallway to Agnes's room, only partly convinced she wouldn't answer back when she called her daughter's name. The wounds were still very fresh.

'It was a beautiful service,' Hazel said sweetly, as she

began to clear the dishes and coffee cups and bring them to the kitchen.

'Yes,' Martha agreed. 'It was.'

'Very Agnes,' Hazel said. 'Filled with love and beautiful reminiscences. Walls of flowers. Everywhere.'

Martha began to tremble and Hazel placed the cups and saucers down on the coffee table and walked over to comfort her.

'Why didn't I listen sooner?' Martha anguished. 'Believe her? Believe in her?'

'She was your child? How could you see her as anything else? Not want to save her? Spare her?'

The gentle and profound words of wisdom from Hazel were unexpected and touched Martha deeply, but not quite enough to relieve her of the guilt she'd been carrying around with her. 'I was trying to spare myself,' she bawled.

'She loved you.'

'God forgive me.'

'He has,' Hazel said. 'And so has Agnes.'

'Do you really think so?'

The sound of a few light coughs came through the speaker of the baby monitor in the kitchen and Hazel and Martha both looked towards it. It was a reminder, to Martha in particular, that it was no longer just about her and how she felt, her needs. There was someone far more important to be concerned about.

'I know so,' Hazel reassured her. 'Why don't you get some rest? I'll go in and check on the baby.'

'Thank you, Hazel. You have been so strong. I don't know what I would have done without you.'

'You can count on me. And Jesse, Martha. We're here for you and for her.'

"You've both been incredible,' Martha praised.

Compliments from Martha had always been hard to come by, but she was a different person now. They all were. Hazel smiled and hugged Martha, who retired to bed. She finished cleaning up and headed for Agnes's room. The child was restless, twitching slightly, coming, it seemed, out of a deep sleep. Hazel lifted her from her crib and walked the room front to back, side to side, bouncing the child rhythmically and singing.

'Sorry I'm not a very good singer, Faith. Now if your Auntie CeCe were here, it would be a different story.'

Hazel hummed and cooed, did whatever she had to do to calm the child and before long she fell back asleep. She laid the little girl in her crib once again and stared down at her for a long while, admiring her. She had tufts of copper hair sprouting from the sides and top of her head and when she closed her eyes tight like that she looked very much like Agnes.

'I can't wait to tell you about your mother, Baby,' Hazel said sweetly. It isn't every day you can say "baby girl, your mom was a saint" and really mean it.'

Hazel walked around the room, looking through Agnes's

closets and keepsakes, making mental notes about things to be kept for the child and things to be donated, depressed at the thought of having to give much of it away one day soon. There was no way that Martha could ever handle that. It would fall to her. She knew it.

She sat down on the bed, her head in her hands, closed her eyes, pondering all that had happened. Their childhood. Their friendship. The things that had been. The good. The bad. The things that would never be. When she opened her eyes Hazel found herself focus on the drawer of Agnes's desk. She stood and approached it, opening the top drawer, and was shocked at the sight of a card in an envelope with her name on it. It was taped to a vintage velvet sack, which she opened first. It was Agnes's Victorian tear catcher. The one she'd admired.

Hazel held the delicate glass flute and put it up to the light, where a million beams of coloured light seemed to bounce off it. At the bottom were the last drops of tears, the last of Agnes. She opened the card and gasped, barely able to contain her emotions. It read:

I Love You

'I love you, Agnes,' she whispered.

Hazel collapsed in a heap on top of Agnes's bed, the one on which they shared their gossip, their secrets, their fears and their dreams.

She opened the cap on the tear catcher.

Hazel cried.

29

Faith Eaters

The rain stopped. The clouds broke gradually over Brooklyn, stretching west from Prospect Park to the Gowanus and across to Red Hook, from Carroll Gardens and Cobble Hill north to Brooklyn Heights and Dumbo, to the bridges, transforming stubborn gray afternoon skies to a pink, purple, and orange sunset. Shadows from high rises, office towers, and church steeples in the gentrified brownstone neighbourhoods seemed to reach down like long fingers across the streets and sidewalks, grasping for the pedestrians below like some gigantic movie monster or like a god. Signs seemed to be everywhere that things were changing.

Catherine and Hazel, who'd been walking from Agnes's

Park Slope neighbourhood, made the turn at the Barclay's Centre from Atlantic Avenue to Flatbush Avenue and headed toward BAM and Downtown Brooklyn, when they heard a loud and compelling voice in the distance. It cut through the rumble of idle truck engines in bumper-to-bumper traffic, the painful squeal of MTA buses braking at their appointed stops, the complaints of double-parked delivery men to overzealous traffic cops, the inane chatter of colleagues talking business along the busy thoroughfare, the happy screams of children running from their schools. All the typical sounds that make up a day in the city.

They approached the young man, scruffy and unkempt in all the right ways, looking like some post-wave John the Baptist, in a thick crowd of passersby. He stood atop a red plastic milk crate, holding a microphone, miraculously keeping his balance and his unfailing erect posture despite the slope in the sidewalk. His voice crackled with enthusiasm. His eyes burned with the passion that only comes from certainty.

'He's hot,' Hazel whispered with a little laugh.

'Shut up,' Cat scolded good-naturedly, elbowing Hazel gently in the ribs. 'Let's listen.'

It was the first light moment either of them had since Cecilia and Agnes had died and it showed on both their faces. The clouds had broken not only above them but within them.

'*Don't* pay it forward!' he shouted, raising the politically correct eyebrows of some in the crowd. 'Don't do something good because something good was done for you. Do something good just to do something good. Without expectation of reward or recognition.'

As one of the earliest apostles of Cecilia's, Catherine was especially sceptical of the sort of bandwagon jumpers that tried to hitch their wagon to her mentor's message. To scam a few sympathetic onlookers to take pity and drop a few bucks in their jar. In fact, she'd come to believe that these frauds and phonies were just part of the larger Cipher plot to mislead potential followers and to discredit the girls and Sebastian. They might have won a few key battles, taken Frey down, but the war definitely continued to rage on. It could be hard sometimes, very hard, she reckoned, to separate the wheat from the chafe.

Despite her reservations, she was also gratifie to see and hear so many authentic followers beginning to craft their own interpretations of the meaning of Sebastian, Agnes, Lucy, and Cecilia's lives and deaths. That was their whole point, after all. To know yourself, accept yourself and most of all, to be yourself. And how you did that was entirely up to you. The more Cat listened, the more she was persuaded that this guy was the real thing.

'Now that's a disruptive message,' Cat murmured under her breath. 'Do good. Just for the sake of it.'

'Kind of old-school just standing up their preaching or whatever, don't you think?' Hazel observed. 'He could just post some videos on his wall. Tweet some pics and cool sayings. 2.0 it, you know. It would be easier.'

The stage performer in Cat kicked in and she tried to explain it to Hazel. Thinking of his impromptu lecture as she might one of her own gigs in front of a live audience. There was nothing quite like winning people over face-to-face. The look in their eyes, the change in their expression. It was a kind of alchemy. Magic.

'Maybe that's why there are so many people listening. There's no filter,' Cat figured. 'It's personal. He's doing it the hard way. One at a time.'

The boy was unfamiliar to them yet his words seemed very familiar. As if he was speaking for someone else rather than for himself. The more he spoke, the more deeply he touched them. He wore a pin, one of the Agnes-Lucy-Cecilia-Sebastian mash up milagros that sold so briskly from nearly every street corner these days. His, however, was obviously not store-bought. It was handmade and he wore it like a badge. On some days, the press reported, you might see as many 'Subway Saint' medals as crosses on people across the borough and even the city. It was one sure sign their cults were growing. One among many. Hazel and Catherine listened evermore intently.

'Look around. To your right and to your left. In front and behind you,' the boy suggested and then paused. 'And forget what you see!'

'Wow,' Hazel exclaimed. 'He really gets it.'

'The answer isn't before you,' he shouted. 'It is inside of you.'

The crowd was completely rapt now and growing larger. Hungry for his message. His insight. Whatever Lucy, Cecilia, and Agnes had initiated Catherine smiled at the boy, acknowledging him with a 'keep up the good work' nod of her head. She was inspired by him. She looked around for a tip jar but there was none. Another good sign his motives were genuine. Cat gestured oward Hazel and the pair made their way out of the throng.

'Drinks on me,' she said with a wink. 'Don't be afraid.'

The boy flashed her bright smile and interrupted his self-help sermon just long enough to shout out,' Cheers, Cat.'

Cat turned back and flashed him a thumbs-up for recognizing her.

'He's brave, standing up there like that, considering all that's happened,' Cat commented. 'Cecilia would be proud.'

'You think that's how it was for them with Sebastian?' Hazel asked.

'You mean getting seduced by a hot guy with a mysterious message?' Cat answered, with obvious sarcasm in her tone. 'I think there was only one Sebastian.'

Hazel smiled weakly and turned thoughtful.

'I guess, but that's not very encouraging for the rest of us.'

'You don't need to be Sebastian. Or a saint for that matter. Find your own way to express it. I think that's what's important.'

'Being so inspired by someone, believing in something, in somebody so much, you'd die for it. That's a powerful connection to make, though.'

Cat thought about it for a second and related it to the only experience she really knew well. Her own.

'Whether its music or spirituality, politics, relationships, whatever,' Cat observed, 'on some level, you have to be willing to give yourself over, suspend disbelief, to be a fan, to commit to the end, to drink the Kool-Aid. It just depends whether you like how it tastes.'

'Drinking from the wrong cup can get you dead,' Hazel said sheepishly. 'I still don't really understand why it all turned out this way. I miss Agnes.'

'But they're not dead, Hazel. Not really. That guy preaching and those people listening are proof of it. Faith is proof of it. Living proof.'

Hazel paused and swallowed hard, thinking of how best to say what was on her mind.

'I see Agnes sometimes. On the way to school. In the backyard of her house outside her bedroom window when I visit Martha and Faith,' Hazel said, looking away from Cat, unsure of the reaction she might get. 'You think I'm crazy, right?'

'Nah. If you're crazy I am too,' Cat suggested. 'I see Cecilia in the audience at every show. Around every corner. They're inside of us. That guy was right.'

'Maybe we should tell Jesse about him?' Hazel said. 'He saounds like he could be one of us.'

'Maybe,' Catherine agreed. 'It's growing. Taking on a life of its own now. The more the better. People are ready to listen.'

Hazel and Catherine strolled back towards 4th Avenue and down Pacific Street to Smith, window-shopping and café hopping. Without realizing it, the girls had walked all the way to Precious Blood just as evening fell. They stood silently for a long while, staring at the entrance to the massive edifice and at the symbols, sculptures, and engravings that marked the stained-glass windows and outside walls of the cathedral. But as striking as the exterior of the renovated building appeared, it was the treasure within Precious Blood that they reflected upon most.

The guard at the door recognized them and stepped aside. Hazel and Catherine bounded up the staircase and stepped inside the vestibule, in awe of the dark and cavernus space awaiting them. The girls lit votive candles to illuminate their path but did not move.

'Hello!' They each called out into the darkness, again and again, like scared children waiting to hear their echo. Or for a friend to call back.

'Do you think they know we're here?' Hazel asked nervously.

'I think they do now,' Catherine joked.

'I know we don't know each other very well, but I hope we can be friends,' Hazel said.

'No, we don't know each other well,' Catherine agreed, 'But we have a lot in common.'

Hazel hugged Catherine hard and long.

'I could really use a friend,' Hazel said.

'Couldn't we all.'

'What do we do now?'

Catherine's answer was short and certain. 'Keep them alive.'

Hazel's eyes wandered toward the ossuary doors at the other side of the church.

'What if they aren't there?' Hazel wondered. 'Like what if their bodies are gone?'

'You mean stolen by vandals or some crazy super fans?' Cat replied.

'Or something else,' Hazel suggested.

'Alive?'

'Yes, what if we went down there and found their dresses and headpieces in their glasskets. Their bodies gone. Walking the streets among us again.'

'I don't need to see if their bodies are there or not to know that they're out there among us. Now and forever.'

EPILOGUE

ICONS

Jesse stood behind his desk and stared out from the floor-to-ceiling windows of his penthouse office across the brownstone blocks and towards the gleaming tower of Precious Blood cathedral, gathering his final thoughts. The expansive view of Brooklyn never failed to impress him. He turned around to face the woman, a respected journalist, sitting across from him.

'And that's what happened,' he said wearily.

Jesse rubbed at his hands as he always did when thinking about them, the memory ever fresh in his mind and in his broken bones and torn muscles. He knew full well he'd relayed a story so fantastical it could scarcely be believed. And if he didn't, the wide-eyed look on the journalist's face and her frantic scribbling on her notepad were sure signs he'd done some mind-blowing. They were both exhausted.

'I'm flattered you chose me to tell this story but why now?'

'It's time,' Jesse replied. 'There have been so many rumours which turned into gossip, then into legend. Or lies. This will be the truth as I know it and have lived it.'

'Some might say you've used the mystery to your advantage. Secrets and lies were your business at one time, weren't they?'

Jesse removed his glasses and rubbed at his greying temples.

'That was a long time ago.'

'I'm not looking to cheap shot you, Mr Arens, but I do want you to understand that I'm not a rubber stamp for you either.'

'I'm not expecting a love letter. Just that you will be fair.'

Fairness was what Jesse sought more than anything. Through the years since the girls had passed, so much had been mis-stated, misinterpreted. Until now, he'd preferred to entrust their legacy to the hearts and minds of their ever-growing legion of followers. They were the ones, he believed, that mattered most anyway, and they seemed perfectly satisfied. But the truth also mattered to him.

'If you don't mind I just have a few follow-up questions.'

'Sure,' Jesse agreed, putting his hands in his suit pants pockets.

'Lucy, Cecilia, Agnes and Sebastian are candidates for sainthood, I understand.'

'True. The Pope began the process and the investigations

before he died. I have no doubt about the result.'

'Subway saints, the papers have called them. First of their kind.'

'Hopefully not the last,' Jesse replied.

'I don't think there's any danger of that. They continue to be an inspiration. Statues, relics spread all over the world. People pray to them, see them. It's an amazing legacy.'

Jesse smiled.

'Elvis, Jesus and the Sackett Street Saints,' he joked. 'I try to keep them alive in my way, but there is a beauty and meaning in the old traditions. Sister Dorothea is our Vatican contact and she oversees those things for us. I can arrange a meeting if you like.'

'I know the Victorian tear catcher that Agnes used has been of great interest over the years.'

'It was donated by her closest friend, Hazel,' Jesse informed.

'She runs the museum about the girls in the Gowanus that your foundation endowed.'

'Yes,' Jesse said enthusiastically. 'She is a real keeper of the flame and probably has the best relationship with Agnes's followers than any of us. You should definitely interview her.'

The writer made a note.

That place used to be the old halfway house Frey set up, right?'

'Born Again. I rebuilt and repurposed the building. Put it to better use, I think.'

'They never did find out who burned it down, did they?'

Jesse replied impassively and directly. 'No.'

'The portrait of your friend Tony that hangs in the entrance there? An odd choice, isn't it?'

'Tony was a doorman and a friend. The best at both. It made total sense to me that his would be the first face you see as walk into that building.'

'A sort of guardian angel you mean?'

'Everybody has a saint inside them. Some just never get the acknowledgement they deserve. This was my way of paying tribute to him.'

'Quite a story you've told,' the writer commented, shaking her head in both disbelief and admiration. 'A real story of devotion.'

'It's their story.'

'You're too modest, Mr Arens,' the writer opined. 'In these twenty years, you've built a communications and technology empire that eclipses even the one created by Daniel Less and you wield even more influence in this city than the infamous Alan Frey. How ironic that you now own this building, operate from this floor, where he did so much damage.'

'Wealth and power and influence aren't bad in themselves,' Jesse opined. 'It's how they are used that matters.'

The journalist looked around at the photos and accolades that hung on the walls of the office; first among them, pictures of Lucy from her club kid days, and platinum album awards for Cecilia and for Catherine, the superstar artist whose sales had helped build his first record label and his first fortune.

'It's hard to imagine that Cat was once a struggling artist.'

Jesse laughed. 'Well, she might be again soon if she keeps giving money away like she has.'

'With a week of arena shows coming up in town I don't think we need to worry.'

'No,' Jesse agreed turning serious. 'Cecilia would be very happy to see that her music and her message live on in Catherine.'

'I saw that they are raising the Milagro logo above the entrance as I arrived today. It must be gratifying for you.'

Jesse thought about that for a moment. It was, but not in the way the writer might have intended.

'It's all about them now. The future,' Jesse said, turning two pictures on his desk toward the writer. 'My daughter Faith and my son Jude. 'Hopefully, they will carry on the work I've started.'

'Lovely kids. Faith looks just like Agnes.'

Jesse stared lovingly at the photograph. She did indeed, he thought, look so much like her mom. Faith's true parentage had of course been the subject of rumour and speculation since she was born. Jesse was always very careful not to get into it too deeply. A self-deprecating quip was usually enough to satisfy inquisitive reporters or nosy neighbourhood gossips. It had to be. The truth was way beyond belief.

'Yes, fortunately for her,' Jesse said with a smile. 'Beauty, smarts, and a loving heart. I'm very proud of her. Proud of them both.'

The writer was satisfied with Jesse's little joke as he'd hoped but wasn't quite done probing.

'What have you told her about her mother?'

'I told her what any child of deceased parent tells them.'

'And what is that?'

'Your mother was a saint.'

The reporter laughed. 'In this case it just might be true.'

'It is true,' Jesse replied.

The reporter, noting Jesse's certainty for the record, cleared her throat and continued.

'It must have been hard for them under the circumstances, both the bad and the good.'

'They know who they are and respect where they come from. A parent can't ask for more than that.'

The writer nodded and continued.

'Why do you suppose Alan Frey was so helpful in the subsequent investigations against his colleagues, those other Ciphers as you called them, after his conviction.'

'Hard to say, but I think he wanted it known. He was proud of what he'd tried to do.'

'It cost a lot of people their reputations, their fortunes, in some cases their lives,' she said. 'Those trials and perp walks of bankers, brokers, board chairmen, university deans, politicos, prosecuters and judges. Totally riveting.'

'Which was all fine with Frey,' Jesse explained. 'He considered Daniel Less as much threat as Sebastian and the girls, maybe even more. He had to have *his* name on their defeat. Any other outcome was unacceptable.'

'His way or the highway.'

'I prefer to think of it as the low road.'

'So ironic. Done in by the Seven Deadly Sins,' she opined. 'Vanity. Greed.'

'Envy too,' Jesse added for good measure.

'What a waste.'

'This may sound odd to you, but he was a true believer in his own cause. Proud of the whole shadow world he'd created. Turning on his own kind wasn't an act of contrition, it was an act of retribution. Admitting to it wasn't a statement of guilt but an act of defiance.'

'A little cowardly I always thought,' she added.

'He didn't want anyone replacing him and he saw to it no one would.'

'Replacing him? You really believe there is a hierarchy in actual war between good and evil going on, Mr Arens?'

'Frey has already been replaced along with the rest of the Ciphers,' Jesse said. 'You can believe that.'

'I'm sure you know there is a lot of scepticism out there. I mean Less and Frey and their colleagues might have been bad guys but turning them into nefarious super villains and leaders of some sort of global cult seems farfetched.'

'Yes, I know there is a lot of scepticism. In fact, Frey and his kind rely on it. It's why I've dedicated my life and my business to uncovering it. Shining a light on it. Providing an alternative to it, fighting it whenever and wherever possible.'

'Pardon me, but it sounds a little archaic.'

'It is,' Jesse said simply. 'A war as old as mankind.'

Jesse's conviction was powerful, if not entirely contagious.

'I don't imagine you shed any tears when Dr Frey died demented and in prison?'

The question seemed strange to Jesse after all that had happened. He'd foresworn his feelings of revenge towards Frey long ago.

'I don't take any pleasure in death,' Jesse explained, 'He was a man of great intellect and ability who wasted it doing harm to those he might have helped. His soul died long before his body.'

Jesse's assistant buzzed in.

'Mayor Murphy on line one for you, Jesse.'

'Thank you Mrs Fremont,' he said. 'I'll return later.'

'A relative of Agnes Fremont?'

'Her mother. She's been with me since Agnes died.'

'My impression was that she was very sceptical back in the day.'

'We had that in common. We both learned differently. And she has been so influential in helping me raise the children. Couldn't have done it without her.'

'So no woman in your life? I would imagine you are quite the eligible bachelor?'

'My heart belongs to Lucy . . . Cecilia and Agnes. Always did. Always will.'

'Sounds like a love story.'

'Yes, it was all a love story.'

She could see that Jesse was spent. But the she did have one more question. Perhaps her most important one.

'One last thing. Why do you think so many people follow them? What was their appeal in your opinion? I mean in the end they were just three girls from Brooklyn.'

'Yes, but they could have been three girls from anywhere. People are hungry for authenticity and honesty. For truth,' Jesse explained. 'There are so many pundits and experts who want to tell us what to think, how to live, who to be but precious view that *show* us. Who live it.'

'I take it you aren't a big fan of the media then.'

'I'm not a big fan of filters. To the people who believe in them, Lucy, Cecilia and Agnes represent vision, courage and love. They lived for it and died for it. No further translation or explanation is necessary.'

The reporter closed her notepad, satisfied she'd gotten what she needed in her sessions with Jesse.

'So see clearly, speak fearlessly and love completely. Is that it?'

'Works for me,' Jesse said. 'The world is a little better today because of them.'

'Only a little?'

'Slow is fast enough,' Jesse said hopefully. 'We're getting there.'

'Well, I don't want to keep you from the Mayor. Your foundation and the charities you fund have been a great boon to the kids of this city.'

'All I wanted to do was to make sure that everyone knew they had a choice about who they could be.'

'And who is that?'

'Themselves.'

'You're very lucky then, Mr Arens. People seem to have gotten the message.'

'Miracles do happen,' Jesse assured.

'I'm not a believer,' the writer confessed, 'but you've nearly convinced me.'

'It's up to you to convince yourself of what you choose to believe. Up to each of us, I think. Life is a sort of Rorschach test. You see what you want to see.'

'Or need to see?'

Jesse smiled with understanding. That *I was once like you smile* he used to resent but found great use for this days.

'Faith is to believe what you do not see; the reward of that faith is to see what you believe,' Jesse recited.

'Augustine?' the reporter asked.

'Yes.'

'Seeing is believing,' she murmured aloud, realizing that Lucy's mantra and the answer to her question were the same.

Jesse nodded, the smile moving from his lips to his eyes as he prepared to say goodbye.

'If there's anything else you need, just get in touch with Mrs Fremont. She'll be able to fill you in on any other details.'

'Yes, she's been very helpful. Well thank you for your time, Mr Arens.'

'I'll look forward to your book,' Jesse smiled.

They shook hands and Jesse grabbed the suit jacket from the back of his chair and put it on.

'Gone for the day?' Martha asked.

'No, just going for a walk.'

Martha didn't need to ask where.

'I'll have dinner ready at home for you.'

'Thank you.'

Jesse strolled the few blocks to Precious Blood as he had each day, acknowledging the smiles, well wishes and greetings from people on the street. Each time he approached the church it was like the first time, with a sense of anticipation for what he might find inside. But now there would be few surprises. He'd entered into a contract with the Diocese of Brooklyn to oversee and staff the chapel. To make sure it remained in pristine condition for as long as he and his children lived, and long after.

Jesse took the steps downstairs, a little more gingerly then in his younger days, and approached the chapel. He paused to run his finger along the inscription.

Omnes Sancti

And entered. He never ceased to be amazed at the sense of peace he felt within the chamber. Of holiness. The scent of incense and roses never got old. Eternal flames flickered, reflecting from bleached-bone fixtures, polished wood, metal and hanging chandeliers, throwing both light and shadows as they always did. The room was alive. Lucy's video played with Cecilia's music as the soundtrack on a never-ending loop, over and over. Even after all this time, he thought, it did not look or sound dated. Agnes's last words burnt into the planter walls still inspired.

There were Lucy, Cecilia and Agnes, surrounding Sebastian's reliquary, as uncorrupt as the day they'd each been laid to rest. And so very beautiful. The chaplets and Milagros that served now as the namesake for his company hung still from their ivory wrists. The girls were there for everyone that wanted them. Needed them. Believed in them. And they would always be.

He brought his lips to each casement and kissed it gently.

'We've done good,' he said simply.

He took a seat in the pew and looked at them for a long while reflecting on his life's journey. Jesse kneeled before his friends, his heart and mind full of thoughts from the past and hope for the future, reflecting on the journalist's observation.

'I wasn't lucky,' Jesse whispered. 'I was blessed.'

The Word According to Agnes

Call me crazy in the head,
I've been called far worse.
But I can't help whom I love,
Evil eyes a curse.
You will not keep me from him,
His heart is my heart.
You think this is the end,
But it's only the start.
So, lock me up, throw them away.
All your hopes and dreams.
Mine, they belong to,
He will burn through me.
Let this bloody scar be a reminder,
When I decided to be free.
You cannot choose whom you love,
It is love that will choose thee.

Agnes, pray for us.